DIME

DIME

EDITED BY BABS LAKEY

Quiet Storm Publishing • Martinsburg, WV

Published by Quiet Storm Publishing
PO BOX 1666
Martinsburg, WV 25402

www.quietstormpublishing.com

Cover by: Dustin Evans

ISBN: 0-9749608-6-1

Library of Congress Control Number: 2004105434

Printed in the United States of America

Compiled by Babs Lakey

DIME INTRO by Babs Lakey

It's coincidental that Clint Gaige, publisher of Quiet Storm Publishing, suggested that we join forces to do this anthology (annually) of short mysteries, and even more so that it be christened, DIME. That title was only a suggestion, he said, but what a suggestion! FMAM began with the simple title Futures, (as in, I put my *stock* in your talent!) followed by one line, *brought to you by writers and artists with the fire to fly*. People tried to say that I'd gotten it wrong, I must have meant to say, fire to write. Well, no. I meant *fly*. HAHAHA! Those were the people that interested me; I wanted to help launch those flights. And, the wonderful thing about FMAM, these past seven years, is that we have been able to help launch many careers for artists and writers with that fire to fly. The coincidence was that Clint chose FMAM and then chose a title for a product that was also originally launched with incredible fire! The DIME novels of yesteryear breathed a passion and fire into novels that made readers over the world take notice. In fact, in 1860, publishers Erastus and Irwin Beadle played a central role in the early history of the dime novel with a romantic novel that sold 65,000 copies in its first several months. What a feat! In 1860! Without the aide of media and Internet! I am astounded by that figure and yet it shows us what is possible when we give people what they desire. And do this with the already mentioned, fire to fly! You're about to read in excess of twenty stories written by creative people with a fire to fly that will astound you!

Our first collection of stories is ready. Dime's murderous, primrose path beckons. Along the path you'll find bodies, ladies and gentlefellows, and more than a few shivers, and above all, stories that haunt, stick in your mind until the day you, yourself, expire. This is one of those collections that will stay with you until you die. This is Hitchcock with a smidge of the *literary*, a smadge of the *horror*, and a smack of the *oldies but goodies* on the FM-AM channel. Get comfy, you'll be in your chair awhile. HAHAHA! Oh! And lock those doors and windows tight. Just a thought… just in case….

Dime I

Crestfallen's Widow
By Simon Wood

"I suppose you know who I am?" she asked.

Crestfallen was a smart detective. He knew who she was. In the San Francisco Bay Area, it was hard not to know Jane Staam. In the week since her millionaire husband, Jack Staam, had nose-dived his car off Highway 1 and down the cliffs south of Stinson Beach, she had become a celebrity.

The Chronicle had reported the property developer's death as suicide. Business worries weren't to blame. You had to be a special kind of stupid not to make money in the property market in the Bay Area. Even Crestfallen was worth a small fortune thanks to his modest home he'd bought a few years back. He could move to Nutsack, Arkansas and live like a king. But who wanted to live in Nutsack, Arkansas?

Something much more devastating than a bad day at the office had caused Jack Staam to end it all. Prostate cancer. Staam was a depressed man who wanted to go out on his terms. He told his wife something cryptic then did the deed. Health was the great leveler. Not even the riches of Solomon could save someone from terminal illness. It didn't care who you were.

So, what brought Jane Staam to his office? She was the grieving wife, but public opinion had done an about-face when Staam's business partner had announced that Staam was planning a divorce and a change in his will. She was a signature away from losing her desirable status as next of kin and the cops had a case. She went from damsel to demon in a day.

"Mrs. Staam, what is it you think I can do for you?"

The redhead from the accounting firm next door drifted by his office. Normally, Crestfallen tracked her progress with avid interest, but not today. Jane Staam commanded any man's undivided attention. God had had a hand in her creation. She possessed shampoo commercial good looks, the kind the plebs would never attain. At forty time should have been eroding her, but, it wasn't. It was adding to her beauty. Maybe Staam's business partner was right and she had killed her husband. She had only to ask, "Oh be a dear, Jack, and drive off a cliff for me." Hell, Crestfallen knew he would have done it, if she'd asked him. The redhead looked distinctly miffed at being neglected, but she'd get over it.

"I need to prove Jack killed himself. The police are building a case against me. I don't have anyone rooting for me."

"What about friends?"

Her laugh was harsh. "Mr. Crestfallen, you find out who your friends are when the only reason they are friends disappears."

"Money?"

"You bet. My friends were friends of Jack's money."

"Well, let's get one thing clear. I'm not doing this out of friendship. You're purchasing my skills. I'll do my best to discover the truth, which might be good or might be bad. But, you don't buy me."

"You'll take the case?"

"It's about time I dusted off my shining armor." Crestfallen's smile was crooked.

"Thank God." She dug in her purse. "How much of a retainer do you require?"

Normally, someone of the Staam's ilk didn't need to put up a retainer. But he'd better get something while he could, in case things ended up going pear-shaped for his client.

"Five thousand. If that runs out, I'll bill you weekly."

She wrote him a check and handed it to him. A file came with the money.

"This is background for you. There's the doctor's diagnosis as well as Jack's psych profile."

"I'm sure it makes depressing reading."

"The divorce papers are in there too."

Crestfallen raised an eyebrow.

She noticed his response. "He never signed them."

"Why were they ever drawn up?" Crestfallen leafed through the paperwork, taking his eyes off Jane Staam for the first time.

"Mr. Crestfallen, every marriage goes through its ups and downs. We were on a down at the time."

"You can't get any more down than driving off a cliff."

The insinuation wounded Jane Staam and Crestfallen regretted the callous remark.

"Jack's cancer depressed him and he got angry a lot. He lashed out at everyone--even me. The divorce papers were a symptom of his illness."

Crestfallen closed the file and placed it on his desk. "Paperwork is great stuff, Mrs. Staam. It keeps desks from floating around. But I'm at my best when I'm interrogating, examining, and reconstructing. Stuff like that."

"Spoken like a true man of action." She smiled.

His face flushed. Stupid really, he was a grown man, not a lovesick teenager, but he couldn't help himself.

She smiled again.

"Where would you like to start?" she asked.

"The crash site."

The cliff was treacherous, but no more than any other lining that part of the Pacific Coast Highway. A smattering of guardrails provided feeble protection for speeding cars. Crumbling hillside ran onto the road. It was surprising more people hadn't been killed. Crestfallen peered over the edge. Scarred earth and ravaged foliage were a reminder of Jack Staam's violent death. Staring back at the lookout point and the highway, he imagined Staam's route into oblivion.

"And?" The sea breeze tugged at Jane's chestnut hair. "You've been silent long enough."

"I can see how a car could go off here by accident, let alone on purpose. Not much to look at though. Tire tracks are history. No way of telling whether his foot was on the gas or the brake when he went over the edge."

Jane flinched.

"Sorry, I didn't mean for that to sound the way it did. How do we get down to the beach?"

"Drive, then walk."

On the beach, Jane took off her shoes for the hike. She had pretty feet, sexy even. He wouldn't have expected anything less. They found police tape cordoning off the area. The car was gone, but oil-stained sand marked its final resting-place. Staam's descent from cliff to beach was very clear.

"Who's got the car?"

"The police."

"Who's the investigating officer?"

Garcia was as round as he was high. He wasn't fat, just unattractively muscular. Evolution hadn't been kind. And like all cops, he wasn't pleased to meet a rent-a-cop.

"Lieutenant Garcia, I'm Peter Crestfallen," Crestfallen said, offering a hand.

Garcia's granite handshake crushed Crestfallen's hand.

"Mrs. Staam's lawyers told me to expect you. C'mon."

Garcia led Crestfallen through the impound. He stopped in front of a red MG roadster that looked to have been chewed by a T-rex. Crestfallen guessed it had been in cherry condition before it lost its fight with gravity.

"Is it okay to touch?"

"But not to drive," Garcia growled.

Forcing the mangled driver's door open, Crestfallen slipped behind the wheel. He examined the car, trying to ignore Staam's blood on the busted windshield. He waggled the stick shift. It was in neutral.

"What a waste of a good car," Crestfallen lamented.

"And of a person," Garcia added, putting the comment in perspective.

"Staam *was* dying, right?"

"Yeah, but he wasn't dead. You might be breathing your last, but if I put a pillow over your face, it's still murder."

"Anything I should know? Cut brake lines, etcetera?"

"Look, Crestfallen. I'm not going to tell you squat. I don't want you spilling everything to your client."

"Lieutenant, I'm honor bound by my state license to divulge any crimes in my knowledge."

Garcia snorted. "Yeah, right."

"Don't believe in honest PI's?"

"Not while I've got a hole in my ass."

Crestfallen grinned. He didn't need to confirm that Garcia's hole was in existence. Garcia was all the asshole he needed to see.

"Are we finished here?" Garcia whined. "I have criminals to convict."

"I've got what I need."

Garcia yanked on the buckled door. It shrieked in pain and Crestfallen clambered out.

"Thanks, lieutenant, it's been very informative." Crestfallen grazed his hand on granite again.

Garcia stormed off in the direction of his office, leaving escort duties to one of the impound guys. Crestfallen waited until he was a suitable distance away.

"Lieutenant..." he called after Garcia.

Garcia stopped and turned.

"I hope to be the honest PI who'll seal up that tight ass of yours."

Crestfallen returned to his office to find a visitor. He was tall, around fifty, with plenty of tan. Crestfallen guessed who he was. It was only natural for him to pay a visit.

"Mr. Crestfallen, I'm Terrance Sykes, Jack Staam's business partner."

"Take a seat."

Both men sat. Crestfallen laced his fingers over his stomach and waited for the obvious to take place.

"The police tell me you're working for Jane."

"That's correct."

"Can I give you a piece of advice?

Crestfallen shrugged.

"Don't, Mr. Crestfallen."

"That's not your decision to make."

"I know Jane looks like a good client, but you're making a mistake."

Crestfallen wasn't so sure. In his experience, working for the underdog always went down well with the public and was good for subsequent business.

"Why should I drop Mrs. Staam?"

"Because you're getting in the way and only helping to delay things."

"May I ask why you're so interested in disinheriting...sorry, slip of the tongue, discrediting Mrs. Staam?"

"I object to your insinuation. Jack Staam was a close personal friend."

Isn't it always the way, Crestfallen thought. The press always receives startling revelations from close personal friends. God knows what a close personal enemy would say.

"I'm guessing you were to be Staam's new beneficiary. But that's not gonna happen now that he's dead and the new will was left unsigned. So, you're trying to stir things up and hopefully sway things your way, that it?"

"Jesus Christ, no wonder she came to you. Only someone as low as you could do her dirty work. And just for your information, no, I wasn't going to inherit everything. Jack told me that I would receive his shares in the company, but his wealth would go to charity. He was involved with a lot of charities."

What businessman wasn't? They all needed a tax write-off.

"Okay, let's ignore that you would become the CEO of Northern California's premier property development firm. Why did Staam have it in for his wife?"

"In facing death, Jack saw what the rest of us have known for years."

"Which is?"

"Jane Staam is a gold digging bitch. Do you know how they met?"

Crestfallen shook his head.

"In a Mervyns, for Christ's sake. She worked in menswear. She flirted and showed a little thigh. Next thing we all knew they were engaged."

"True love works as mysteriously as God. Not all millionaires find trophy wives at the country club."

"Screw you, Crestfallen. You don't know her. I do. She wanted a meal ticket and she got one."

"When did Staam have doubts?"

"After he told her his cancer was terminal, she started winding up shop."

"What do you mean?"

"A realtor in Hawaii left a message for Jane about some luxury house on Maui and a competitor contacted Jack directly regarding the sale of the business. Jane had said Jack was retiring." Sykes sneered triumphantly. "Am I convincing you, Mr. Crestfallen?"

"What about the divorce? The papers weren't signed. Anybody could have put them together. You, for instance."

Sykes snorted. "It was to be Jane's birthday present. He was going to serve her the papers. So, you see."

"See what?"

"She must have gotten wind and seen that she'd be out on her ass in a few months."

"But California is a no fault divorce state. She would have gotten half in the divorce settlement. Half of Staam's wealth is enough to live on in luxury."

"You don't get it, do you? And you're supposed to be a detective. The divorce papers were a joke."

"Not a very nice one."

"It wasn't meant to be. The divorce was to piss her off. The will was the important thing. He'd be dead before the divorce went through but the will would cut her out without a cent."

Sykes' cell chirped. He checked the display on the phone, but didn't answer it.

"I'm late for a meeting." He put the phone away and tossed a business card on Crestfallen's desk. "Call me if you drop the case. I'd be interested to hear why. You might impress me."

When Sykes was gone, Crestfallen made two calls, one to Jane and the other to Jack Staam's doctor. He made appointments to meet both the next day.

Staam's doctor was the opposite of Sykes. "I can't believe what they're saying about Jane. She doesn't seem like a murderer," Lehman babbled.

"That's probably why the police haven't arrested her."

"Good point," the baldheaded doctor acknowledged.

"I'd love to talk about Mrs. Staam, but I'm here about Jack Staam."

"I'm sure you're aware of a patient's right to privacy."

"Yes. I'm not after a case history, more your impression of Mr. Staam. Basically, in your opinion, do you think he was capable of suicide?"

Lehman tapped a finger against his top lip and exhaled. "Jack Staam was a very vital man. Highly active."

"So, you're saying, no?"

Lehman shook his head. "That's who he was. But the prostate cancer was ravaging his spirit as well as his body. We tried procedure after procedure, but once I told him medical science had done all that it could, it was like I pulled the plug. I hate to say it, but yes, I do think he was capable of suicide."

"Thank you, doctor." Crestfallen rose and shook Lehman's cool, dry hand. "You've been a great help. I'll leave you to your patients."

Lehman held the door open and Crestfallen thanked the doctor again.

"Really, it's no problem, but for a true evaluation, you should really talk to Jack's doctor."

Crestfallen froze. "Excuse me?"

"Jack's doctor."

"You're Jack Staam's doctor, aren't you?"

"I was. I referred him to a specialist, Doctor Tanaka, about four months ago."

The garage door crept up, revealing a red, chrome-bumper MG roadster. The car was in cherry condition, just like Jack Staam's should have been.

"Jack bought them as a pair," Jane explained.

Walking to the driver's door, Crestfallen ran a finger over the gleaming paintwork. "Well, it saved you some money finding another one."

"So, you want to recreate Jack's drive?"

Crestfallen nodded. "I like reconstructions. There's a lot to be said for them. And I doubt Lieutenant Garcia has done one."

Jane smiled and tossed him the keys. "Should give us the upper hand."

Crestfallen gunned the engine. It rasped. Echoes of a bygone era filled the garage. He smiled. Sometimes being a PI had its perks.

It didn't take long to get out of San Francisco and onto Highway 1. The road seemed entirely divorced from the overpopulated and overdeveloped city. It wasn't as convenient as the freeway, but the winding road that mimicked the Pacific Coast was refreshing. In a time of automatic this and electronic that, driving a classic sports car reminded Crestfallen there was a reason why cars needed drivers. He wished he didn't have a job to do.

"Terrance Sykes paid me a visit last night," Crestfallen announced after a lull in the conversation.

"What did he want?" she shouted over the howl of the wind that ripped through the cockpit and yanked at her perfect hair.

"He told me to drop the case. You weren't to be trusted, etcetera, etcetera."

"I'm glad you didn't listen to him."

"But I did listen."

A storm brooded in her stare.

"He helped put things in perspective." He paused. "The same way Doctor Lehman did."

"Doctor Lehman?" She couldn't mask her shock.

The road folded back on itself. Crestfallen threw the MG into the bend. A cautious driver, even a wise one, would have eased up on the gas. Crestfallen didn't. His foot became leaden on the accelerator. Protesting tires squealed. The back end fishtailed, but he kept it in check.

"The good doctor gave me his insight into Jack's fragile mind. In his opinion Jack was a broken man only a hint away from suicide."

"What did I tell you?" She was smiling but lightning flashed in her eyes. "Jack was unbalanced. He said he wanted to go out on his own terms. I told him not to talk like that. Life was life and I wanted to spend as much of it with him as I could."

"Touching."

They came out of a right-hander and the road ahead was a series of sharp S-curves. Oncoming vehicles whistled past in the opposite direction. Door mirrors were in danger of eloping with each other.

"Did you ever meet Doctor Tanaka?"

Her blank look was answer enough.

"He's Jack's other doctor."

Her mouth opened to deny the claim but she closed it to hear more. Confusion ruled her rich, emerald eyes. Her hair blew across her face and she didn't look so indestructibly beautiful.

"Lehman referred Jack to Tanaka when everything was at its bleakest. Tanaka is a marvel in cancer research. There was a documentary about him a couple of months ago. Do you ever watch PBS?" Crestfallen didn't give her time to answer. "Jack underwent radical treatment, as part of a clinical trial."

"And Tanaka couldn't help Jack either?"

Over the engine noise, Crestfallen couldn't tell if it was a question or a plea.

"He could and he did. Jack's cancer was in remission when he died. Tanaka didn't know how much time he had given Jack but it was enough for him to re-evaluate his life. Suicide wouldn't have been an option, I think you'll agree?"

"It seems out of character." Her words caught on the way out.

"You're right, Jane. It does seem out of character. But do you know what really seems out of character is that he didn't tell his loving wife about the treatment." Crestfallen looked away from the road and directly at Jane. "And that screws up a whole bunch of facts."

Speed limit signs paled against the speed Crestfallen wrung out of the MG. The bends seemed to tighten with every squeeze of the gas pedal. Tire squealing was commonplace. It was crazy driving. Other road users acknowledged their agreement with blaring horns. Crestfallen had to correct for the car's shortcomings.

"Do you think Jack drove like this, the night he drove off the road...a well man?"

"You're scaring me."

"I'm scared too. Scared that I'm sitting next to Jacks' murderer."

She whirled on him.

"You should have chosen a car with automatic transmission."

She tried to protest. He didn't let her.

"The stick shift gave you away."

"What do you mean?"

"When I was examining the car, I found it in neutral. Jack wouldn't have gotten far driving like that. I'd suspected you'd done it and Sykes, Lehman and Tanaka provided me with the motive. Because of Tanaka's help, his institute became the major beneficiary in the new will. You should have examined it. If you had, maybe you wouldn't have played the suicide angle."

"You still don't have any proof. It's all circumstantial. You're going to need a confession."

"I might not need one." Crestfallen pointed at the familiar lookout point at the end of long downward section of road. "Look familiar?"

"Expecting me to break down at the scene of the crime, Crestfallen?"

"No. I'm going to drive this car over the edge. If the car remains in gear, the jury will have a little extra to chew on."

Jane stared straight at Crestfallen. Her eyes bored into him, trying to read him. He didn't turn away. He let her see the truth.

"You really think this is going to work?" Jane hissed.

"I'm willing to find out, are you?"

"Stop the car now and you'll never have to work again."

"I like working. I just don't like being made a fool of. Besides, I don't think you're in a position to make a promise like that."

"You're pretty proud of yourself, aren't you?"

Crestfallen shrugged. "I have my good days."

"You're right; I didn't know he'd been cured. If I did, maybe I would have killed him differently."

"You still wouldn't have gotten any of his money."

"The money doesn't matter." She sounded like she meant it. "Do you know how Jack Staam made his fortune? Off the backs of others. My father learned that and our family paid for it. Jack sold him land that couldn't be developed. That broke my father. I grew up poor while Jack got richer. Then thirty years later, we met and I saw my chance. We married. I was going to ruin him from the inside out."

"But you were married five years."

Jane couldn't hide her shame. "I got to like the money too much. I enjoyed not scrimping and scraping."

"Until you found out about his cancer."

"No, when I saw him plan to do to someone else what he did to my father, I told him who I was and told him I'd bring him down. Then his cancer made anything I'd planned pointless and I decided to let him suffer awhile."

"But not once you found out about the will change."

"I didn't want him screwing my family twice."

"Has it all been worth it, Jane?" Crestfallen asked.

She smiled at him like he was a simple-minded child unable to comprehend the simplest of concepts. Crestfallen knew he would never understand her bitterness and loathing. That kind of hatred could never be comprehended. It originated from a unique place known only to the damaged.

Crestfallen hadn't been looking. He'd run out of road. The lookout point was dead ahead. He slammed on the brakes, the wheels immediately locked. The MG left the road for the lookout's unpaved surface. The car shook on the loose ground. Jane gripped the windshield, bracing herself for an impact that would never come. The roadster stopped inches from the cliff edge. It was a minute or so before Crestfallen could speak again.

"How did you get him out here?"

"I hit him across the head. I figured that no one would be able to tell after the crash. I drove him out here and pushed the car over the side."

"How did you get back to the city?"

"I had a car stashed nearby. Simple really."

Then the tough lady act fractured. Her façade shattered into a thousand pieces and she burst into wracking sobs. She threw herself into Crestfallen's open arms. He held her tight. He would do his best to help her, but he couldn't save her. He went to say something to comfort her, but the dry snap of the hammer being pulled back on his .357 that had been neatly lifted from his shoulder rig stopped him. He drew back from Jane and found the gun jammed under his chin and no tears on her face. Without being asked, he raised his hands.

"Get out," she commanded.

"Come on, Jane. Don't be stupid. How far do you think you're going to get now?"

"I'll get far enough, don't you worry."

Crestfallen believed her. Something in those cool emerald eyes told him she had a plan. She ushered him out of thc car with the gun. He did as he was told and she slipped into the driver's seat, keeping the gun trained on him.

"Keep the retainer, Crestfallen. Cash it while you still can."

Jane put the MG in gear and winked at him. He realized a fraction of a second too late what she was going to do. She floored the gas pedal and the roadster leapt forward. Crestfallen dove at the car, but it tossed him off like a novice bull rider. He hit the ground hard. Gravel ate through his jacket and flesh. The MG disappeared over the edge, taking Jane Staam with it.

Crestfallen stood, massaging his wounds. He tottered over to the cliff edge and peered over the side. Jane lay on the beach. The totaled MG, on its roof with one wheel still spinning, smothered her body from the waist down. He decided this ending was probably for the best. Everything else had been on Jane's terms, why not her death?

Crestfallen removed his cell and dialed the police. He asked for Garcia and got him. "Lieutenant, how's that ass of yours?"

"Is that you, Crestfallen?" he barked.

"Do you want to realize a dream and meet an honest PI?" Crestfallen asked and picked a chunk of gravel from the heel of his hand. "If so, meet me at Jack Staam's crash site."

Simon Wood is a California transplant from England. His current book is *Dragged Into Darkness,* a short story collection from Medium Rare Books. Readers are welcome to visit *http://www.simonwood.net.*

A House Divided
by John L. French

The phone was ringing when I got into my office. My machine picked up before I could. A woman's voice came on.

"Matthew, I need you. Call me right away."

I knew the voice. The woman it belonged to was tall, very attractive and financially well off. And she needed me. Every single man's dream. Except that this woman's interest in me was solely professional.

Sharon Manchester was a lawyer, one of the best, no, *the* best defense attorney in Baltimore. We had a past, she and I. A case I was working ended with her being forced out of her corporate practice and into criminal law. A break for both of us. It turned out she had a talent for keeping people out of jail, and, once she'd forgiven me, she called on me whenever she needed the services of a good investigator.

I called her private number.

"About time," she barked into the phone without greeting. Caller ID has ruined telephone courtesy for some people. But not for me.

"And good morning to you too, Ms. Manchester. What's the problem and how can I help?"

"Murder," was all she said before hanging up. She always did know how to get my attention. Twenty minutes later I walked into her office.

Sharon was at her desk. As the man sitting across from her stood up I saw the scratches on his left cheek and a mark by his right eye that would be a bruise in a few hours.

"Matthew," Sharon said, again ignoring the pleasantries most of us use to get through life, "this is ..."

"I know," I said, recognizing him from the papers. "His name is Legion ..."

The man smiled and completed the phrase, "For we are many."

His name wasn't really Legion, it was Doe. First name, well, that depended on just who you were talking to.

Starting life as Brian Drake, in his twenties Doe was diagnosed with Multiple Personality Disorder. Putting it simply, his mind, his psyche was fragmented into many different personas, each with its own purpose, each with its own role to play in how Drake dealt with the world around him.

The diagnosis came as a relief to Drake, whose behavior up until then had been considered the result of anything from drugs to paranoid schizophrenia. "I was glad to know," one article quoted him, "that the voices in my head were just me talking to myself, that they really were there."

Once diagnosed, Drake began the usual therapy for such patients, that of gradually merging his various personalities into one unified whole. It was a long process, taking up many hours of therapy. A year after it started, Drake was down to five main personas.

That's when the fun started. One of the personalities decided that he liked things just the way they were. During a time when he had conscious control of Drake's body, he hired a lawyer, our very own Ms. Manchester. In court, Ms. Manchester argued that her client, who for the purposes of the trial used the name "William Doe," was a person in his own right and that integration would cause this person to "cease to be," in effect, killing the entity known as William Doe.

The other four personas fought the suit, claiming that "William" was merely part of a fragmented whole and therefore had no individual rights.

But you know all this. How could you have missed it? Reporters from magazines, newspapers and every local and national network in the country descended on Baltimore, everybody with cable access watched the trial on a daily basis - they all wanted to see a man sue himself for custody.

Everyone had an opinion, and those with degrees made money renting themselves out as experts to the media outlets. Attorneys discussed the possible legal ramifications of having two or more people inside the same body. Political experts argued whether Drake/Doe was entitled to one vote or five. And the only thing the army of psychologists that were paraded by us agreed upon was that Drake's condition was *not* schizophrenia.

Aside from watching both the "right to life" and "right to choose" groups trying to figure out whose side they were on, my favorite part of the whole mess was the sight of Drake changing seats in court. Ms. Manchester would question a witness. Before the defense could cross, Doe would leave the plaintiff's table and walk over to the defense side, his expression and mannerisms changing subtly as he gave way to one or another of his other personas.

The ease with which Drake switched personalities amazed some mental health experts. Some argued that this was evidence that he was faking the whole thing. Others said that it was a tribute to the treatment he had received so far that the different facets of his mind were able to cooperate to such an extent. In fact, this was a key defense point - that Drake's ability to "change his mind" so readily argued in favor of the fact that he was nearly wholly integrated, and should be allowed to complete the process.

In the end it didn't matter what any of the experts or special interest groups thought. It came down to the opinion of one woman in a black robe.

Ruling from the bench almost immediately after closing arguments, Judge Gertrude Devereux ruled that "It is this court's decision that the persona of William Doe, currently housed in the collective body of Brian Drake, is a legal entity in his own right." She then enjoined the remaining personae from continuing any treatment that would lead to William's melding with the other four.

After her ruling, Judge Devereux waited for the inevitable "Notice of Appeal" by the defense. Instead, the defense presented the court with a petition to name "Brian Doe, Drake Doe, Charles Doe and Brenda Doe," (that's right, one of the personas was a female) legal entities as well, all residing with William Doe in a collective body. The judge agreed and five people walked out of the courtroom on one pair of legs.

In his press conference afterwards, the defense attorney explained what had happened. "My clients, having just sustained the expense of hiring two legal teams, simply could not afford to continue with an appeal. Their petition to be named as persons in their own right was done simply to protect their interests."

It should have ended there. After the books and the movie and the failed sitcom loosely based on their life, the Does should have faded from public consciousness. And they would have, if William hadn't decided to run for a seat on Baltimore's City Council, his slogan - "Five for the Price of One."

The other four stopped William the only way they could, they all ran against him. With the vote split five ways, their opponent won easily.

And now here I was standing in a lawyer's office with the Does, and the subject was murder. It looked very much like they were going to be in the public eye again.

"So who'd you kill?" I asked Doe as he sat back in the chair. I took the one next to him.

Before answering, Doe took a pack of cigarettes from the left inside pocket of his suit coat. Lighting up without asking either of us if we minded, he inhaled and let out a puff before answering, "I didn't kill anyone."

I took a guess based on what I'd read about the Does and saw during the trial.

"And what about your roommates, William?" The look he gave me told me I'd been right. Before he could ask, I added, "I am a detective."

"Let me tell it, William," Sharon said from behind her desk then turned to me. "Last night William had a social engagement with a young lady. He spent the night, or rather, he fell asleep in her bed. Charles woke up first. When he did he saw that the woman was on the floor. She'd been beaten to death."

"Any chance of an intruder? Husband, jealous boyfriend?" I didn't think there was, but it's best to get the obvious questions out of the way first.

William shook his head. "The door was bolted. Besides, Drake's a light sleeper. He would have woken up. It had to have been one of us."

"And you don't know which one?" Another shake. "Why not? Don't you all look out the same pair of eyes?"

"It's not like that," William said. "We're not always conscious all at the same time. At times, the only one aware is the one in charge of the body. The rest of us are - well, it's like a light sleep, call it dozing. Other times, one or more of us are awake but just watching."

"And who's awake now?" I asked.

"We all are. It takes an effort, but we can do that when it's something important going on."

"Like now?" He nodded. "And what about last night? Any onboard voyeurs?"

"It's hard to tell just who's awake, but we do try to respect each other's privacy. No one likes an audience. I really don't care, but it bothered Doris."

"Doris was the ..."

The look on his face - sadness, regret, guilt? It came and went so fast I couldn't tell. "The ..." he paused for the word.

"Doris Randall, the victim." Sharon said matter of factly.

"And how'd you find out she was dead?"

"Charles woke us all up."

"And you didn't kill her?"

"No!"

"And you don't know who did? Nobody let anything slip while you were all waking up?"

William sighed. "No. We had dinner, we went home, we made love, we fell asleep. That's all I know. I cared for Doris. If I knew who killed her I'd tell you."

"Let me talk to Drake. Wait." I turned to Sharon. "They're all your client now?"

"Yes. All of them, even if I only get one fee from the lot."

"Okay, Drake. Come on down."

Doe changed. Slowly, William gave way to Drake. His face became softer, less angry looking. His whole body relaxed. He gave me an amused grin, "Like I haven't heard that one before." Drake's voice was higher than William's, much higher.

He looked at the cigarette in his right hand. "Nasty habit," he muttered, and stubbed it out in the ashtray on the corner of Sharon's desk. He smacked his lips, grimacing at the taste left in his mouth. Reaching into his right coat pocket, he took out a mint and popped it into his mouth, throwing the wrapper next to the butt.

Legs crossed, hands cupped on his knee, Drake "For the record, I didn't kill the girl. In fact I had nothing to do with her. My tastes don't run that way."

I shrugged. Big deal. "Must be nice then, living with three other men."

Drake smiled, "They certainly don't enjoy my nights out. Brenda does, however. As I do hers. We share."

"Your bed partners don't mind?"

"Who tells them?"

I changed the subject back to the murder. "What do you know about last night?"

Drake gave me a look of disgust and a small shoulder shrug. "Not much. I had the body that afternoon, I had some work to finish. William took over for his date and I went offline. I did wake up briefly last night."

"What time?"

He shrugged again. "Couldn't tell. It was dark and I was in a strange bed."

"Alone?"

“I'm never alone, but I know what you mean. There was a body in bed with me. Knowing who it was, I went back to sleep. The next thing I knew, Charles was waking us all up."

"What did you do then?"

"Got dressed and left right away."

The key to interrogating suspects in a murder is to question them apart, then compare stories, see what doesn't match. I thought about this while I was talking to Drake. They were all in there, watching and listening, no doubt editing their versions of what they did and saw based on what each one said. Still, you played the hand you were dealt even when the deck was stacked and hoped you were the better cheat.

Brian Doe wasn't any help. Aside from spitting out Drake's second mint and lighting up his own brand of smokes - menthol versus William's unfiltered - he claimed to have "gone away" right after fixing dinner that night. (It was his turn to cook.) Like Drake, he was unaware of the murder until alerted by Charles.

Saving the one who found the body for last, I next talked to Brenda. Like the others, her appearance was accompanied by a complete change in mannerisms. Passive to William's aggressive, features animated compared to Brian's complete lack of expression, she was most like Drake. But where his effeminate movements and body language seemed affected, Brenda's were much more natural. Talking to her and listening to her high-toned voice, I briefly felt like the only man in the room.

"I really wish I could help you, Mr. Grace, I do. But I really was not paying attention that night. What William and that woman were going to do, well, despite the situation I find myself in I'm not really into women."

"Drake says you and he sometimes share."

"Drake's a horrible gossip and more than a bit of a bitch." That said, Brenda's eyes rolled slightly back into her head. "Yes, I meant that," she said to herself. "Well then, go ahead." When her eyes rolled back to me she said, "He's sulking. We probably won't be hearing from him the rest of the day."

"Did you hear or see anything last night, Ms. Doe?"

"I did wake up once. Not in control, just for the ride, mind you. William and that woman were, well, let's just say they weren't sleeping. I went right back out. And the next thing I knew, Charles was shouting us awake."

"Okay, let me talk to him."

Another complete change. When Charles took over, Doe became the kind of man you trusted right away. Leaning back in the chair, he relaxed completely, looking me right in the eye, nothing to fear, nothing to hide.

"It's about time," he said, but with a smile to let me know he was just joking.

"Saving the best for last. Did you kill Doris Randall?" I gave him a smile back. If he thought I was joking, fine.

"No," he said simply, not taking offense at the question.

"Do you know who did?"

"If so, you wouldn't be needed."

Good point, which reminded me of something I had to ask Sharon. But I wanted to finish with Charles first.

"How did you find the body?"

"Dead. Sorry, poor joke. I woke up early, I often do - I'm the morning person of the group. When I woke up, the first thing I noticed was that the bed was wet. Now I, or rather, we, haven't wet the bed since the age of seven, when our body finally got tired of the beatings. I switched on the light and saw the blood. Doris was on the floor. She'd been beaten rather badly." Charles held up his hands, showed me his knuckles. They were badly bruised, with partly healed lacerations. "No question that one of us did it."

"I take it that's what you're hiring me to find out--which one?" I asked Sharon.

"Exactly," she confirmed.

There were a number of questions still open, I'd get to them later. But first I asked, "What's the police view on this?"

Sharon sighed, "They haven't been called yet."

"What!" I shouted loud enough to startle whoever was in the next two offices. "Why the Hell not?"

"Matthew," Sharon said calmly, "my obligation is to my client, or clients as it were. We all know that as soon as the murder comes to light, the investigation will lead back to the Does. They'll be arrested, despite the fact that only one of them is guilty. If you can discover which one did it, this can all be resolved quickly, and without another media circus."

"Resolved how?"

"Just go to the scene, find out what you can. When you come back, we'll talk more."

Lawyers. If they weren't such a source of steady income, and if I didn't need them to keep out of jail myself from time to time, I'd have nothing to do with them.

On my way to the crime scene, I tired to figure out just why Sharon needed me. Doris Randall's body was bound to be discovered sooner or later. Hell, there was a better than even chance the police were already at the scene. After Randall was found, it wouldn't take the police long to connect her to the Does. And the circus Sharon was worried about would start.

There was no way the Does were not going to be arrested. I knew the head of the homicide unit and had matched wits with him several times. Detective Lieutenant Joshua Parker would not listen to Sharon's "You can't arrest the guilty person without locking up four innocent people." To Parker, they'd all be guilty. He'd lock them up and let the courts sort it out.

In court Sharon would, no doubt, make the same argument, that it's better for a guilty man to go free than for four innocents to be jailed. The great State of Maryland would argue against Judge Devereux's civil ruling - that the Doe collective was legally one person. With that Sharon would have the Does pull out five drivers' licenses, five voter and library cards and five social security numbers. With that the state's argument would fall apart, and the Does would go free, killer and all.

Which led me back to why Sharon needed me. Surely not knowing was better, reasonable doubt and all that. Maybe she thought my discovering which persona was the killer would give her an edge. If so, that was okay. I had an edge too. I already had a fairly good idea who it was.

To my surprise, there were no patrol cars surrounding the Park Avenue apartment where William and his friends had left Doris.

Using the access code Charles had given me I let myself into the building. His key opened the apartment door.

Taking out my digital camera, I snapped photos from the doorway. I wanted a visual record of what the apartment looked like before Parker accused me of tampering with evidence. Once I had the living room recorded I did the same for the dining room and kitchen. No signs of disturbance yet, but I knew the main show was in the bedroom.

It was as advertised. The bedroom was neat, clean and well ordered, except for the body on the floor. After taking my photos from the doorway, I walked over and took a closer look.

Before becoming a private investigator, I'd been a crime lab technician for the BPD. In the ten years I worked crime scenes I'd seen many a horrific sight - burned bodies, dead children, slaughtered families. For shear savagery this was right up there - her face battered beyond recognition, the bruises on her torso and arms telling me of the beating she'd taken while still alive.

I knew then what I had to do. I took one last look around the apartment, photographing what I saw - Doris's body, the spatters on the wall, the blood covering the sheets. That done, I called the police.

I know what you're thinking - good little PI's aren't supposed to do that. They're supposed to wipe down all surfaces, remove the one critical piece of evidence that would convict their client, then get the Hell out of Dodge, leaving the police to find the body on their own. Well, maybe on TV and in the books you read, but in real life that kind of behavior only gets you the top bunk in the Grey Bar Hotel.

But what, you ask, about my responsibility to my client? Which one, the killer or the four who just may be lying about knowing what happened? Or the lawyer who was going to use me to see that a killer walked free? No, right just then my responsibility was to the girl on the floor, to see that somebody, somehow paid for her death. Right or wrong, that was what I was thinking when I took out my phone and called Parker's office number.

It would take time for Parker to have a patrol unit respond to the building, even longer for them to get from the lobby to the eighth floor. Time enough for what I had to do. When the uniforms came in, I was sitting at Doris Randall's desk with my hands neatly folded in my lap. The two cops checked my ID, searched me for weapons (I didn't have any), then proceeded to make certain that the rest of the apartment was secure, stopping to look at the dead body along the way. Besides asking who I was and could I prove it, neither talked to me.

Parker showed up with his detectives twenty minutes later.

"Good morning, Lieutenant," I greeted him when he arrived. (It was still slightly shy of noon.)

He gave me a head nod and uttered a surly "Grace" then went into the bedroom. When he came out he looked at me and asked, "You touch anything?"

I tried to look shocked and insulted. "I know better than to disturb a crime scene."

"I know you know better, Grace. That doesn't mean you wouldn't do it."

The man knows me all too well, even if this time I was innocent. "Lieutenant, I called you, remember? If I was going to fiddle with evidence, I wouldn't have hung around."

"We'll see," he grudgingly acknowledged. "Tell it."

I gave him the digest version. "I was called this morning by a lawyer whose client reported that a murder had taken place in this apartment. The lawyer hired me to check things out and proceed accordingly. Things checked out, and I called you."

"And the names of the client and lawyer are ..."

"Privileged." Parker gave me an "I might have known" look and was deciding on how mad to get with me when I added, "for now."

"What do you want?"

"I stay and watch your investigation. What you learn, I learn. Afterwards, I'll tell you everything you need."

"And if I decide to take you downtown and put you in a little room until I get back?"

"Then this, and any further conversation we might have are over. And a killer just might go free."

Parker didn't like me very much, but he knew me, had known me from when I worked scenes as a crime lab tech. He decided I wasn't bluffing.

"Okay," he agreed, "you can stay. But first," he held out his hand, "give it over."

"I'm unarmed, ask them," I said, pointing to the uniforms that had first responded. "They do a nice frisk."

"You may not carry a gun, Grace, but you're never without a camera. Give it over." Parker's hand was still out. Reluctantly I handed him my digital.

By now the lab techs had arrived. I didn't recognize either of them, new hires I guessed. If they had heard of me at all it was probably the cautionary tale of how and why I left the department and would have been warned to stay away. Parker called one of them over and handed him the camera.

"What's on here?"

The tech powered up the camera, pressed the right buttons to display any photos I may have taken. None showed.

"Empty, Lieutenant."

Again Parker held out his hand. "Don't make me ask again, Grace. Or I will have you strip searched right here and now.

The last time Parker caught me on a crime scene and confiscated my camera he settled for removing the flash card, not stopping to think that I may have switched it for a new one. It seems he learned from his mistake. I took an envelope from my jacket pocket and handed it to him. He passed it on to the tech.

The lab tech took out the flash card and loaded it into the camera. She then displayed all the photos I had so carefully taken. "Nice work," she said, handing me the camera back but keeping the card. Parker had trained her well.

"Nice try, Grace." To the lab tech he said. "Mr. Grace is going to watch. If he touches anything, shoot him. Or rather, call me and I'll shoot him."

Parker left me to see what, if anything his detectives had come up with. I followed the crime lab techs around. They photographed and sketched the scene. Then one of them dusted for prints while the other started to collect evidence. Using tweezers he carefully picked the cigarette butts from the bedroom ashtray and put them in small envelopes. Small pieces of clear plastic from the floor went into a separate envelope. He looked around, except for the bedclothes and the blood samples, there wasn't anything else. That was okay, I'd seen everything I needed to see.

An idea had started forming when I saw the tech collect the butts. Things gelled when he picked up the plastic. I suddenly had a clear idea of what had happened last night, and why.

"Lieutenant," I called. Parker came into the room. "Let's take a ride." I hoped I was in time to prevent what might be another murder.

On the way back downtown, much to his surprise, I leveled with Parker - about Sharon hiring me and who her clients were.

"Damn," he swore softly. He knew as well as I did the legal difficulty of convicting twenty percent of somebody and the national press coverage the attempt would bring.

"Hey, at least your job is done with the arrest. It's the State's Attorney's office that's got to win in court."

"Grace, you should know my job isn't done until the killer's locked up for good. And from where I'm sitting, the only time the s.o.b.'s going to spend in jail is however long it takes for him to make bail."

"Maybe not." And I told him what I thought was going to happen, what, in fact, had probably happened right after I left Sharon's office. Then I told him what he could do about it. It was enough to make him almost like me.

We walked into Sharon's office without waiting to be announced. The Does were still there. I thought they'd be.

"Matthew," Sharon said in surprise when I walked through the door, "what are you ..." Surprise changed to anger when Parker followed me in. "What is he doing here?"

"Sorry, Sharon, couldn't help it. The good lieutenant twisted my arm."

Parker, who I've never known to tell a lie, remained silent. Sharon looked at me doubtfully. I don't think she bought my attempt to hide the fact I'd changed sides.

Ignoring them both, I went over to our clients. Coming up close and looking them in the eyes, I said, "I want to talk to William."

I watched as a variety of expressions passed over the face in front of me - Brian's nearly blank stare, Drake's amused superiority, Brenda's animated features, Charles's directness - all of them went by at least once. It was as if they were trying to decide who was going to talk. Nowhere did I see a trace of William.

They settled on Drake. "So you guessed it, William was the killer."

"It was no guess, gentlemen and lady," I said, knowing they were all listening. "I knew before I left this morning."

"I don't see how." Still Drake.

"Matthew," Sharon said in warning, nodding towards Parker.

"It doesn't matter, let him listen," I told her. Then to the Does I said, "William said that he and Doris shared dinner, then her bed. Afterwards, he fell asleep and didn't wake up until Charles sounded the alarm. Yet Brenda said that during the night she woke up to find Doris and one of you having sex. If that someone was William, there was no reason for him not to mention it. Since he didn't, it must have been another one of you."

"So someone got a freebie, big deal."

"So it gives us motive. Maybe Doris knew who it was, maybe not. But while she was with whoever, William woke up, didn't he?"

Not waiting for an answer, I went on. "William woke up, and didn't like what he found. Doris was his, and one of you took her from him. Since he couldn't take it out on himself, he took it out on her."

This time I waited. Eventually Drake said, "Hard to prove."

"Then let William come out and deny it."

There was another long pause. "He can't," Drake finally said. "He's gone."

"What!" Sharon shouted. There was no reaction from Parker. I'd told him to expect this.

"Explain."

Drake sighed. "Of course we knew it was William. Like he said, I'm a light sleeper. I woke up when he started beating her. I tried to stop him, but he was too much in control. I woke the others but even together we couldn't stop him."

"So you came here, hoping Ms. Manchester could find a way out, lying to protect William, right?"

"Right, we thought if no one knew which of us it was, the police couldn't make an arrest."

'The rest of you," I said, trying to look past Drake, "is that true?"

Drake faded, Charles came out. "Speaking for all, yes."

Parker, who had been uncharacteristically silent through this, finally spoke. "So what happened to the William part of you?"

"We thought that by keeping quiet we'd stay out of jail. After Mr. Grace left, Ms Manchester pointed out that …"

"Just a minute," Parker interrupted. "Anyone mind if we do this by the book?"

"What do you mean, Lieutenant?" Sharon asked.

"Well, since it's clear that your client, or part of him, anyway, did kill someone, I'm going to have to arrest him. So I think Miranda would be a good idea right about now."

"As a matter of law, Lieutenant," Sharon replied, "the killer may no longer be here. If so, then any arrest may subject you to a civil suit."

Parker smiled. I'd seen that smile before. Sharon hadn't. If she had, the interview would have been over. "I'll take my chances, Ms. Manchester." He then read the Miranda warnings. To be absolutely sure, he read them four times, insisting that each persona come out and acknowledge that he or she understood the rights as read.

"Are you done?" Drake again, obviously the group spokesman. "Well, as Charles was about to say, Ms. Manchester told us we would be going to jail no matter what, and that it might be some time before she could get us released. That changed things."

Drake paused. Collected his thoughts. "Before William sued us, we were close to unification. Only the court order forced us to live together. When it became clear that it was either all of us or William …"

I finished for him. "You ganged up on him. The four of you used his guilt combined with your strong desire to be one and what, divided him among you?"

"Something like that. Anyway, he's gone."

"And so is your killer, Lieutenant," Sharon added. "So go ahead and arrest them. I already have the writ of habeas corpus drawn up for Judge Devereux. With William gone, all you have left are four innocent people."

"Maybe," I said quietly, "maybe not."

"What do you mean, Matthew?"

I stood, walked over to her computer. "May I?" She nodded. I logged on to the Internet, then to an online email service. Entering my user name and password, I brought up the mail I'd sent myself from Doris's apartment and downloaded the attachment. Thumbnail photos of the crime scene came up.

"Grace!" Parker was none to happy with me.

"Before you ask, Lieutenant, I had some time before you guys arrived. While I was waiting, I downloaded the pictures from my camera into Ms. Randall's computer, then emailed them."

Parker gave me a cold stare, realizing that there was no way he could stop me from doing the same thing the next time. "I should have just taken the damned camera," he muttered, loud enough for me to hear. I got the message. I could have my fun, but it would cost me.

Clicking on the photos, I gave Sharon a tour of the crime scene, talking as each image came up. "As I said, I had William pegged as the killer from the start. I went to the scene thinking I might find something that would change my mind. I didn't."

I brought up a picture of Doris's beaten body. "This was done in anger. A stranger couldn't have done this …" a close-up of her face "… or this …" zoom in on her split lip and broken teeth, "… or this …" around the eyes …

"Okay, Matthew, we get the point." First time I ever heard Sharon get emotionally upset. I guess lawyers don't like to see what their clients are capable of.

Back to a general shot of the room. "Yeah, that's enough. You can see why I didn't want anyone from this group to get away with anything. But while waiting for the police to arrive I started thinking about the one who had sex with Doris - the other one, not William. Why? Why would one of them do something that he or she had to know would upset William to such a degree? And granted, maybe one of them couldn't have stopped him, but surely all of them working together could have. And we know I was right about that."

I pulled another series of shots. "This ashtray," I zoomed in, "There's William's brand, but those other two, they're Brian's menthols, aren't they?" Another photo, zoom in to the floor. "And aren't these candy wrappers from the mints Drake eats to kill the cigarette taste?"

I looked at the client, wondering which one was running things now. It didn't matter.

"You planned it, probably had been planning it for some time. What did you do? Watch William and Doris get it on, then wait until they fell asleep? The rest of you stayed up - long enough for a few smokes and a couple of mints. Then one of you woke Doris, and while he was having his fun another one woke William."

"How could we know how he'd react?" one of them asked, Charles maybe, it was his tone of voice.

"Because when everything's considered, he was a part of you. You knew where his trigger was, and you pulled it."

"But why would we?" Higher pitched voice, nervous, Brenda. If they were truly different people I'd separate them and work on her. She'd break first.

"Because you're tired of living in a time share. You want unity, and William and the court order kept you from achieving it. But now, William's gone. You used his emotional distress and your collective will to do what otherwise could only have been done in therapy, therapy the law would not allow."

I gave that a moment to set in, then went on. "And all you had to do was provoke William into killing someone, then wait to be arrested. That would give you an excuse to get rid of him, and the law couldn't touch you, because the 'person' responsible would no longer exist."

"A nice theory, Matthew," Sharon said once I'd finished, "but of course there's no way to prove it. And even if you could, so what? Regardless of the provocation, it was William Doe and William Doe alone who killed Doris Randall."

It was time to drop the big one "A nice summation, Sharon. If I were a juror, I'd acquit. But you forgot one thing. Everyone in this room heard your clients admit to destroying the persona of William Doe who at the time was legally a separate human being, entitled to the protection of the great State of Maryland. Lieutenant?"

Parker did the honors. Standing up and walking over to where they were sitting, he said, "Charles Doe, Brenda Doe, Drake Doe, Brian Doe - you are all under arrest for the murder of William Doe." Five minutes later, he was leading them out of the office.

Much to the dismay of every paper, news magazine and TV network, there was no trial. Faced with being tried as four people for the "death" of William Doe, or as one for the murder of Doris Randall, the four plead out on the condition that their therapy be resumed. And soon there was one - Brian Drake, together again, looking forward to a new life, which he'd be able to enjoy in about ten to twenty years.

French is a CSI supervisor for the Baltimore PD. He oversees the preservation and collection of evidence from crime scenes, an interest he builds on in numerous short stories. Look for THE DEVIL OF HARBOR CITY by John L. French, Wild Cat Books http://my.lulu.com/wildcatbooks.

The Girl in Apartment 2A

By G. Miki Hayden

Carol Ann prided herself on sleeping through the night, which she achieved by never drinking liquids after 8 p.m. But something had awakened her that morning, so she got up and looked east out her window through the visual alleyway formed by the back of buildings on St. Mark's Place--where she saw…my God…the rosy fingers of dawn themselves.

Ah, that was what the classical poet--whoever he might have been--had meant. Those were they, the fingers, exactly rose pink, as explicitly promised. What a marvel! In a moment, she lay down, went right back to sleep, and didn't get up again until the radio began to play at 9:35, precisely the time she was slated to awaken. Perfection.

As she was eating two eggs she had scrambled in a small enamel saucepan--she had never gotten around to buying a frying pan and didn't really like the word "frying," anyway--her doorbell rang. That was inexplicable.

"Who is it?" she called. Maybe she ought to buy that frying pan. She could bop bad people on the head with it. They called them skillets, too, she suddenly realized, and she could get one in traditional iron.

"Police," came a nicely timbered male voice.

Putting her eye to the peephole, Carol Ann peered out, then opened the door, though still leaving on the chain. She pulled her red silk, Chinese houserobe together at the top. "How do I know you're the police?" she questioned cautiously. But she liked his looks and nodded when he flashed a badge, then thought the better of it and reached out, steadying his hand to study the NYPD shield. "Nice," she concluded. They must make those things in some kind of metal press. She tried to imagine the process (they would set the machine to number sequentially), while observing him again.

Cute, she had to admit. He was deadly cute and, interestingly enough, both of them were blond. Also, he wasn't any taller than five foot eight, while she just about hit the five-foot mark. She took off the chain.

"We're investigating an incident that occurred sometime this morning at the back of the building, ma'am. Did you hear anything?" He gazed at Carol Ann intently.

She didn't have to smile at him because she was already smiling--who wouldn't at the sight of a hunk like him? He was young, too, not that much older than she--and she was 26--so maybe he wasn't married yet. She could *not* go out with a married man. Not after the last time.

"Hear anything? What happened?" She paused. "Oh… the rosy fingers of dawn…"

"Excuse me, ma'am?" He didn't flinch, but she could tell what he was thinking.

Carol Ann shook her head as if ridding him of his wrong-minded notion. "That helps pinpoint the time, you see," she explained. "I didn't look at the clock when I got up because I keep it on the opposite side of the room, but I looked out the window."

His eyes were still wide upon her and she knew she wasn't detailing the matter entirely right. Precise communication was so very important. "The clouds were lit by the rising sun, so all we need to know is what time the sun came up this morning and how many degrees above the horizon it usually is when the clouds appear rosy. This way we'll know the time that I woke up."

"Fascinating," the handsome policeman murmured empathetically. She liked the way he was dressed, too, businesslike in a suit, but not *looking* like a guy wearing a suit, so to speak.

"Yes," she agreed eagerly. "Because I never ordinarily wake up until the radio comes on. That means I did hear a commotion in the back--but without knowing I had. And it establishes the time. For the trial."

"The trial, ma'am?"

"Supposing one was held, of course." Should she invite him in for an espresso? She wasn't sure how much coffee she had left. "What happened, anyway?"

The policeman sighed. "A man was murdered behind the building. Joseph Olesku, who ran the tattoo parlor on the ground floor. Know him?"

Carol Ann stopped smiling and took a step back, away from the door. "Oh my God…well, I…I didn't know him, really… Oh, how awful. I…I said hello to him sometimes, if he was standing outside on a really nice day. He didn't do a very good business, I don't think, but I don't know. How did it happen?"

"Ma'am, I'm going to give you my card, in case you think of something definite, or if you can recall what you heard in the alley last night." The look he presented to her with the card demonstrated some doubt as to that possibility.

She almost went to get her own card from her bag, but then realized that the phone number on it wouldn't be right. She was living a new life now, anyway, and didn't need reminders of her past floating around in her present. "You have a notebook, I suppose," Carol Ann said. "I'll give you my name and number and you can write that down."

When she came out of the building at 10:43, the sidewalk was cluttered with police, and an ambulance was parked alongside the curb. She didn't see Detective Edward Green, only uniformed cops. She wondered if they called him Ed--or Eddie. Eddie was better, maybe. Ed sounded too husky.

She was going to be nearly on time for work today. Amazing. Despite stopping to chat with Eddie when he had come by. Now, she didn't dawdle, but clacked her way to the corner in a pair of brown sandals she had bought at a thrift shop near Thompkins Square Park. Waiting for the light to change on Second Avenue, she thought she recognized the man to her right. She turned and smiled and said "hi"--such a small town thing to do. She reddened.

"Oh," he responded, startled. "I didn't think you'd remember me."

"Of course," she assured him, although she didn't. "How are you?" Someone from her old life, was her best guess.

"Well... I..."

The light turned and she rushed off, waving at him enthusiastically as she hurried, nearly tripping in the strange new shoes. She had never been a sandal person.

She didn't have to punch in at work, but Barry, her boss, always noted any deviations from the set schedule, and, when she was late, she had to make up however many minutes she lost. But, obviously, an expectation of that sort was entirely fair. From an hourly employee, one expected the hours, full and complete.

She took a sip of the green tea she got as a perk of the job and went online, pulling orders from their website, then processing them, laying bottles of hard-to-find herbs and other special supplements into the proper-sized boxes, then carefully billing the credit card numbers while making up invoices. Not a complicated operation. Tedious, actually. That was what she had been looking for, in fact: work that didn't place an intellectual demand on her and which was routine. But she wouldn't have minded if the job paid a whole lot better.

Her thoughts kept straying back to the murder. Snatches of memories of minor interactions with the tattoo artist came to mind. She couldn't recall anything special, which seemed a shame.

Murder. The most prohibited and horrific human act.

If she'd waited a while, she probably would have seen them bring him out in a zippered, black polyethylene bag, but she was glad she hadn't, because even the thought of such a thing made her shudder. Yet how had he been killed?

She left about three after finishing the orders from the day's mail and, though nearly faint with hunger, she'd made up her mind. She headed straight for the precinct house nearby on 5th Street. She didn't want Eddie to forget her and she thought she looked much better now in a brown, terribly short mini skirt and beige tank top than she had in her robe--although the red silk went quite nicely with her pale complexion.

Luckily, he was in front of the building when she arrived, so she didn't have to ask for him by name. He even knew who she was without being reminded. She followed him upstairs.

Quite obviously at home here, he took his seat at a shabby desk that looked as if a generation of police officers had written phone numbers on the surface, not wanting to mar the scattered papers lying everywhere around the room-- flowing from both *in* and *out* boxes and spilling over half-open filing cabinet drawers… She refused the chair that he offered her and continued to stand.

"Did you remember something?" Eddie prodded.

"Remember something?" Carol Ann repeated blankly.

"About what you might have heard this morning." He had that expression on his face again, as if he thought she wasn't normal. Funny, because she always imagined she had a crisp style of address, yet sometimes others didn't grasp what she was trying to convey.

"Oh, that, no. I wondered, for one thing, if you'd made any progress in the case." She didn't care for the way he continued to look at her, but she did like the face in general, an Ohio kind of face. He reminded her of home. "Most people don't like living in a building where someone was killed," she added sharply. "People have normal concerns about such things."

"Of course." His expression didn't waver.

"Any progress?"

"We're working on several leads right now. Are you a reporter?" A fantastic moment--his eyes narrowed. She had read the phrase recently and here it was directly before her. Remarkable, two in one day--the rosy fingers, and, now this…

"Good heavens, no," she refuted at once. "I'm… in supplements. But actually…" She took a breath. "I've been thinking for some time now of joining the police."

He was back to that look again, that passive signaling of incredulity. What was wrong with this man? She glanced at his fingers. No ring though.

She waited for him to say something and when he didn't, added quickly, "I thought you might have some advice about my getting into …" What did one get into to become a policeperson? "The academy."

Eddie Green cleared his throat. "Uh, maybe you don't realize it, but the competition is exceptionally fierce. First, high scores are needed on the test, and then… Then they usually take the candidates with college degrees."

"I'll do well on the test." She dismissed any problem on that account with a single blink. "As to college degrees--that's all right, too."

His eyes went bigger, several notches more skeptical than before. "You aren't old enough to even be out of high school, yet," he practically snorted.

Of all the condescending… "Because I'm short? I don't think the police have a height requirement, do they?" She scanned the room for officer height, but the only cop standing was a black guy who reminded her of Michael Jordan,

"Well," Eddie protested. "You do look awfully young and you must weigh under 90 pounds. Criminals come in all sizes, too, and that means we get them six foot four and 300 pounds. What are you going to do when you're faced with one of them?"

This was completely prejudicial of him, probably illegal. "Take out my gun and make him lie down flat on the sidewalk," she answered, trying to sound menacing and tremendously capable. "Anyway, I'm a brown belt in karate." Her voice had risen a decibel or two and she tried to rein it in a little when the black detective threw her a glance. "As for a college degree, I have a Ph.D. in religion from New York University--NYU. Until very recently, I was on the faculty there."

She knew, even as she said the words that she shouldn't have brought the old life into play. *Men don't make passes at girls who wear glasses.* She didn't wear glasses, but men didn't care for intellectual girls. That's what it all boiled down to, usually. She was peeved with herself for letting her ego flap her lips. "So if I help you solve the case, will you write a recommendation to get me into the academy?" she demanded.

"Oh, no," said Eddie, rising from his chair in a defensive gesture. "Please don't help me solve the case. That is... please don't."

Fine. He could be that way. She didn't care, exactly, although her sense of pride was sorely aroused. She went home and cooked some ground turkey in her saucepan and ate that with a few leaves of organic red cabbage. Then she walked to her old department at NYU. Professor Melovsky had given her the summer to continue using her old computer for various studies she was working on.

Waving at the department secretary, Amy Chin, Carol Ann entered her old office and booted up.

Whatever she intended to do in the world of academic research, and she wasn't entirely sure just what that was, she simply felt she couldn't do it in an academic setting. Teaching classes even a few hours a week spoiled her focus. She was a scholar, true, but a creative one, and she needed a break from the mental stresses that had been on her since she had been 17, starting here as an undergraduate.

She scrolled through some of the ideas on which she was working and stopped to read, "The effect of the immigration experience on the practice of xxx." In other words, fill in the blank. The actual topic of the study would depend on which group was most accessible for her to interview--the Jains, the Sikhs, the various Moslem populations in the city. Hell, even the Tibetan Buddhists, as over-examined as they had been, were worthy of a small article in a journal like *Religion and Culture…*

But that wasn't where she was headed at all today. She wanted to find out as much as she could about the murdered man, or at least discover how she could get details about his life and business. Everything was on the Internet, right? Wrong. In this day of the information highway, ploughing through the New York City dot-gov site was like being on a bicycle trying to get to LAX. If she wanted the records of Joseph Olesku's business licenses and so on, the webpage said, she'd have to send in a request--not to mention money to pay for the photocopies--and then wait six weeks. Six weeks and the killer could be gone from the country…or Eddie Green himself might have tracked down the perpetrator. Hmmmph.

She couldn't decide on a thing to do except go home, hang around the stoop and gossip with the neighbors. So she did just that, exhausting herself with idle chatter, until she gave up and went inside to meditate and then watch *Law & Order* for investigative tips. The one thing she had learned from the old ladies in 2C was that Joseph Olesku had been stabbed to death.

The next day was like any other, as if the murder in her building had never occurred and as if she hadn't met a man whom she might possibly date. Didn't short men--and, face it, five foot eight was not exactly tall--didn't short men usually like woman who were petite? Was the problem the damn Ph.D., again? She rued her outburst.

Setting that aside, she performed her work while silently chanting the name of an Indian yogi. Another project she was working on was a book about her own use of spiritual techniques and the outcome. Carol Ann saw the idea as something of a bestseller in the making. She looked carefully for the results of her several hours chant on the way home. No specials at the fish market on First Avenue and nothing else spectacular, either.

Except that when she got back to her building, she saw that the police tape was gone and someone was inside the tattoo shop. Maybe Eddie? She squinted to see through the dirty window. No, not a blond. She opened the door and entered, anyway.

That someone was sweeping--an older guy, but his eyes were bright as buttons when he looked at her. Bright as buttons? Were they really? No, she didn't think so…but they were alert and pretty aware.

"Hello," Carol Ann said. "I'm an upstairs neighbor." She pointed up, as if to heaven.

"Joseph is dead," the man informed her. Quite a bit of rubbish went into the dustpan and she wondered if he was inadvertently getting rid of evidence. But maybe Eddie and the others had given up on the case.

"I know," Carol Ann said. "His parents were from the Ukraine and they went to the big Orthodox Church on 7th Street. They're dead, though, but he grew up here." Give a little information to get somc, shc hoped. Of course, she always found out people's religious affiliations, if nothing else.

"Oh, so you knew him?"

"Yes." She peeked at the litter he had dumped into the wastebasket. A cigarette butt. Those were generally clues, with

DNA on them--and the brand alone could be significant. Oh well. She had no forensics lab at her disposal. "Can I look at the books of tattoo designs?" she asked, spotting them on the counter.

He nodded and continued to sweep while Carol Ann searched for a graphic that would tip the scales on the case. "Oh, look," she said, "a svastikah." The swastika, or, more properly, svastikah had been used by the Nazis as their symbol, but was really of Hindu derivation (not to mention Buddhist, Jain, and Navaho). Maybe Joseph's killer had been with the Jewish Defense League, or some group like that.

The man came over and examined the design, then picked up a pen, to mark heavy lines through the Nazi cross. "I'm Rom," he announced. "I don't do those."

"Oh," she admired. "A Gypsy." *The effect of the immigration experience on Gypsy religious practice*?...no, not a good one. "Are you taking over the store?"

He nodded. "What do you have?"

"Huh?"

"What tattoos?"

"Oh, gosh, none. I was just a personal friend of Joseph's, that's all. Because I live in the building." Tattoos weren't good for you. She'd read about it. The ink poisoned you and you came down with a fever at first. Could someone have killed Joseph over a tattoo gone wrong? A tattoo that spelled death for a loved one because of an immune system disorder? Or simply a tattoo that had been badly done? Her mind clicked through the possibilities.

Then again, maybe Joseph had been killed to steal a great location on St. Mark's Place. "Were you a friend of Joseph's, too?" she asked.

"I knew him from the TAA, our Tattoo Artists Association. I'm Felix, by the way--that means happy in Latin. I'd been looking for a place."

Ah ha! A good space in Manhattan would be hard to find. She gave him an encouraging and interested look.

"This neighborhood is lousy, though. Two tattoo parlors across the street and more further east. I'll stay here, for Doris's sake, until the lease runs out in about seven months." Felix shrugged and stashed the broom in a corner, standing it on the handle to preserve the wisps. The broom was new. Obviously Joseph hadn't set much store by cleanliness.

"Doris," Carol Ann murmured thoughtfully. Doris was either Felix's wife or had something to do with the shop.

"Yes, poor Doris. She called me up because she knew I was looking for a spot. The problem is I live in Brooklyn. Oh well, you gotta try to help out when you can, don't you?"

A nice sentiment. She wondered if it derived directly from some religious practice and was about to ask, then thought the better of it. Felix took up his expected station at a stool beside his needles. Oh, God, maybe someone had gotten AIDS from them, another reason to kill the tattoo artist.

"Doris," Carol Ann repeated again, with a tad more enthusiasm. "I need to write her a note. Good Lord. Do you have the address?"

"Of course." He stood and went behind the counter where he searched through some papers, then wrote the phone number and address out for her, as she watched. He did have a fine hand, but the idea of those fingers scrawling with a needle and ink against her flesh was not a pleasant concept. *Mutilation as a religious act* came to her as another possible study title. She'd have to go primitive on that one, however, unless she wanted to take the tack that Hell's Angels bikers comprised a religious cult--a possibility.

After talking to Felix, Carol Ann sat on the steps outside, searching in her purse for her key, wondering if she had left it at work again. As precise as she was about nearly everything, little details still slipped through the cracks.

Instead of her key, she pounced on paper and pen, and sat writing down the possibilities she had thought of as to who might have killed Joseph Olesku. A disgruntled client, or the relative of one; Felix, in order to move into the store--not likely--or Doris, who had turned out to be Joseph's wife. Maybe Doris. Perhaps to live with Joseph Olesku was to loathe him--or a financial matter was involved.

Carol Ann's fingers didn't find the house keys and she walked back toward work, still valiantly searching. At the corner of 7th Street and Second Avenue, she flashed on Eddie, Detective Eddie. True she had been walking more in the direction of the police station than she was accustomed to, but seeing him was rather a miracle, nonetheless. To think that she probably had passed him dozens of times in the neighborhood, never noticing, never knowing what--if anything--fate had in store. He saw her, acknowledged her vaguely, and headed east. She trotted and caught up with him.

"I'm not following you," she said at once. "I'd say you're probably the one following me." She had meant it as a joke, anxious that he not imagine she was chasing him, but the words didn't come out very funny at all. Her brow wrinkled. She couldn't think of a thing to say after that, since she really didn't want to refer to the investigation--either his or hers.

"How are you?" he asked at last, glancing at her sideways, but not altering his rapid stride so that she had to rather hurry to keep up.

But what could she even reply to that? She had nothing interesting to say that wasn't about a paper or book she had in mind to produce. "Oh fine. How are you?"

"Great," he answered.

She felt a bit as if she were running a race. "Could you slow down?" she requested, expecting a harsh retort and for him to rush off. Instead, he obediently reduced his speed and they sauntered with a few comments from each of them about the weather.

A couple of farmers had tables out by Thompkins Square Park and Carol Ann and Eddie bent their heads to examine the produce. Plump red cherries were selling for $5 a pound, which she found outrageous, nearly the price of gold--or maybe silver. She stared covetously at the luscious looking fruit.

He bought a pound. "Are you going home? I'll walk you over," he offered.

She agreed, her heart beating just a little faster and her hands once again plunging into her purse, trying to find the missing key. Well, she'd let him walk her home, then she'd have to walk all the way back to the office to see if she'd left the key there. She hoped Barry would still be at work, otherwise... She wondered how much a locksmith would cost.

"Any luck with the investigation?" she asked at last.

"These things take time."

Be that as it may, she knew the trail was going to grow cold. The common, or television, wisdom was that one had to catch a killer inside of 48 hours.

Bingo! She hit upon her keys in a zippered compartment she never used. What a relief.

As they stood on the sidewalk by the stoop in front of her building, Eddie handed Carol Ann the bag of cherries. "What's that for?" she cried, truly taken aback for the first time in a long while and not reaching out her hand.

"Cherries. Humans eat them."

Slowly, she accepted the peace offering. "Only if you come up to have them, too," she said. "And for a cappuccino."

The next day at work, half her mind was occupied with chanting the yogi's name, while half mulled over Eddie's suggestions for success in applying to the academy--all volunteered spontaneously. The third half busily charted out her new career as the foremost police expert on urban cults. Some tiny, dim portion of her convoluted brain was, meanwhile, left to muddle through entering and fulfilling orders for oxygenated magnesium--Oxy Mag--and Ayurvedic amla paste.

For some reason, she finished up later than usual and walked just about as close to the precinct house as she dared go, but didn't see Eddie. The main thing she must not do at this point was look too interested. She had to avoid appearing eager, at all costs.

Doris Olesku lived in a rather ordinary old building on East 15th Street, where, shifting the flowers she had bought to her left hand, Carol Ann rang the buzzer for 3D with her right. Since she had called from work to say she wanted to make a sympathy visit, she was actually rung into the building, and she climbed to three.

A woman with grief-reddened eyes stood in the hall waiting for her. Oh, no. Suddenly the murder and the investigation became too real. "Mrs. Olesku," said Carol Ann softly, "I'm so, so sorry." She couldn't imagine how to console this stranger. She offered the bunch of goldenrods, lilies, and baby's breath.

"You knew my Joseph?" Doris was a gone-to-seed brunette, not a surprising wife to the late Joseph Olesku, also a bit on the bulky side and a Slavic-featured, dirty blond.

"I live in the building where he had his shop."

Doris led in Carol Ann as if the act were a somewhat natural one and Carol Ann perched on the end of a sofa covered with newspapers and the litter of last week's grocery flyers.

"I don't know what I'm going to do," Doris Olesku began to sob, while reaching for a pack of cigarettes. In fact, the apartment smelled like a dirty ashtray. When Doris got up to fill a jar with water at the sink for the flowers, Carol Ann followed. "The kids," Doris continued, "the bills..." She then saturated Carol Ann's ears with the most intimate details of her financial life, which soon had Carol Ann urging her to move in with her also-widowed sister in Floral Park.

Carol Ann felt dazed by her own helplessness at offering succor. A few words quoted from the *Bhagavad Gita* seemed inadequate and had less than a calming effect.

"At least you got Felix to take on the lease," Carol Ann added, recalling her goal. She still held out a fragmentary hope that the lease was the key.

"He got a bargain," Doris declared. Aha! "I could have added two hundred or so over the landlord's rent, if I'd held out for someone else to take the space." She shrugged. "But the lease is almost up, anyway. I wanted to get the damn thing off my hands."

"Yes, of course," murmured Carol Ann. "But in one day? Was Felix eager to move in so soon?"

"I begged him," said Doris. "I don't think I was taking advantage."

"No, of course not."

"I threw in all of Joseph's stuff, worth three or four hundred."

In another 20 minutes, the phone rang and Carol Ann leapt up and blurted out some mannerly excuses. Descending the stairs, she felt wrung out entirely.

On the street, she ran straight into Eddie Green, whose blue eyes appeared to have a life of their own. Those eyes gave her a piercingly nasty look. "What are you doing here?" The man managed to turn those few words into a damning accusation.

"Making a condolence call," she answered coolly, as if she had never had a lustful thought about him in her head. She sailed off to study the schedule at both the Friends' meeting house and St. George's Church--so long as she was in the neighborhood.

In actual point of fact, despite the two interviews she had conducted with such phenomenal élan, Carol Ann still didn't have a single clue that could point to a killer. Neither Felix nor Doris frankly seemed more than indifferent suspects at best. Felix hardly appeared to care about being in the shop and Doris was probably too neurotically self-concerned to actively plan her husband's murder. She surely hadn't gained financially from his death.

Carol Ann was stymied. Although she had momentarily had the vision that she was being divinely led to a new career in law enforcement, maybe investigation wasn't her forte.

In St. George's thrift shop, she picked up a couple of old hymnals--always worth collecting for an eventual comparison of hymns sung by various denominations--and studied a secondhand wood end table priced at $35. Not bad, but did she really need it? The hymnals were only 50 cents each.

By the time she arrived at the building along Washington Square Park that housed NYU's religion department, she was unusually fatigued. Amy Chin explained to Carol Ann that she was working overtime, preparing the fall schedule for Professor Melovsky to approve next week.

"Look at the hymnals I bought," Carol Ann offered. "Two different editions. "From the 1950's."

"Very nice, Dr. Morris," Amy said. But Carol Ann noted that the secretary's lack of enthusiasm was tempered only by politeness. Furthermore, Carol Ann was always embarrassed when Amy--Miss Chin--called Carol Ann Dr. Morris. She had several times begged the woman to call her by her first name.

"I'll work a while," said Carol Ann. "I have some thinking to do."

The secretary gave a nod of acknowledgment. "Oh, by the way, someone came by to see you last week. I kept meaning to tell you."

Carol Ann raised her eyebrows to show she was listening, but she wasn't really. She wondered if Eddie could actually be angry at her, or if her being so independent had piqued his interest in the slightest.

"I told him you weren't teaching this semester and he was disappointed. Said he wanted to write you a note. I know I shouldn't have given him your home address, but I did. He seemed pleasant enough."

"Of course," agreed Carol Ann as if unruffled, but she didn't like the idea of a student having her address and was rather surprised that Amy could have done such a careless thing. Then she recalled that she had gotten Doris's phone number and address from Felix in exactly that same way. "What did he look like?" she questioned Amy.

"A red-headed boy--in your Christianity as Society Maker class from last semester, he said." Amy gave Carol Ann a somewhat apologetic smile. "I didn't get his name, but I'm sure he'll write."

Carol Ann shrugged it off, bid Amy Chin good night, and went into her old office to boot up. Staring again at some of her ideas for studies, she was disconcerted by the thought that one of her former students now knew where she lived. She brought up the class list and meticulously went through it one by one, calling up the university student database with photo IDs to examine the pictures. She couldn't remember ever having seen half of these people in her class. Yet the fact that she had given all a grade, except for one incomplete, was a sign that they had all attended with fair regularity. In a school of 50,000 students, some anonymity was guaranteed.

Hmm, here was a face that looked familiar. And probably because she had seen him very recently. That was right! He was the man she had run into on the street. She printed the picture on the department ink jet at Amy Chin's desk. When Carol Ann came out to look, Amy was examining the reproduction.

"That's him," she said. "That's the man who was looking for you." She blinked at Carol Ann in astonishment, then read the identifying information out loud. "Daniel Nurham."

Carol Ann went back in to her cubbyhole office and scrolled through Daniel's records. Now she remembered him. Not by his appearance, but by the grade she had given him and her documenting comments to herself. The man had been a raving lunatic, his opinions the far opposite of well considered. She had flunked him on his final essay and denied him credit for the course.

No, the problem wasn't that she disagreed with his ideas (which she did), or even his atrocious grammar--she gave students Cs who could barely spell their own names. He simply hadn't seemed to absorb a single concept from the selections they had been given to read and that they had discussed in class. Pro or con, if only he had commented upon the course content, she would have given him a grade high enough to earn him credit for the hours. But the work Daniel had produced consistently and on the final, in particular, showed him to not only be of an obviously deranged mindset, but, worse, not to have read the assigned material.

As Carol Ann sat confounded by the recollection of his work, a chill went directly up her spine. Good golly, she had never had a chill run up her spine before. And, according to the idiom, wasn't the chill supposed to go *down* the spine? How odd.

She felt as if she could see the scene unfold before her eyes: Daniel Nurham had her address. He had cased the apartment house and figured out that her apartment was in the back. That night, he went through the narrow alleyway between the buildings, where he stood trying to figure out how to pull down the fire escape. At the same time, the tattoo artist, having heard a noise, came out the back door. Daniel already had the knife in his hand, so he stabbed Joseph Olesku and fled.

Hearing one sound or the other, Carol Ann had woken up and looked out her window to view those indescribably lovely, blushing, fingers of dawn. Just one floor beneath her on the concrete in back lay the man who had unwittingly saved her life.

Daniel didn't leave the area but had stuck around to see the results of his handiwork--or to see *her*. Perhaps he had gone into one of the restaurants along St. Marks and had an early morning coffee. He had come out again and watched the police, watched Carol Ann leave the building, and then had walked alongside her to the corner.

Maybe she was crazy to think any such thing. But she believed she owed Joseph Olesku her life. She sat a while and thought about what she must do. Reality, and a nasty reality at that, had her in its grip, nearly paralyzing her. Finally, overcoming her great reluctance and fear, she dialed her former student's telephone number.

Glad because of her nerves that no one answered, when the machine gave the signal, she forced out her message. "This is Dr. Morris, Daniel. I've put two and two together and I know what happened. You wouldn't want this story to get around. I'll call tomorrow and let you know what you can do about it."

Trembling and her stomach roiling, Carol Ann hung up. She had sounded tough, hadn't she? She sat and chanted silently for a while, a desperate prayer.

Sitting across the desk from Eddie, Carol Ann must have had a serious enough expression on her face for him to make an effort to listen. "What if," she said, "the killer wasn't after Joseph Olesku, after all, but Olesku happened to come out when someone was back there--someone on his way to hurt a very different victim?"

"It's possible," acknowledged Eddie.

"I've done something to guarantee that, if I've pinpointed the killer correctly, we'll be able to catch him trying to murder his real, intended target."

"Who is?" Eddie asked.

"Me," answered Carol Ann.

He probably hated her by now and this was the only time she'd ever get Detective Edward Green into her bedroom, but here he was, sitting on the old wooden milk crate she used as a dressing chair.

"Take off your shoes," she ordered. "You can't sit there. You'll have to get in bed with me."

"I will not," Eddie refused, as if assaulted.

"Well, for goodness sake, I know it's a sacrifice, but you'll have to. Otherwise he'll see you sitting there. And, believe it or not, the sheets are clean."

He took off his shoes and crawled into bed beside her, fully clothed. He drew his gun.

"I'm not going to hurt you," Carol Ann said.

"Shut up."

For a change, she did as told and they both lay there silently. After a while she began to drift off. She jerked awake. Maybe she was wrong. Even she had to acknowledge the possibility.

The hours ticked by. At about four, she got up and went to the bathroom. Funny, too, because she never, ever did that. But then, tonight she hadn't been sleeping, really. Her metabolism was in gear, busily processing.

At about six, the sky started to lighten and they both looked at one another. "I'm sorry," she whispered.

He shushed her.

Ten minutes later, she got up and looked out the window. This morning she didn't see the rosy fingers of dawn as on the day Joseph Olesku had been killed, but the few clouds out were colored pink, the same pink as then though in a more diffuse coloration. Only by luck had she seen the fabled fingers.

She lay down and Eddie took her hand in his. Then a minute later, they both at the same second jumped at the sound of someone or something on the fire escape. Eddie pulled the sheet over himself and she, acting according to their plan, feigned sleep.

Carol Ann felt terrified, as if death was only a moment away, which it might well be. True, Eddie was beside her, a trained police officer with a weapon, but fate often had more twists prepared than one could imagine. She felt sick.

The window, already partially open, slid up with a slight creak, and she could sense a presence stepping into the room. Oh God.

Eddie was up and Carol Ann opened her eyes. Eddie's pistol pointed at the intruder, who turned to flee. Carol Ann sprang out of bed without thought, her fear dissolving as she moved. She tugged at the intruder who hung out of the window.

"Get out of the way," Eddie ordered, pulling, yes, Daniel, back into the room, allowing Carol Ann to kick her former student in the shin.

In an instant, Eddie had him down on the floor, where he handcuffed the boy.

"Because I failed you?" demanded Carol Ann hotly. "Because of that you kill someone? You nitwit. All you had to do was go over the assigned reading. No one asked you to agree with it." She wanted to kick the idiot again.

"You ruined my life," Daniel charged, while Eddie hauled him to his feet. "Without those credits, I couldn't graduate."

"Nonsense" refuted Carol Ann. "If you had the slightest intelligence you could have taken another course and passed."

Eddie radioed for a squad car.

"I'm coming with you," Carol Ann told him. She went to the mirror to comb her hair, then put on those dubious sandals of hers. "You can take my statement."

She smiled and Eddie actually smiled at her in turn.

"Okay, Officer Morris," he said. "Then I'll invite you to my house and make you pancakes. Let's see if we can bulk you up for your training."

Pancakes? Mmmm. Well. How could she break it to him that she didn't eat carbohydrates, especially grains? She pondered that one all the way to the precinct house.

G. Miki Hayden's *Writing the Mystery,* received Agatha, Anthony, and Macavity nominations, winning the Macavity. Miki's latest novel *New Pacific* is from Silver Lake Publishing. *New Pacific* is the sequel to *Pacific Empire*, which received a spot on the *NYTimes* summer reading list.

Before The Flames
By Seymour Shubin

I've told myself over the years that I should have known something was terribly wrong, that I should have tried to talk to Conrad, or even more told my folks. I know, I know, I was only a kid then, just nine, and I wouldn't have gotten anything out of Conrad anyway, and as for my parents they certainly wouldn't have suspected anything.

You see, the Willigs were the aristocrats of our neighborhood. The father had built the houses on our block, solid twins, the long row of them separated in the middle by their own house, a single, not particularly large as I look back, but a mansion in comparison with the others, with a full-width sunporch and a number of gables on its second floor. He was a tall, distinguished-looking man, his wife dark-haired and so pleasant. Conrad was their only child. He was my age and we played together, but there was a difference: he went to private school while I went to Phipps Elementary, just a few blocks away. We were next door neighbors, though in a sense a whole world apart. It wasn't just that it was the Depression and that they didn't seem to feel it. It was as though they had been born into a certain way of life.

Mr. Willig and his wife were the first people I ever knew, for instance, who golfed. And not only golfed, with Mr. Willig in plaid knickers, his wife all in white, but one of their two automobiles actually had a lidded aperture near the rear tire to store the clubs. And Mr. Willig hunted a few times a year, climbing into his car with their two dogs yapping around him, and coming back with a deer or two, or limp birds, which he hung in their large backyard that bordered the alley along our house. Conrad started going with him when he was about seven.

And that house, that house. There was a richness even in the smell of it as you walked in. It even had a billiard and gun room, with racks of rifles behind glass, and lines of cue sticks against the walls and scoring markers on long wires overhead; and staring fixedly at it all were antlered trophies on the walls. But these had become too many for that room alone, and so one of them, the mammoth head of a stag, was in the living room and another out in the sunporch, near where their Christmas tree would go.

And what a place for Christmas. Their trees were so tall and fat, reaching to the ceiling and hovering over the hooting and flashing train, with its village and bridges and tunnel, that you could watch winding around even from outside on the sidewalk. And that alone was a totally different world to a little Jewish boy, the child of immigrants, who was sure that Santa Claus must have spent plenty of time there, just next door, to leave so many gifts before flying in a high arch over his own house.

I don't remember if my father and Mr. Willig ever had a conversation, though I imagine they did. In fact I don't remember Mr. Willig talking to anyone in the neighborhood, though he was not a scary guy to us kids. Impressive but not scary. Mrs. Willig and my mother, though, were really friendly. They were sort of built alike, somewhat stocky; and though she had a maid she would often, like my mother, hang out the wash in the back yard and would even occasionally sit out on a windowsill to wash a window. And I distinctly remember the time Conrad came over to our house for dinner and Mrs. Willig asking my mother the next day what was it she'd made, Conrad had loved it so.

"It's brisket. You're not familiar with that cut?"

"No, in fact I've never heard of it."

And a few weeks later she tried it, only she called to say Conrad said it wasn't the same, it wasn't the same.

Conrad was a stereotypical only child, spoiled by his parents with toys I wouldn't even dream of. Sandy-haired and rather short for his age, he also had the kind of good looks that made his mischievousness forgivable to neighbors. Like, during this one snow storm he massed together an igloo in his yard and told fat Harry Gilbert to try it, it was so warm in there, and then with a shovel smashed it all down on him: Harry's folks never came complaining though poor Harry, encrusted with snow, ran home crying. And though Conrad was forever knocking off sparrows with his BB rifle, it was something the neighborhood accepted. Which was quite a contrast to the one time he handed me his rifle to shoot at a blackbird on the back driveway, the first time I'd ever even held a gun, and I popped it and, as it flopped over, I immediately took off in panic. One of the mothers witnessed the assassination from her kitchen window. Soon kids in the neighborhood were huddled around in a vacant lot for the funeral, and they weren't allowed to play with me for weeks.

If a kid of nine can be charmed by another kid, then that's the word, I was charmed. And how I envied him, not only for his wide variety of things but his magic---how everyone instinctively liked him. But there was nothing I envied more than his model airplanes.

I was always trying to build one that would fly, would work for days amid a tangle of balsa wood and tissue paper, only to have them veer immediately from my hands to the ground. But Conrad's father made a number of them for him that not only were things of beauty, but flew--taking off from the driveway gracefully, soaring as long as the rubber-band driven propeller turned, then gliding down while all of us kids raced after it. Then one day Conrad came out of his house with a brand new Fokker tri-plane in his hand. Bright red. The Red Baron's. True even to the machineguns.

It was so magnificent that even Conrad, usually so cool about these things, was in awe of it. Instead of letting us crowd around him as usual, he yelled us away. And as he tightened the propeller and held the plane trembling on the ground, he warned us over his shoulder not to run along under it when he let go.

"Stay back, hear? Stay back."

And then he released it, rising to his feet and following it as it sped along the driveway behind our houses and then lifted up gracefully and curved over the adjoining vacant lot. We followed, though a way back, as he ran after it, his hand up in the air should it suddenly swerve down. And when, its propeller finally motionless, it did glide down, heading into a rough portion of the lot, he caught it gently on the run.

I never saw him play with anything longer than this. Every day for at least a couple of weeks he'd be out there flying it and chasing after it. And then one day it struck me that I hadn't seen him for at least three or four days. I remember thinking I should go up and ring his bell but I didn't. I was always in awe of his parents, no matter how often I saw them. And I told myself that if he wanted to play he would play.

And then one day maybe a week later I saw him standing outside his kitchen door. He looked over at me. It was, as I remember it, a long, long look.

"You want to see something?" There was something defiant in his voice.

"Sure."

"You want to see something?" he repeated. He sounded angry.

"Sure."

"Okay. Okay."

He turned and ran into his house. A few minutes later he was leaning out of his bedroom, holding the plane. He held it high in the air, then lowered it, then disappeared into his room as though he'd been testing something. He was back after several moments, holding a lighted match to the tail while the propeller whirled. I couldn't believe what I was seeing. He held the burning plane even higher, then with a little thrust released it. It rose against the clear blue sky, the tail and now most of the fuselage in flames. It straightened out, then curved, then I remember it rising again, only to turn and now dive at an angle to the ground.

I stood there, frozen, a part of me loving the sight of the flaming plane in its death throes, of the Red Baron going down, but another part wishing weakly he had given it to me instead. And the wish grew stronger as I stood by the little smoldering mound on the ground. I looked up at his window but he wasn't there. Nor did he come out. I stood there alone as if at a stranger's grave. And that night, it must have been a couple of hours before I could fall asleep.

It was the next morning that I woke to voices outside and police cars. My mother, as though waiting for sounds that I was awake, walked into my room crying and took me in her arms. What had happened, what was happening, came out in bits and pieces. Mr. Willig had shot his wife dead last night, and then himself. They'd apparently been quarreling off and on for days, over a woman he was seeing.

Thank God, thank God, he didn't hurt Conrad, my mother kept saying.

Didn't hurt Conrad?

To this day I see him by that window, the flaming plane in his hands.

I never saw him after that. He was raised, I understand, by an uncle and aunt. And years later someone told me that he was married and was working for an accounting firm. I've often tried to picture it. But somehow it is still hard for me to think of him at a desk--or anywhere but in those golden days, before he stood at that window.

Seymour Shubin is the author of thirteen novels, one of which, ANYONE'S MY NAME, made the New York Times bestseller list. Another, THE CAPTAIN, was an Edgar nominee. His thirteenth novel is THE MAN FROM YESTERDAY (Academy Chicago, Spring, 2004).

Dime I

Looking for Philip Marlowe
By Ben Plotkin

My office had just been refurnished. What had been the upstairs of Señor Goldberg's Authentic Tortilla Factory was now replete with sleek, ultra-modern, Zen furnishings that my designer assured me would attract top-tier clients. Clients I wanted. Clients who actually had money. Clients that could get me a new Range Rover—my 2000 was getting old. I was tired of low rent nutcases bursting in and insisting I find their lost poodles. Hardly the reason I'd gotten into this racket.

I leaned back in my Spartan black suede chair and waited for the money to walk through the door.

What I got was Stan.

Hardly had the last piece of raw tuna slid down my throat before Stan bombarded me. "I'm behind the eight ball. I need your help bad."

I put down my chopsticks and gestured at the minimalist block of wood that functioned as a chair for clients.

Stan sat and frantically continued his monologue.

"My babe set me up. I just got out of the big house. Nothing big you know, no bindles or blow downs, I just got bopped for some bent cars. I was lucky though, I just did a bit. I'm not a boozehound--just liked them fancy boilers and couldn't keep my hands off. But that's not my biff. Can you help me? You got to. This button man is gonna bump me off if you don't help."

I stared blankly. My sharp detective's wit told me his name was Stan. That's what the nametag on his mechanic's jumpsuit read. I wanted to hit the speed dial and demand a refund from my designer. This was not the clientele I'd laid out 75 G's to attract. I couldn't even understand this guy.

Stan sensed my indecision.

I leaned back in my chair. "I'm sorry, could you go over that again." I hoped for a more logical explanation.

"I catch you," Stan said, shaking his finger at me. "You're worried about the cabbage. You think this cat just crawled out of the can and can't cough up. You think I blew it all at the can house, because some canary canned me. I got case-dough just for this though. I got cars cheesed between here and the big T. I got you covered. So don't you worry about cash." He pulled out a wad of hundreds and threw it on my desk.

I was getting a headache. I picked up the cash. It looked real. I had nothing else to do that afternoon, so I tossed the cash in the drawer. "What *exactly* can I do for you?"

"You're a dick right?" Stan said, while carefully studying my office furnishings. "Even though you got this daisy office, you're still a dick. What I want is duck soup, you find the droppers that are after me while I lay low in some dive dump and dip my bill. I'd do it myself but I'm in Dutch with this dame and I don't wanna get filled with daylight."

It was obvious that Stan needed extensive therapy. I let him stew for a moment. He fidgeted, anxiously working the grease from beneath his fingernails.

Finally I said, "So, you want me to find someone for you—is that it?"

"Eggs in the coffee man…eggs in the coffee. I don't want to end up with no electric cure."

I was catching on to Stan. I still couldn't understand a damn thing he was saying, but I was getting the gist. I think he wanted me to find someone. I tried to keep the questions simple. "Who do I find?" It was as simple as I could make it.

"I want you to find Philip Marlowe. They were always talking about him up in Folsom. I heard all kinds of flimflam about Philip, but I know for a fact that it wasn't fake. They say he used to be a flattie but found some frail and faded away. Philip's from Hollywood—got an office out there supposedly, but I can't find it. I gave you the fry, so you can find Philip for me—that fair?"

I let his lexicon of arcane alliterations fade before I spoke. "Philip Marlowe? You want me to find Philip Marlowe?" He had obviously been reading too much detective fiction.

"I didn't want to gab over this to no gumshoe but I'll tell you anyway. I lied before. I set Phil up. That's why they're gunnin' me. These greasers that are after me—Phil set them on me. I'll tell you why. I glommed a gam of his. I didn't mean to. You gotta understand that. It was at this gin house. I was gulping a little too much giggle juice when this girl with great getaway-sticks gloms on to me. She asks me for a gasper and starts gabbing away. She tells me she's Phil Marlowe's girl and that he's this guy with a gift for the gat. She tells me he once gunned down a greaser who just gazed at her. She wants to know if I'm still game. What was I to do? She had great globes, so I groped her."

I reached into my desk found a bottle of Aleve and tossed down five of the little blue pills.

"Philip Marlowe—the detective, lives in Hollywood," I said.

"Now you're hot hombre. See I hooked up with his hooker and now his hatchet men out to send me off into a Harlem sunset. I got to find Phil and set it all straight."

"Chandler's Marlowe—that's the guy you're worried about?"

He didn't answer; he was visibly shaking now. I worried that if he managed to make it through the alphabet he'd explode.

"If you don't help me I'm gonna ing-bing all over the rug," he said and stood.

Whatever ing-bing was I was sure I didn't want it happening on my long-haired, Moroccan ibex rug. Stan bobbed up and down excitedly, he was shaking worse than one of those quarter-operated vibrating beds in a dive motel. He was obviously a nut case. Of course, he was a nut case with a stack of cash, which made him a player in Hollywood. Judging by the heft of the bills, it would pay for at least one or two of my *Feng Shui* counseling sessions. I had visions of redecorating my apartment.

"I'll take the case," I said. "You want me to find you Philip Marlowe, fine."

"That's jake, Jack," Stan said. "Really jake! I'd stay but I gotta jot—go get me a jorum of skee, it makes me less jiggle-brained. You gotta find Phil for me." Stan bubbled out the door.

I leaned back and tried to will his nervous energy out of the room. Just being in proximity with the guy left me feeling like I had just downed a triple espresso. I prayed the Aleve would work fast.

Find Philip Marlowe—simple enough right? My library card was as good as the next guy's. I was oscillating between formulating a plan to confront Stan with the collected works of Raymond Chandler and calling my designer with new ideas when there was a knock at the door.

"Come in," I said.

No one came, only another knock.

"Come in," I said again. I was going to have to get a new building; despite the assurances of my Feng Shui therapist, this place was only attracting nuttos. I got up and opened the door.

"I said you could come in…" I didn't get a chance to finish my sentence. The big guy in the doorway raised his gun and whacked me like I was a fastball headed for far left field. It was goodnight gonzo.

When I came to, my head felt like it had volunteered for crash test duty. I needed a personal airbag. And another Aleve. I was still in my office, but the place was a mess of smashed glass and broken furniture. It was awful, full of bad energy, just like the big guy with the gun standing over me. A permanent snarl was tattooed on his face. He wore a thick wool suit and fedora that seemed out of place for both summer and LA.

"You got any analgesics?" I said.

He whacked me across my temple with the barrel of his gun. Maybe it was the only thing he could do; maybe he didn't know what analgesics were. My vision got less blurry and I saw the bottle of little blue helpers lying on its side atop the shattered remains of my titanium desk.

The big guy with the gun noticed me eyeing the bottle and picked it up and dumped the remaining pills into his hand.

"Knock it off kitten. These won't do you no good by the time I'm done kicking you around," he said, scattering the pills across the floor. He walked over to where one had fallen and maliciously ground it into blue dust. I wondered if the stain would come out of my ibex rug.

"I got your kale too," he said and held up the wad of hundreds Stan had given me. He was obviously an acquaintance of Stan—maybe they both belonged to the same twelve-step program. I was beginning to think a nearby loony bin was having a field trip. I should call them; tell them where their patients were. I had just about enough of unintelligible urbanites for one afternoon. I was going to tell this guy how I felt, gun or no gun.

I tried, but it was then I noticed that I was tied to my chair and trying to get up only caused it to rock back and tip over. I fell backwards and was left staring up at the ceiling. The guy with the gun laughed, walked over and stared down at me. I was looking right up his nose. He sniffed.

"You're lucky I'm laughing or I'd have to give you lead-poisoning. No one lams out on Louie, least of all some lollipop the likes of you." At least I knew the guy's name. I'd be sure and mention it to the police. "I see you're lost in thought—you ain't gonna call no law in on Louie. It's only me and you."

"Lucky me," I said. "You a friend of Stan's?"

"That meddling mark? You could say I know that moniker. That dumb mug had to go get mixed up with Marlowe's moll. But I got his mazuma now," he said taunting me with the cash. He paused for a moment then said, "How'd you know I was here about Stan?"

"Let's just say you talk similar. Look, you mind helping me up?"

He thought about it for a moment then pulled my chair back up. It was an improvement.

"Look, Stan's not here. Besides, I hardly even know the guy. What do you want?"

"I want the package that Stan nicked from Marlowe's dame."

"What?" Why did Marlowe keep popping up in things? I knew I hadn't kept up with current events, but to the best of my memory, Marlowe was as real as Peter Pan.

"I don't buy your act. You want me to think you know nothing, but I know Stan gave you the nickels to look after the package he nabbed from the newsie—Marlowe's newsie. Stan did a number on her while she was hooked on nose-candy. You look like a nance, so I know you'll give it to me before I have to get too nasty."

He sneered; this seemed to be the part of the job he enjoyed best.

"What was in the package?" I said. I was stalling, but I needed something and Stan hadn't given me any package. The thought of Louie smashing more of my office furniture terrified me. I needed to keep him talking while I tried to wriggle out of the chair.

"The oyster fruit. The dame had the oyster fruit. Problem was Marlowe was holding them for me. He got careless; let some nice pins he had been poking pack them out. Now I look like a patsy. That peeper Marlowe hasn't got my pearls and perhaps he's setting me up to do time in the pen. So that punk Stan comes along pitches some woo to Marlowe's pro skirt and palms the pearls. Now, I'm tired of waiting so unless you open them pipes of yours I'm going to plug you."

I could only assume this was some kind of subtle threat. Maybe I should have been more frightened but I was fascinated by his ability to rant without ever having to stop for breath.

"Pearls?" I said. Louie nodded. There was a knock at the door.

Louie looked at me and for a moment was speechless.

"Queer, isn't it?" I suggested. "I wasn't expecting company." He didn't say anything but cautiously walked to the door and flung it open—Stan stood on the other side his face filled with fear as he stared down the barrel of Louie's gun.

Louie sneered at Stan. "Just the rube I been looking for. Get in before I let my roscoe start talking." Louie waved Stan into the room with the gun. Stan looked like he had just wet himself. I guess he hadn't been expecting Louie. "Now we'll see if this roundheel you thought was going to rescue you rates for radishes. Maybe I'll just rub you both out," Louie said, his face beginning to redden.

Here we were, one big, happy family. Now that Stan was here maybe he could translate for me. If nothing else, Stan's arrival had given me a chance to partially wriggle out of my ropes. Despite Louie's tough guy act it was obvious he had never been a Boy Scout—he couldn't tie a knot.

Louie shut the door and came over to study both of us. He seemed pleased with his handiwork.

"Nice to see you again Stan," I said. "Maybe you can explain a few things?"

Stan looked angrily at me. "You're the shamus. I'm not going to sing to no stoolie. I just came back for my spinach and that's square." Well, that cleared things up with Stan. Maybe having two of them around wasn't any better. The situation was not improving. Here I was, trapped with two raving alliteratives. Between them, I figured I had about seven letters left in the alphabet to end this thing one way or another.

"You didn't see me tail you did you Stan? You thought I was just some tough triggerman, but I don't take to having no tart tarnish my trousers. Now I got you, you're taking the fall for your tomato unless I get what I came for. I didn't make this trip for biscuits."

With all this talk of spinach, tomatoes and biscuits, I was getting hungry again. I tried to put it all together in my head. Stan had swiped some pearls from some woman who had swiped them from some fictional detective who may or may not be Philip Marlowe. Marlowe had been holding the pearls for Louie as part of some pay off. Stan had looked me up—he had wanted me to find Marlowe so he could give him back the pearls and get Louie off his back. The only problem was, Louie was very much over Stan's back at the moment, busily berating him with the butt of his Beretta. Apparently, alliteration was contagious. If I could have, I would have slapped myself out of it.

"You're going under!" shouted Louie and whacked Stan upside the head with the gun knocking him to the floor. I was still a little worried but I had a few things going for me: for the moment, they were entertaining one another, I had managed to wiggle free from my ropes and finally, I was hoping they'd peter out somewhere around W.

I wiggled my way out of the chair, picked up one of my minimalist wood stools, and whacked Louie over the head. Louie sprawled forward onto the floor and lay there—silent. His head lay a few inches from one of the Aleve's. He might need it when he came to.

Stan stared up at me with a look of amazement.

"What?" I said.

"Va-va-va-voom—out like a light!"

"I've had just about enough of both of you," I said. I bent down and picked up the wad of bills that had rolled out of Louie's hand. "I'm keeping this for my troubles. Someone's got to pay for this mess."

Stan wiped some blood off his head with the sleeve of his jumpsuit. He seemed relieved. "For a moment I thought you were just some weak sister and that I'd end up in a wooden kimono. That Louie's a wrong gee. You whacked him good though—all the way to Xanadu."

"Thanks," I said. "Now hand over the pearls." Stan looked terrified again, he blanched and shook but finally reached into his jumpsuit and handed me something wrapped in a greasy, brown paper bag.

"What's the use of shutting my yap anymore. Take 'em. I'm yellow. I know. Give 'em back to Marlowe."

I looked inside the bag. Sure enough, there was a long string of perfect pearls.

"Pretty, but not worth getting zotzed over," I said to Stan. He looked up at me and smiled, like I finally understood.

"Not worth getting zotzed over," he said.

"Stay here. I'm going to get some law." I walked downstairs to call the cops. They were going to love this one. I used the payphone outside the building. The dispatcher said they'd be here in a few minutes. I leaned against the wall to wait. All this trouble over a handful of deep-sea baubles.

I looked up. For a moment, I thought I saw a figure in a fedora lurking in the shadows across the street. It was a hot day. Maybe it was just my imagination.

Ben Plotkin is currently a medical student. In between studying, he still finds time to write. In a previous life, he lived in Hollywood and worked on movies. It was glamorous.

A Budgeted Life
by Bill Capron

Josh Ehrens death was a mystery to no one else. Just me.

That's not so unusual. My entire life goes against the logic of things, like some sort of metaphysical oxymoron. It's a bit like my vision; I am profoundly color-blind, so I see a lot of things others miss. Where the rest of the world is cued by color, I have to search for shapes. It's the basis for what makes me different, but I didn't know it until I had my eyes forced open. Even after six years, that experience is about as painful as vision can be.

Like the visible part of an iceberg, most people focus all their attention on the world of the good. It is, with good reason, an exclusionary kind of vision, selectively discriminating. Lately though, it's the other five-sixths that floods my senses, a ghostly nether land the average citizen can ignore until it crosses over to do him some pain. Even then, he usually closes his mind to it, and gets on with the good life, eyes wide shut. I don't do that. My past and future are enmeshed in the warped space between the worlds of good and evil, where cops and criminal lawyers are the prime human species, and the animals run wild. Yes, I live there, visually, if not physically, just below the smooth surface, and it's a bit scary sometimes, and a lot too mean. And I can't avert my eyes, so I can't escape all the nastiness. Still, when it comes right down to it, that's my business, confronting nastiness. Sometimes it happens to my friends.

I'd known Josh Ehrens for twenty years, ever since we worked together for a cable television company in Philadelphia. In many ways he was a throwback to a more mature time. But mature is the wrong word. Maybe more measured. Josh appeared to be from a harder era when men hoarded their dollars, conserved their feelings, and measured their words. Where Josh, if he ever thought about it, might say he never wasted his feelings, others would say he never gave them the light of day because he didn't have them. It's possible they would both be right. I'll side with Josh.

From my perspective, Josh had no extremes in his life. He almost never smiled or frowned, keeping a placid 'I'm listening to you' look of expectancy on his face when I was speaking, or a 'held in suspense' look when he wanted to say something. But he was a happy man, it's just that one had to look hard to see it. And he was happiest when today was just like yesterday, or when someone else paid for lunch, or when no one made any demands on him, mental or physical.

It took me a long time to figure Josh out. Back twenty years ago, I'd thought him secretive, unhappy, scheming. That was only because we weren't that close, and the then-me, well, I didn't see deep enough. We later went our separate ways, and after fifteen years of traveling, I settled in Portland, Oregon, my final stop. I'd become rich, lost what mattered most to me, and took up my profession to deal with my loss, or maybe my new vision. Anyway, four years ago I was working a stakeout in the city, when I saw Josh eating lunch in the corner of a small cafeteria-style restaurant off Front Street. He looked secretive, unhappy, scheming, just as I remembered him. I forced myself to say hello. He recognized me and smiled. It was a nice thing. At the time I recalled wondering if it was a nice smile because he had changed, or because I had changed. I've since learned it was me. Josh never changed. That was one of the great things about him.

Josh came to Portland because his wife, Jocelyn, was transferred by Delta Airlines. It was a big deal to him, moving, that is. He didn't look forward to the new challenges, especially a new job – he'd worked for the same company where we'd met since college. For Josh it was just change, and he didn't much take to it. When Delta wanted her to go to Atlanta. Josh said no. Back to Philadelphia, maybe. Atlanta, no. It had been seven years since the family left him. So Josh sent out his two sons for a couple weeks every summer. It was enough for him. It was enough for them. In fact, it was the same day I saw him that he'd dropped them at the airport. I didn't know that then, because Josh didn't tell me. After a while I learned about the kids, in dribs and drabs, the only way Josh tells anything.

Thinking back, I wonder if a man can really love his children if they're not like him. I don't mean not like him at a given moment, I meant not like him ever, and never going to be like him. I know this is probably true of every generation, except with Josh, it was as if two or three generations separated him from his sons.

Josh was more like my grandfather on my father's side of the family than like me, as if he'd lived through the Depression. But I don't think it was any one thing. Maybe the first time he got excited about something, it was taken away, or the first time he got caught drinking, he got a beating, or he was arrested. He was a guy who considered seriously every bad thing that ever happened to him, recorded it in a ledger, then never did it again. It was certainly a learned behavior, but I'm sure the genes played a part too, though it might be one of those generation skipping traits. I'd have to know more to verify it, and even then I might miss it. There's no way any psychiatrist could ever dig it out, but then Josh wouldn't want him to, because it wasn't important to him.

Josh was one of my regular poker guys. He had a beer, maybe two, won or lost a little, never smiled or frowned at his hand, never regretted losing, never flaunted his wins. He had a favorite baseball team, the Mariners, but you'd never guess it to watch him at the game. And he always had a girlfriend, but never for long. He was really a good-looking guy, same age as me, forty-seven, in good shape, so the women were pretty. He made good small talk, responded like a regular human being, but they usually needed more, so in a month or two they were gone, replaced by an equally attractive stand-in. It didn't bother him any. I mean that, it didn't bother him any. If she'd stayed for a month or a year, it wouldn't have meant a thing to him, or, at least, not that anyone else would know. I knew, just like I knew that I was his best friend, and it was important to him, but that realization was a long time in coming.

I know what you're thinking, Josh was an unhappy guy. He wasn't. He didn't care enough to be unhappy. Everything in his life was good. He had a good job, a nice house in a quiet neighborhood, lots of money, which he never spent. He fished, and went out for a drink, and went to museums, and friends' houses, and birthday parties, and weddings, like they were line items on a schedule written by someone else, someone who cared. But it wasn't someone else, it was Josh, and he did care, though in his world he didn't let on. It wasn't on purpose, it was just the way he was.

There was a time when I thought Josh lived an unexamined life, but since then I've become convinced it was a too examined life. He never did anything without scanning it from every side, reducing its impact on his world. I figured it was a reflex, maybe I was wrong, it might be on purpose at that. It was still the way he was.

As I said, I learned all this in bits and pieces. One might ask, why did I care enough to find out. Well, Josh was a nice guy, easy to like, but overtly standoffish. It's not an expected combination, but it worked for him. I wanted to know why, it was important. Let's just say, I'm a nosy guy, and I'm in the right business for it. So I made Josh a project, and on the way he became a friend.

So, back to the sons. They're identical twins, and about twenty now. And they are nothing like their father. Where Josh was budgeted, Jim and John were profligate. In everything. They shared nothing with their dad other than their time, a paltry two weeks a year. I didn't learn this from Josh, I learned it from my time with the three of them, mostly fly-fishing, or eating on the way to or the way back from fishing. They were nice kids, well mannered, but something important was missing. It might be that examined life thing, that they had no introspection in them. They lived to the moment, spent every second, every dollar, even emotion, like there was no end to it. It might be a gen X thing, that they didn't take anything personally, as if life was a Hollywood movie and all would be fine in the end. Well, life isn't, and it wasn't.

The last time I saw Josh, a month ago, he told me he'd just gotten back from his wife's funeral. He wasn't openly sad, but I could see the edges of it. I think I was the only one who could see it. Because I'm the only man who really knew Josh. Because, unlike the women who came and went, who all could see deeper than I could, just because they're women, I knew from looking so long. He told me she died in debt, that she'd spent every penny she'd earned, and a lot she hadn't made yet. And the boys hadn't had a clue. She had always planned on having tomorrow to replenish the account, but a car going the wrong way on the highway finished that. And the driver was an uninsured illegal, and dead. And Joce had no life insurance. And she'd let the car insurance lapse, accidentally. And the boys were pretty much penniless. He was taking over their living expenses in addition to the college tuition at Penn he was already paying. He'd told them they had to get jobs, to show their good faith, so to speak. He wanted them to budget their lives, if only just a little. This was all stated to me as a matter of fact, nothing like the angst I'm sure the boys expressed to their expressionless dad. Talk about a lack of communication!

It was the last time I saw Josh. A day later he was dead. He was mugged in the Southeast, supposedly picking up a whore. I didn't for a second believe it. No, I didn't know everything about the man, but what I knew, I knew well. Sex for Josh was not important enough to make an outward show of it, and, add to that, he never paid for anything he could get for free, like that last time I saw him, when I picked up the tab. Just like always.

I also knew that Josh wouldn't have taken the occasion of his death to make so public a show of his feelings as to hire me. It wasn't in him. So .why do it? Because I'm made that way. Because I work for justice. Because my friends are important to me. Because I was picking up one final tab.

Now the cops assigned one of their best detectives, Maureen McMartin, a girl I could learn to want, if she was available, which she isn't. We share a long history, not always good. She knows how I work, and she doesn't like it that I don't let the bad guys off the hook, no matter what the legal system decides. I'd say that was because she's angry she can't make them pay herself. Except it's deeper seated than that; she's a 'by the book' kind of person, and I'm not in the book. That's why she's a good cop. Still, she had no reason to think Josh's death was anything more than it looked to be, and she concentrated her efforts to take a murderous hooker off the streets. Me, I wasn't swayed by the facts, if you know what I mean.

I knew it was the kids, but as with too many crimes, knowing and proving are two different things. Still, if I was going to exact a retribution, I'd have to be certain. Sure, I know, what makes me think I've got a right to make justice happen. I don't, and no matter how certain I think I am, I might be wrong. No, what I do is create a situation where if they're guilty, they will do something to cook their own goose. That is, I let justice happen. I'm not often wrong, and when I am, then it's no harm, no foul. But Josh's case wasn't that complicated.

Jim and John flew in the next morning, interchangeable as always. I crossed paths with them at the funeral home while they were making the final arrangements. I'd started the ball rolling with the undertaker, so it wasn't as if I was unexpected. They shook my hand, shyly, despite them being as close to me as anyone else's kids have ever been. I read more into it than I should have. Still looking back on it, it was really there, the reluctance.

I called my lawyer son in New York. Robin went to Penn. My story tickled his interest, so he and his wife, another alum, took the rest of the day off to investigate. Traci, his wife, worked in admissions up until her graduation from the law school two years ago, so she still had contacts. She called me around seven that night.

She verified my caller ID, "CB, it's Traci."

I asked her if she'd had a good day and we discussed the little things my son and I never seem to get to. Then I asked, "So, what do you know?"

Her voice sort of ululated, like she was swinging her head, "There's not a lot to know. They're pretty good students, B plus, with a lot of friends. They're party boys, but that's not unusual for juniors." She thinks everyone grows up by their senior year, like she did. I know better. I didn't. "They're known for using their identities to play practical jokes, like swapping girls, and some of the teachers think they take tests for each other."

"That's it?"

"Well, there was one other thing. John got arrested for drinking his freshman year, got into some kind of hormone driven brawl. He was a week from eighteen, and he had a license in another name that he'd used to get service at the bar. Well, he was booked under that name, but he used his real name when he filled out the release documents. No one noticed at first. Then the cops talked to someone in admissions, and they tried to get the fake ID from him, but he said he'd destroyed it. That's the reason it was in his records."

With my usual insightfulness bordering on rudeness, "So, the other name?"

It didn't phase her any. "Cameron Swayze, like the news guy from the fifties." She surprised me with, "It takes a licking and it keeps on ticking." She's only twenty-six, but she's the kind of girl who'd know that kind of thing. Robin wouldn't have a clue. I'm not being mean, since he's more like me than Traci.

I made quick thanks, and told her she could name her first child after me.

"Yeah, right, CB, like any kid wants the moniker Caleb Black Green. Come on, already. Anyway, my kid's not going to be color-blind." On that note, she hung up.

It used to be you could fly under any name, but those days are gone. Now you need a picture ID. So on short notice you return to the old chestnuts. And they were broke, so I guessed they'd flown Delta after getting a family discount, then called in and changed the name. I mean, why not, they never expected anyone to know about Cameron Swayze.

I took Maureen McMartin out to breakfast. She was her usual suspicious self, but she wrote it all down. She called me two hours later and said a round trip ticket in the name of Cameron Swayze had been used to fly from Philadelphia to Portland the day before Josh's death, and the return at midnight the night he died. She said the boys were arrested at the funeral home, and the cops in Atlanta were searching their apartment in Philadelphia. Two hours later she called me to say they found the tickets and the ID.

I called the funeral home and told the manager that I'd be there in an hour to pay for Josh's funeral and cremation. It was the least I could do for a friend. Anyway, it was the end of the final tab.

I got the urn two days later. I paid for a funeral mass. I'm an atheist, and Josh wasn't much of a Catholic, but he'd have wanted it, even if he'd never have asked for it. There were about hundred people there, ten of us were in the regular poker rotation, the rest from his work. He didn't make many close friends, I think just me, but a lot of people liked him. It made me feel good, them being there.

I've since heard the sons have made a claim on Josh's estate if they beat the rap, or when, and if, they get out of prison. I hired a lawyer to make sure that didn't happen. I don't leave justice to chance, ever. His parents are long dead, so I don't know where Josh would have wanted the money to go. He didn't have a will, and I figured he wouldn't care enough to deny the money to his kids, but I did.

I don't plan on going to the trial, which starts some time early next year. You never learn that much at a trial. And you can never know everything. Life is a first person event, and you can never know anything about motives and intentions for certain beyond yourself, and even that has to be qualified. Anyway, they so seldom dish out justice at trials, though this time I expect the right thing will happen. If not, then I'll have to think some more on it.

I knew Josh Ehrens better than anyone else in the world. I see in black and white, but I think Josh lived in between those, the gray middle. He had no ups and downs, no happy and sad, but he lived a good life in his budgeted way. In fact, it was the profligacy of his children that thought nothing of taking his life. They would say they valued life more than he did, even as they denied it to him. I think they had too much, it was too easy, and they valued it too little. I hope that over the next fifty years they learn the value of a budgeted life, but I'm not betting on it.

Bill Capron is a fifty-six year old who retired when he sold his company in 1998. He has published many Color-blind Detective stories which can be accessed from his website, *www.thecolorblinddetective.com*.

The Pills - A Very Short Mystery
By Tim Wohlforth

"Your hair looks nice," he said.

"Thanks," she said.

"Did you just come from the beauty parlor?"

"Yes."

"For me?" he asked.

"Maybe."

"Are you ready?"

"I'm not sure. Don't know if I can actually go through with it."

"It's easy," he said. "The pills dissolve instantly in any liquid. Just drop them in his nightcap tonight. He'll die in his sleep. No pain. No fuss. Then you call me. I'm the family doctor so I'll sign the death certificate."

"Sounds simple enough but I'm the one doing it. He's my husband."

"That hasn't bothered you for some time now," he said. "Don't you see? No more sneaking around. You and I marry. His wealth, my medical practice. We'll have a beautiful life together. That's what you want, right?"

"I guess," she said.

"You love me, not him."

"Sometimes I don't know how I feel."

"But I know," he said. "Trust me."

"I'm trying to."

He slid a small bottle of pills over to her.

"You haven't touched your drink," he said.

"Feeling a little nauseous, and anyway, I shouldn't."

"Why not?"

"You know why," she said. "You're a doctor."

"That's something we need to talk about."

"What do you mean?"

"We don't want to start out together encumbered."

"Encumbered?" she said. "That's what you think?"

"It's a simple operation. I'll perform it myself. No need for anyone to know."

"It's yours, you know," she said.

"I know," he said. "Still."

"You don't care."

"I care very much," he said. "Now don't cry. It's ruining your mascara. We've got to keep our heads. Be practical."

He looked away as he reached into his pocket to find a handkerchief. She opened the pill bottle, poured its contents into his drink, and placed the empty container in her purse.

Wohlforth has published thirty-five short stories. Quiet Storm has published a noir novel, No Time To Mourn, in 2004.

My Kind Knows Regret
by Robert Morrish

Settling into his usual shooter's position – legs shoulder-width apart, elbows and knees bent, leaning slightly forward, left hand braced around his right wrist, right index finger curled gently around the trigger – Brad Votek took aim at his target. He inhaled slightly and squeezed the trigger.

I can picture it as if it was yesterday.

The first shot was a heart shot, but he kept pulling the trigger, again and again and again, until the clip of his Sig P228 was empty. None of the bullets impacted far from the location of the first shot. The last of his spent cartridges clinked, hollow and harmless, on the concrete floor.

"Nice grouping," I said. "I can see you haven't lost your touch."

"Always could out-shoot you," he replied. "That'll never change." He ejected the clip, set it down, and popped in a fresh load.

There'd been a small wall between us ever since Brad joined the Marines out of high school, and I'd joined the Army after community college. Personally, I didn't give a shit; we were all supposed to be on the same side. Except I'd seen far too many fierce fistfights between guys who were supposedly allies to completely accept that school of thought. Enemies were wherever you found them, and Brad had bought into the Semper Fi thing, tooth and nail. To him, it wasn't the Armed Forces, it was the Marines against the world. Sometimes it seemed like that "us vs. them" mentality – or more specifically, *me* vs. them – was at the very core of what Brad was about.

It was an old sticking point between us, but one I had long ago tired of getting snagged upon.

"You rule, Marine. Buy you a drink?"

"Don't see why not."

Under other circumstances, his air of superiority would have been a little too thin for me, but this was Brad we're talking about, and that simple fact bought him a lot of slack. Thirty years, damned near, of friendship could make up for a lot. I overlooked his insults for the latest time, packed up my guns and ammo, and led him out of the range.

Thirty minutes later, we were a few miles closer to home and a few steps closer to peace. At least it felt that way, with our second round – drinks this time, not ammo – in our hands.

The waitress bent over the table next to us, wiping down the surface and picking up leftover glasses, the backs of her upper thighs peaking further out from beneath a barely-there skirt. I was a happily married man, but I couldn't help but appreciate that taut twenty-year-old flesh just inches away. Brad never even looked in her direction. His gaze was locked on a horizon that only he could see, a future where his wife's wandering path would converge once again with his blindly loyal trajectory.

"So have you signed up for the class reunion yet?" I knew it wasn't something he really wanted to talk about, but then again there wasn't much that he *did* want to talk about, and the silence was starting to stretch between us like a tight rope on a high-wire act.

"No." He went back to peeling the label from his bottle – Black Label, as a matter of fact, the same brand he'd drank since high school. For a moment, I thought that would be the end of his response, but then he continued. "Why the hell would I want to go to that? Bunch of overweight women and balding men – has-beens and never-weres – all getting sentimental about people and classes that they hated at the time; comparing clothes and bank accounts and kids' pictures, everyone trying to out-do everyone else; convince them that they're happy and successful. What a crock."

"You don't have to beat around the bush with me. Tell me what you really think." I laughed, help up a hand to stave off another outburst. Brad had always been cynical, but he'd slipped over the edge into bitterness the last few months. "Believe it or not, you actually used to like some of those people. And I distinctly recall you having a good time at the 10-year and 15-year reunions."

"That was then and this is now." He slumped back in his booth seat and looked up at the ceiling. "Everyone there, even people I haven't seen in the last five years, they're all going to ask me where Christine is. And I don't want to have to say, a hundred and fifty times, that she left me, OK?"

He had a point. There would definitely be some awkward moments. But that had to be better than sitting home, staring at a television set, and drinking himself to sleep every night, which is exactly what he'd been doing since his wife walked out. So I worked on him, I admit it. I had his best interests at heart, and thought I knew what was good for him. By the time we left the bar that night, I'd managed to pretty much swivel him around to my way of thinking.

Of course, it probably didn't help matters that I was going home to my wife of two years who I was very much in love with. Brad had been married to Christine for seven years, and with her for close to ten, and for most of that period I'd been single, dating here and there, sometimes in medium-term relationships, but often a third wheel when getting together with the two of them. Now the tables were turned, and it was obvious he didn't like the view from his new seat.

It was about two weeks later when O'Donnell pulled me aside in the hallway.

"You need to talk to your buddy."

"Who, Brad?" I asked stupidly. I had a fair number of friends on the force, but everybody knew that Brad and I dated back to grade school together. And besides, he was obviously the prime candidate to be a source of concern.

"Yeah. I know he's got a lot of shit on his mind, but he needs to pull himself together. Damned near got himself shot this morning. Could've wound up taking his partner with him. For starters."

"What happened?"

He shrugged, nodded towards the locker room. "Ask him."

Brad was sitting in front of his locker, stripped down to his underwear. He was a damned good-looking guy – short-cropped, wavy dark hair; chiseled features with just enough flaws to indicate some character; a perpetual five-o'clock shadow; a wiry, muscular build – who'd have no problem attracting women if he would just put his mind to it. Or at least notice when he *was* attracting attention. At five-eight, he was a little short for some tastes, but he nonetheless got more than his share of second glances.

I sat down and shot the shit with him for a while, knowing better than to jump right into a topic that he wasn't likely to want to talk about. A couple other guys came and went while we were sitting there, with the "went" part happening pretty quickly after I managed to make eye contact with them, a little detail that escaped Brad while he continued to perfect his thousand-yard stare.

I finally got to talking about work, telling him about how my shifts had gone the last couple of days, and so it wasn't too much of a leap when I said to him, "I heard you had a close call this morning."

He looked me in the eye – the first time in a while he'd done so – and held that look for a long, long moment. Brad wasn't stupid, just stubborn. He knew I'd simply taken a roundabout way, through the back alleys of small talk, to sneak up on this topic. Finally, he just said, "I figured you'd get around to asking about that."

You might wonder what the point of surreptitious behavior is when the underlying agenda remains hidden to no one. What can I say? It was Brad, and three decades of friendship had taught me that the direct route led nowhere fast.

It took a mild apology and a couple more promptings, but he finally got around to telling me about it.

"We got an armed robbery call about 11, one of those Korean markets down on San Pablo. We got there just as this kid, couldn't have been older than 15, comes running out, a paper bag in one hand and a big Colt in the other. We chased him in the car for a couple blocks, then ditched it when he went over a construction fence, and got after him on foot. Belliard fell behind, since he's not in such great shape. I finally cornered the kid in an alley off of 21st, right by where they're going to demo those old apartment buildings.

"He falls on his hands and knees like he's out of breath, then when I'm about twenty yards back, he turns on me with his gun out... by all rights, I should've squeezed on him then. Lords knows it would've been a righteous shoot.

"But you didn't...?"

"Nope, I didn't. I lowered my gun. Walked right up on him, 'til I was less than ten feet away. I guess he thought I was daring him to fire, and he looked like he thought pretty hard about it. He was talking shit at me, *saying* he was going to shoot, every step of the way." He sighed, a simple sound that captured all the world-weariness filling up his soul.

"I could tell you that he was just a kid, and that he didn't look like he wanted to shoot, and that he hadn't done any shooting during the robbery, at least as far as I knew. I could tell you all that, but...I guess, when you get right down to it... I just didn't care, Jason. You know? I just didn't care. If he'd put a bullet through me, at least I'd be out of my fucking misery."

I didn't say anything right away; didn't know what *to* say. My friend was clearly in a worse spot than I'd suspected. While I struggled for words, a pair of lonely tears trailed down his cheeks, keeping pace. In all the years, I'd never seen him cry before. For a macho guy like Brad, it was tantamount to cowardice, surrender. I tried to play that card — I started talking about his obsession with Christine, trying to make him see it as a weakness, something that made him less of a man, something to be shunned and abandoned. But if trying to convince Brad that he should leave his wife to her affairs, grant her a divorce, and get on with his life was the equivalent of bashing my head against the wall, my forehead should have been a battered, bloody pulp by then. No matter what tack I took, no matter if I tried logic or emotion, friendly advice or bald-faced descriptions of her behavior, I couldn't get him to see her for what she was – manipulative and materialistic and completely callous to Brad's feelings. This latest attempt was no more successful than its many predecessors.

"Say whatever you want about her, I just want her back." He looked up at me. "I still really, really love her. There's got to be some way I can get her back."

How do you reason with somebody who's not just looking at things through rose-colored glasses, but through a kaleidoscope that shifted prisms and distorted realities until the resulting perspective was theirs and theirs alone?

"When I see her with somebody else, it just drives me crazy. It's all I can do not to go ballistic on the guy. And lately, ever since she left me, it's been this guy Todd. I don't know what she sees in the guy. I could maybe understand it better if he was a rich guy, driving a Porsche or a Don Juan type. But he's just a regular guy, regular job.

"I keep seeing her with him – I run into them at the grocery store, on the street... it's like I can't escape them."

I had an urge to ask him if he'd really just been "running into them," or if he'd actually been stalking his wife and her boyfriend; but I bit it off. Instead, I tried to convince him to take some time off, maybe even see a counselor, but he wasn't having any of it. I knew he might be a threat to himself, at least in some sense, but I couldn't bring myself to talk to his Sergeant, or anybody else in the chain of command. He was my best friend. I couldn't turn him in. I resolved to keep a close eye on him, spend as much time with him as I could, to keep trying to get him over his fixation on Christine.

A couple weeks went by, then a month. No more red flags. Brad didn't undergo any miraculous recovery, but he at least seemed to move from scratching a festering wound to a sort of numb acceptance. My wife thought he needed more time, a lot more time, before he could start thinking about other women, but I talked her into trying to set him up with a couple friends of hers. Neither one worked out. Brad sleepwalked his way through the dinners and the women walked away wondering what the point had been.

As the class reunion approached, I finally convinced him to attend, with me and Suzanne. I think he gave in just to get me off his back. By the time the night finally arrived, he was resigned to his fate.

Outside of our respective stints in the military, neither of us had ever strayed far from San Leandro, where we'd grown up. We'd both wound up as cops in Oakland, Brad immediately after leaving the Marines and me after a two-year stint out in Walnut Creek – possibly the most boring 'burb a cop could work. I'd joined Brad on the Oakland force for a lot of reasons: we'd hung out a lot in "Oaktown" while growing up, and I honestly wanted to try and make it a better place; it paid better; it was less of a commute; but probably most of all because it gave me the opportunity to work with my best friend. It was no guarantee that we'd wind up in the same precinct, but as a result of a little luck and maybe a little string-pulling by an influential acquaintance of his, it happened. In the years since, we've drifted apart at times, but never for long. Some event, good or bad, would always bring our lives back in orbit and crystallize our friendship. In this case, it was Brad's dissolving marriage that had reined us back in from personal lives that were gradually pulling us off into the day-to-day void.

The reunion was on a Saturday night and neither of us had pulled a shift the next day, so we settled down to some serious drinking before we'd even left the house. Susanne was the designated driver, and by now she'd learned how to put up with us, so she largely left us to our own devices, save for the occasional knowing smirk. Once we actually got there, it started out like a mediocre Woody Allen movie, with far more awkward moments than I could comfortably stand. Everybody and their brother managed to ask Brad where Christine was. You'd think somebody would've had the good sense and social graces not to ram their foot down their throat, but our classmates were a veritable loose-limbed chorus line.

Along about eleven, with a good portion of the crowd having filtered out to rescue baby-sitters and loosen the clothing they'd squeezed themselves into, we found ourselves talking to Walt Murphy, who'd been our class valedictorian. Besides his brains, Murphy was a genuinely nice guy, a pretty decent athlete, and the product of large and respected family. But he'd somehow managed to get a girl pregnant during his junior year, a scandalous event in those days, especially to the "good Catholic" family to which he belonged. Walt was hardly allowed to see the light of day, and certainly not the neon of night, after that. It was probably about as close as you could come to a two-year grounding of a 17-18 year old kid. His lack of experience during those formative nightlife years seemed to rob Murph of whatever social graces he'd had, leaving him forever foundering on the rocks of awkwardness when it came to the shores of the opposite sex.

Murph had gotten the obligatory faux pas query about Christine out of the way early in the evening and then wandered off to embarrass himself elsewhere. Now he'd returned, perhaps seeking to make amends. The three of us were engaged in idle wonderings about the disposition of various classmates who weren't in attendance when Sheri Simpson — at least that had been her name in high school, although I think she's been married at least twice since then — walked up and said hello. Murph had been in our midst long enough to add a couple shots to whatever he'd drank before then, so maybe it shouldn't have surprised us when, after the usual "what's new" pleasantries, he looked at Sheri's burgeoning midriff and asked "are you hoping for a boy or a girl this time?"

To which Sheri replied, in a voice dripping icicles, "I'm not pregnant."

Brad and I mumbled something about getting another round of drinks. We made it a few steps away, just far enough to feel safe, then exploded in laughter. In fact, we got downright hysterical. It was just the sort of absurd moment we needed to wash away the somber undertones. Brad laughed so hard he had tears in his eyes – good tears this time, I remember thinking. I was happy to see him like that. It had been a long time. I thought maybe he'd finally turned a corner, left Christine dwindling in his rear-view mirror, and was on his way to a happier place.

It was a couple days later before I realized just how wrong I was. It was a little after noon when I got the call. A pencil-lead gray sky hung so low I almost wanted to duck my head.

"246 in progress," came the dispatcher's voice. "Shots fired, 1187 Franklin. Possible hostage situation."

I was close, about three blocks away. I swung my bike around and hit the siren. My adrenaline was double-timing it by the time I hit the parking lot. I'd been on the Oakland force for more than ten years, working some bad areas, but I'd been lucky when it came to shots-fired situations. Only three in that whole time — and none where I'd ever actually been shot at or, in retrospect, been in any real danger.

The 1100 block of Franklin was one of those faceless industrial park complexes, filled with anonymous businesses destined to live on the edge or die altogether. 1187 was near the rear of the complex, which spanned all the way to the back of the block. I came through the linked parking lots hard and quiet, killing my siren before I got too close. There was a small cluster of people out front of the building, their car-crash curiosity leading them to gather closer to the scene than they should; their fear keeping them from getting *too* close. I stopped long enough to find out that none of them really knew anything — they were all from the surrounding businesses, none from 1187, which I could see was the home of something called Innovative Kitchen Concepts. They'd heard the shooting and screams, someone had called it in, and now they were hanging back and waiting for the show to begin. I verified the unit was like every other one of its kind, with loading docks in back; told them to clear the area; and drove around back.

There weren't any rubber-neckers in the back. Apparently they'd all figured the best vantage point was out front. However, there *was* one of our cars there. I was happy to see we already had somebody on scene. But then I saw it was car 37, and my heart sank.

Brad and a guy with a gun – that had nearly been a recipe for disaster the last time that pair was drawn. The way he'd been acting lately, it seemed like he now had less interest in putting himself in harm's way, but who could tell for sure? The dispatcher said shots had been fired. God knew what might have already happened.

I parked my bike behind a dumpster at one end of the rear lot, radioed my 10-97 and waited.

But then my mind started flipping into overdrive. There had been shots fired, but there was no shooting when I got there. There was no sign of Brad or his partner Belliard; no indication the situation was *over.* Did that mean they'd been hit? Or were they laying low, holding fire because of a hostage situation? I was driving myself crazy with the wondering while I was supposed to be focusing on the situation. It's amazing how love — the concern for someone you love, the way I loved Brad — can cloud your senses. I guess that's how it was with Brad and his love for Christine.

I knew I had to wait for back-up — protocol didn't allow for any other course of action. But, in the end, I was only able to stay still for a minute or two before it became too much. Hearing sirens approaching in the distance convinced me they were getting close, and that I'd waited long enough.

The loading dock entrance was closed, so I headed for the adjacent door. My heart was racing as I crept closer and inched it open.

A wide, short hallway with three doors off it led to a large, unlit warehouse. I edged my way inside and eased the door shut behind me. As it closed, the darkness regained command. For a few seconds, I couldn't see a thing.

Once my eyes began to adjust, I tried the doors, but they led me nowhere — two bathrooms and a janitor's closet, all empty

— so I moved to the corner of the hallway and peered out into the warehouse. It was even bigger than I'd first thought. They'd apparently leased two adjacent units and taken out the wall between them, so the space extended well off into the darkness. Straight ahead, I could just make out a wall about a hundred feet distant, where the warehouse gave way to offices. A faint rectangle of light trickled in, framing a closed door. Between that far-away wall and me were row upon row of floor-to-ceiling shelves crammed with what looked to be cabinets and sinks and the like, further reducing visibility. As my eyes began to grow accustomed to the darkness, I made out a pool of blood and an outstretched hand, reaching plaintively beyond the end of one row of shelves.

I crab-walked over to the body. The rustle of my clothing seemed deafening to me in the echoing quiet of the warehouse. It was a guy in jeans and a T-shirt; I couldn't tell much more since the bullet had taken the upper half of his face with it when it exited. I'd just about convinced myself to sit tight and wait for the cavalry when I heard a sound come from the front offices, a sound somewhere between a scream and a whimper.

I'd been swimming in fear and indecision but that sound brought everything rushing back into focus, like a movie special effect. Another rush of adrenaline rode with it and the next thing I knew, I was up and moving down the row.

As loud as the sound of my movements seemed to me, the shots, when they came, were much, much louder. I must have seen the muzzle flash first, but at the time it seemed as though that explosion of sound came first; then the sensation of being punched backwards into the shelving. At some point, pain joined the party.

At first, I thought I'd been hit twice. Somewhere up around my collarbone or shoulder was one. That's where I'd felt the body blow that knocked me down. The other one seemed to be in my face. I felt a sharp, stabbing pain there, and could feel blood running into my mouth. I reached up to assess the damage and felt something sharp protruding from my cheek. Without thinking, I got my fingers around it and yanked it out, not wanting anything in my body that didn't belong there. Pulling it out seemed to hurt worse than it had going in. I may have cried out; I'm not sure. I could tell almost immediately that the extraction had made the bleeding worse.

I gazed dimly at the piece of bloody plastic in my hand for some time before I recognized it for what it was. The shot I'd taken in the shoulder had shattered the radio microphone mounted there, sending a piece of shrapnel into my cheek.

I know now that I had slipped into shock as I sat there, staring stupidly at a plastic shard in my hand. Otherwise, I would've had the sense to find my gun, which I'd dropped somewhere, and find a defensible position. As it was, I lay there, feeling my life leak out of me, completely at a loss as to what to do next. There were instants where I flashed on the fact that I needed to take action, to *do something*, but they were fleeting, my attention span reduced to the faltering beat of a heart.

It could have been thirty seconds later, or five minutes, when my eyes focused on a pair of shoes and I realized someone was standing over me. The whereabouts of my gun suddenly seemed very important and I think I started scrabbling and clawing and gasping — a not-very-pretty picture of panic — when Brad reached down to try and settle me. I looked up, saw his face come looming out of the gloom, and felt the hand squeezing my heart suddenly unclench.

He crouched and whispered to me, "How bad you hit, buddy?"

"Just here," I said nodding towards what felt like a drive-through window in my shoulder. "Hurts."

"I bet it does. Looks like hell, too. You're losing a lot of blood. We've got to get you out of here."

"Where's the shooter?" I managed, but I must've been talking too loud, because Brad put his finger to his lips, looked back over his shoulder. "I'm not sure. He keeps moving around."

He paused. "He's got some hostages locked in the offices in front. I got a glimpse before he saw me and started shooting. I think they're OK. Most of them, anyway."

"Not that guy over by the door," I said, looking in the direction where I'd seen the body.

"No, he's definitely not OK."

"How about Belliard?"

He looked at me; swallowed. "Got hit in the leg. He's in that far corner over there," he whispered, nodding. "Once I get you out of here, I'll go get him."

"Don't get yourself killed, buddy."

"Don't worry. I'm not looking to do anything stupid."

He moved around to my left, got underneath my good arm, and hauled me up. It was all I could do not to scream. A little must have slipped out because he hissed at me to be quiet.

The dozen or so steps between where I'd fallen and the back door seemed like an IronMan contest. I'd lost enough blood that it was getting hard to keep my eyes open. I wanted to stop, to rest, maybe to just give up, but Brad wouldn't let me.

Then we were at the door. He opened it a crack, letting in a ray of sunlight. "You've got to take it from here," he said. "Just a few steps and you're home-free."

"Come with me," I said, worried like a brother and willing to ignore, for the moment, Belliard's plight.

"Can't. Gotta get my partner. I'll be along in a minute."

He peered outside, then opened the door a little further.

"Go now," he said, opening the door and giving me a little shove to start me on my way.

I stumbled against the frame, the slight impact sending lightning bolts into my shoulder and across my chest. The sun had come out from behind the clouds and it seemed overpowering now, my eyes drawn down to slits against the blinding light. I staggered forward a few steps, seeing only needles and pins of mirrored brilliance.

I made it out into the parking lot and damned near got my head blown off. There were enough cop cars out there to make it look the precinct parking lot, with a couple SWAT units front and center. And there were enough guns pointed my way to ventilate me in a heartbeat. Fortunately, no one's trigger finger spasmed.

When I was about halfway across the open area, a couple guys in vests ran out to help me. They half-carried, half-dragged me back behind their perimeter, my shoulder shrieking every step of the way.

A doctor started poking at me and somebody forced some water on me. Once they figured I wasn't in danger of imminent death, a couple higher-ups, including the SWAT team commander, started spitting questions at me. They were all talking at once – or so it seemed, in my state – and so I only caught snatches.

"...did you see..."

"Are there dead..."

"...did you talk to him..."

"Are there wounded...."

"What's he want..."

I coughed up some blood then, which caused them to hold their fire for a moment.

"Brad's OK," I finally managed. "He's not hit. He said Belliard took one in the leg, but it's not bad. I didn't see him, though. There's at least one dead guy in the warehouse. Don't know if there's other dead or wounded. Brad said..." I had to catch my breath, "that the shooter keeps moving around. He can't get a bead on him."

The SWAT leader just looked at me as if I were brain-dead. Nelson, the shift Captain, looked nervous. I didn't understand what the problem was. I tried again to tell them what I knew, but I was having a hard time talking; slurring my words like a 3 a.m. drunk. I heard the doctor say something about getting me to the hospital.

Finally, Nelson seemed to get his nerve up. He crouched down to where he could look me in the face. "There's no other shooter in there," he said. "It's Votek."

I stared at him, not comprehending what he was saying.

"Belliard called it in, but... he was hit and now we can't raise him on the radio. He said Votek's wife's boyfriend worked in there; said Votek went in and started shooting."

Just then, with exquisite timing, the sound of one more shot rang out from inside the building.

"You think you know somebody,
You think they know you.
You think you know somebody,
Man, you never do"
— Todd Snider, *"You Think You Know Somebody"*

Robert Morrish is the editor of *Cemetery Dance.* His short fiction has appeared in many anthologies, and a collection is forthcoming from Subterranean Press. His non-fiction work is published in books such as *The Encyclopedia of Fantasy* and periodicals including *Publishers Weekly,* and *Rod Serling's Twilight Zone Magazine.*

Out of Time
by Paul D. Marks

The weather ratcheted up one degree. Ricky could feel even that one-degree as the sweat trickled down his back. Still the heat was one thing, the humidity another. But the sun was shining, the palm trees rippling in the breeze, and the ocean sparkled only a few yards off. Who could ask for more, especially when you've spent the last seven years in exile, waiting out the statute of limitations? South Beach had changed quite a bit in that time. From a slum to an art deco neon jungle.

He took a room at the four story Deco Echo Hotel, the same place he'd stayed at when he left SoBe all those years ago. Only then it was a dive renting for a few bucks a week. Now it was a fancy hostelry with streamline modern railings and pipes in a rainbow of colors circling the balconies and it cost more per day, probably per hour, than it had for a month.

Plastic palm trees swayed and pink flamingos danced. The sky was midnight blue and sparkled with stars that never went out, unless a light bulb blew. The Pyramid Lounge of the InterNational Hotel. A new piano player, Eddie Taylor, was going through some riffs, a little Sinatra, a little Ellington. And then she came in, as he knew she would sooner or later. She almost looked the same - surfer girl blonde hair against tan skin - a little rounder, but in all the right places. Come you-know-what-me heels, short skirt, shiny low cut top and shinier diamond necklace with matching bracelet. She was alone, which surprised him. He did a quick fade on the song he was playing segueing into the Beach Boys' *Surfer Girl*. It had been their song, even though it predated them by a couple of decades or more. The beach crowd they hung with knew all those Beach Boys oldies. And it seemed the Pyramid Lounge crowd enjoyed them too, especially Lynn.

Would she recognize him? He didn't think so. His appearance had changed. Demeanor too. It was a chance he had to take.

She walked up to the piano, stood there a moment, not so much looking at him but through him, dropped a dollar into the tip tray. She started to walk off, turned back. Did she recognize him? She looked him over but nothing registered on her face. Maybe he looked like someone she had known, reminded her of someone. But he was dead, wasn't he? Figuratively if not literally.

Ricky looked different than he had before leaving Miami seven years ago. He was gaunter and had a goatee or chin thing as he called it. His hair was shorter, slicked back a la Alec Baldwin. It was also darker - that was on purpose. And the name on his driver's license was different too. Instead of Richard Donovan it now read Edmond Taylor. The Taylor seemed bland and innocuous enough. The Edmond he'd borrowed from an old black and white movie that he'd watched late one night in his West Coast crib. Between that old flick and *The Godfather,* he realized one was nothing in this world without power and money.

She went to a nearby booth where a man soon joined her. Him? It had to be. Tall, broad shouldered. Shoes without socks. Brown hair with blonde highlights. Also shorter than when they had known each other.

"*Surfer Girl*," the man said, sitting down. "Your song." He called the waiter over, ordered drinks for both of them as Ricky segued into *You Took Advantage of Me.*

"I like the Beach Boys' version better," she said, twirling a ringlet of lustrous hair - not looking toward the piano player.

The next night Eddie was back at the piano. It wasn't long before Lynn showed up. Would Pat come in behind her again? Lynn sat by the piano. He saw her staring at him from the corner of his eye. He smiled at her quickly and only once. He played favorites from the swing and early rock eras. Torch songs. Ballads. A hot tempo boogie roll. She asked him to play *Surfer Girl.* It was like Ingrid Bergman asking Sam to play *As Time Goes By,* play it once, Sam, for old time's sake.

"I played it last night," he said, barely turning up the corners of his mouth. "I try not to play a song two nights in a row. But if you weren't here last night maybe I can break my rule. Customer's always right, you know."

He played *Surfer Girl,* singing along. His voice was mellow, soft and he could carry a tune. Probably not good enough for the big time, but good enough to make a living in a piano bar, if that's what he'd had in mind.

When the song was over she put a five-dollar bill into the tip tray. "Do I know you?" she said.

He looked at her. He wanted to say something else, but said, "No, I don't think so.

She looked at the printed card on the piano with the scrolled writing that read "Edmond 'Eddie' Taylor."

"My husband and I are having a party next Saturday. We have a piano. Can you play for us? I can pay you well."

He thought a moment. "I'm supposed to work here Saturday night and since I just started...."

"We know the owners. I'm sure they'll give you the night off - a favor to us."

He bowed his head.

"Who is this piano guy? Pat said. She knew he was pissed at her for coming home so late, staying out without him. His face was red. His neck bulging. "There's something about this piano player that doesn't sit right with me. Does he look familiar to you?"

She didn't respond. Her mind was someplace else. On a beach not that far down the coast from their house in miles. Very far in time and memory, *Surfer Girl* spinning round her head.

The scent of oleander wandered into his room from outside, same as in the old days - the more things change.... He looked at the bands of color circling across his walls. From them to the mirror. He put on the bedside radio, found an oldies station. The Gin Blossoms came on, followed by Nirvana. He liked the songs he grew up with. When he was a kid his parents forced him to take piano lessons. He hated it, was embarrassed - it was for sissies, so he never let his friends know. Now he was glad that he could play fairly well. When he'd auditioned for the manager of the Pyramid Lounge piano bar he'd gotten the gig right away.

Ricky was just about to turn thirty. Did he still want to be a Ricky at thirty? Or an Eddie? He sat on his balcony, smoked a cigarette, the ocean shimmering in the distance, the beaches empty at 4am. When he'd left the first time he thought of Lynn as the one who got away. He'd wanted to marry her. Since then he hadn't wanted to marry anyone, even though he'd been with a thousand women one way or another. He thought he'd probably never get married, unless Lynn and him got back together. So far everything was fine. He'd made contact. A good start.

He thought about the past. The future. He thought he wasn't someone who nursed a grudge. He was happy to be home.

"Son-of-a-bitch checks out," Pat said. "So, who is he?"

"Well, his name's Edmond Taylor."

"Tell me something I don't know," Lynn said.

"He's really a nobody. Tried to make it in Hollywood - Loser. Broadway - Loser. Music biz - Loser. Piano player in small bars, well, he's doing okay there. Never married. Bounces from place to place. No permanent address. No permanent babe. Nothing permanent about him except Loser. Loser. Loser." He was triumphant.

"I'm sorry to bother you," Eddie said, deferentially, clutching the shiny silver object in his right hand as Lynn opened the door. "I thought I'd better check the piano, tune it if it needs it." He held up the tuning fork. She led him to the living room. The room was as big as a banquet hall in some hotels and more lavishly decorated. It was Frank Lloyd Wright modernized for the 21st century, with higher ceilings. But he knew that. Just like he knew the house stood on three acres of prime beachfront real estate and would be a soft peach color. It would have an original Picasso on the east living room wall, a collection of Faberge eggs in the china cabinet.

He walked three paces behind her, his head bowed, a servant in the presence of royalty. The piano cut the huge room diagonally. He even knew where it would be and that it would be a Bosendorfer grand. He also knew it would be perfectly in tune, as it was tuned every three months, even though no one played it.

"Here it is," she said.

"Nice instrument," and he meant it. He'd played them before. He ran his fingers over the highly varnished surface that he could see his face in. A face he barely recognized, but one that he was getting used to.

He began to tune the piano.

"It's in perfect tune. Perfect," he said, looking straight at her.

Some things in SoBe hadn't changed. There were still the old men on the boardwalk playing chess and checkers and penny ante poker. Ricky lit a cigarette, sat on a whitewashed wooden bench near the gaming area.

A couple of kids were building a sand castle in the wet sand just above the tide line. It was tall, with a moat and parapets, towers and tunnels.

Ricky thought about the tunes he would play on Saturday. Couldn't decide if he'd play *Surfer Girl* or wait for her to request it. He wanted to meet their friends. See what their lives were like today.

He thought about how he hardly recognized himself and didn't think anyone else did either. Besides, it'd been seven years, he probably wasn't even a blip on their radar screens. But he'd been waiting for this day for 2,555 days, plus a few extra thrown in for good measure, just in case.

A big kid came up to the two little kids building the sand castle. They said a few words, then he pummeled the castle with his foot, walked off laughing. Ricky thought about going after him, but changed his mind. The kids should learn to fend for themselves.

For the party the piano had been moved onto the veranda. Seated behind the piano, Eddie could see and smell the ocean. He wore a tuxedo for the occasion, as he had been requested to do. A monkey suit for a monkey on a string.

He opened with a jazzed up version of Beethoven's *Moonlight Sonata.* That got the people who recognized it excited. They'd never heard Beethoven played like that. He was already in, from the first note he played.

The wine and liquor flowed. The food nonstop. The beautiful people talked about stock portfolios, 401Ks and asset allocation.

She walked toward him as he sat on the steps that led to the beach. He was taking his break and was still worried that she recognized him. If she did she said nothing.

"Hiding out?" she said, sitting next to him. He offered her a smoke. She declined. "You should mingle. Some important people here. They might be able to give you a break."

"Thanks, but I'm not looking for a break."

"You just like to play your music and move on."

"Something like that."

"You remind me of someone I used to know."

"Really?"

"An old friend. You look like I thought he might look today. I haven't seen him in a long time."

"Well, they say everyone has their double. I guess I'm his. Did he play piano?"

"No. I don't know what talents he might have had. He was just a kid really. But fun to be around."

He could feel her wistfulness carry to him on the balmy breeze. It almost made him feel sorry for her. "Do you know where he is?"

"Oh, I haven't seen him in years. I hope he's okay."

"It's like Proust says, you don't really know the past when you're in it, and you can't know it today because of the meanings you give it from your present. So my advice is to just forget about him and move on."

They talked for several minutes. She hadn't changed much. Still looked good and her only ambition was to have money, however she could get it. Live a life of parties and luxury. Live fast, look good, die young and leave a good-looking corpse, was what she always said. Looks like she was getting what she wanted. She headed down the stairs to the sand. At the bottom she turned to him, beckoning. He walked down the stairs.

"I'll get sand in my shoes," he said. He knew saying that would allay any thoughts she might have that he was Ricky. Ricky never minded sand in his shoes. He was the surfer boy to her surfer girl. "It'll ruin the patent leather's finish on my rent-a-shoes."

"Don't be so prissy," she said.

He jumped onto the beach, sand rushing over his shoes, spilling inside. She took off her white high-heeled sandals, dangling them over her shoulder by the straps. They walked toward the shore break. Breakers crashed gently at their feet. Ricky's tuxedo pants got wet and clung to his legs. A sliver flame of orange sun fired off its dying rays. Here and there a flare of sunlight sparked the upper edge of the water, making it look magical. Mysterious.

"What're you looking at?" she said.

"The ocean."

"Looks like you're looking beyond the ocean."

"Remembering." He hesitated. They walked further down the beach. Past what was left of another huge sand castle. But now the ocean itself had overrun the moat and the castle was melting back into the sea. Like Shelley's *Ozymandius*' paean to himself, little was left of the once mighty castle in the sand.

"A girl?" she asked.

"A girl. A boy. Another life. Another lifetime."

"It's funny how things like that happen. We think our lives are all set and then poof - in a puff of smoke - it's all gone. Nothing lasts forever.

"Do you wish it could?"

"Don't you? I mean sometimes, don't you wish you could just capture a moment of time and keep it forever, like that old song *Time in a Bottle*?"

"I used to," he said. He looked out across the water. "Not anymore."

"You've been hurt. You'll get over her. We all do. We all learn to live with the choices we make." She took his hand. Her skin was the soft pampered skin of a wealthy woman.

"Your husband."

She put her finger to his lips. She kissed him. The sweet night air filled him with desire. He pulled her to him. It wasn't long before they were on the beach, half dressed, making love under the moon-shadow of a rippling palm tree. She felt so natural in his arms. It felt so natural to be inside her. It was like coming home. Or was Thomas Wolfe right when he said you can't go home again?

A cloud bisected the moon, turning the water dark.

* * *

On his balcony later that night, cigarette at his lips, he replayed the evening in his mind. Making love with Lynn was the peak. But he knew it was all downhill from here. Either that or he should just pack his bags and leave Miami for good. And he would, just not quite yet.

Pat. Lynn. Ricky. The Three Musketeers. All for one. And one for all. Lynn always in the middle, shuffling back and forth from Pat to Ricky. She liked Ricky better. That was obvious, but Pat had more ambition.

He tossed the cigarette off the balcony, its crimson embers fell like shooting stars to the ground below. He went inside, passing the mirror. Stopped. He recognized himself, but didn't recognize himself. He wasn't sure which he liked better, the goofy innocent kid caught up in things bigger than himself or the cunning worldly-wise man whose whole life was a lie. Or was it?

"You lie so much you believe yourself," he said to the face in the mirror.

* * *

Ricky stood in the shore break outside his hotel. The water rushed against his feet and ankles. He dropped a cigarette into the ocean. Heard it hiss itself out. It ate him seeing Lynn with Pat. He was almost angrier with her than him. How could she? The sun was just coming up but already there were kids playing on the beach, dodging in and out of the water. He and Pat and Lynn were those kids - in another lifetime. They had grown up on the beaches of Miami, building castles made of sand. Body surfing, boogie boarding and surfing. When they were teenagers they smoked their first joint together. Both boys liked Lynn. Pat got her first, but it didn't last. Lynn and Ricky were an item. None of them had much in the way of goals except, of course, to be rich and famous. How they would get there they hadn't a clue. Until something fell in their laps.

"I've got the deal that'll make us," Pat says, brushing his dirty blonde hair off his twenty-two year old face. He pulls a small packet of white powder from his pocket.

"What's that?" Ricky asks.

"Baby powder. For a baby like you." Pat laughs. "Coke, you dope. I've got a deal for some coke that will make us rich."

And he did. Only problem was The Law. Pat made the deal. Ricky was to be the lookout. The lookout got busted - with a small portion of the dope. Set up. He didn't rat Pat out, but he jumped bail. So Pat took the money and Lynn, and turned the money into more money. A money machine. And Ricky had to split. And stay split for at least seven years, until the statute of limitations ran down. And even though it had, he didn't want to come back as himself. A joke to Pat. The wiser, all-knowing Pat.

Pat had set him up to be the fall guy. He knew it. Pat wanted Lynn.

Ricky didn't know where to go. What to do.

He bummed. Landed on the other coast. Money. Goddamn money. Everything revolved around it. He needed it to buy a fake I.D. on Alvarado in downtown L.A. He landed in Silicon Valley just in time to get rich on stock options at the startup he worked for. And he ditched out just in time to miss losing it all. His luck was changing.

In his exile he'd had a lot of time to read and educate himself and catch up on many of the things he'd missed when he was younger and a party kid. He took piano lessons.

He would show them. He vowed he'd go back to Miami. Not as some surf bum dweeb, but as someone who'd made something of himself. That plan morphed into one of pure revenge. He came across an old saying that stuck in his mind: "revenge is a dish best served cold". It was seven years cold now. He'd changed his appearance and his identity with his money and computer knowledge. He created several new identities for himself. Tinker, tailor, soldier, piano player. They would all come in handy some day.

He hired a detective to check out Pat and Lynn. He knew everything about them. Their mansion. Their money. Sure they owned the club, but that was just a money-laundering gig for their real business, drugs. But Pat got what he wanted - Lynn. And Lynn got what she wanted - a lifestyle of the rich and famous.

Did they ever bother to think about him? Revenge, Ricky thought. Breakfast of champions.

Edmond was his Miami identity. His *real* new identity was someone else altogether. But Ricky was dead, as Edmond would be soon too. He thought about pulling back, knew he couldn't. His dish of revenge would be cold, but it would be sweet.

Lynn liked Edmond's playing. She invited him to the house several times to play. Pat was always there. No second takes of their beach scene. He wondered how they could not recognize him. True, it had been seven years and he had changed his appearance. But do people really forget that quickly? Or do they want to forget?

Pat and Edmond were on the veranda. Eddie watched the palm trees and the breakers. Lynn was inside with the cook, making sure the dinner was perfect. Pat and Eddie made small talk. Then Pat said:

"Don't you have greater aspirations? I mean, I'm not putting down what you do, but don't you want something more?"

It was the opening Ricky had been waiting for. "Sure. But if you mean do I want to be Elton John or Billy Joel, no I don't care about that. You lose your freedom."

"So what do you want?"

"I just want enough money to not have to worry about money anymore.

"You won't get that playing piano in bars.

"Don't I know it." Eddie paused, sipping his mai tai. He wore a look that said should I open up to this guy?

"Looks like you've got something on your mind. Don't worry, I know musicians don't always deal in the up and up. Smoke a little weed. Score a little coke."

"That's it," Eddie said, near breathless. "I've got a chance to score big on some coke. But I don't know if I should take the chance." Eddie stuck his hands in his pockets. He said, "This is my big break, but I'm scared shitless - I don't wanna do time." He sounded the total nerd, which is exactly what he wanted.

Eddie stared out to the ocean. Its endless waves crashing the shore break, tearing off little pieces of earth, washing them out to sea. Kids jumped in the surf. Ricky hoped they'd grow up happier than he had. Pat took his time before answering. Ricky knew it was a game. He could see the machinations in Pat's mind: play Edmond out. He's just a stupid piano player, in over his head. Then offer to help, a deal. I'll save you, for a nice cut, of course. And maybe leave you in the lurch like I left that schmuck Ricky all those years ago. But this time Edmond and Ricky was ready for Pat.

Then it came. Pat had his hand on his chin. "I do understand that you enjoy the piano gigs but you want to be a little more financially secure."

Eddie smiled.

"The risk factor is holding you back."

Eddie nodded. Pat put his arm around Eddie's shoulder.

"Good money, quick score, but also a large downside."

Eddie sighed. Pat had played into his game.

"How much are we talking about?" Pat said.

"Half a million dollars' worth," Eddie said. "I know, you're wondering how I got into this. Friend from the club scene. He's Colombian. And he's looking for a new outlet here. Someone who's untainted."

"Someone like you."

Eddie smiled a soft, sweet smile. Those acting classes he'd taken were paying off.

"I might be able to help you. Cover the downside at least. I know some people who might be able to unload the stuff for you, take the lion's share of the risk. And after all, who cares, right? People should be allowed a little pleasure. Should be allowed to do what they want with their own bodies."

Eddie nodded again. Shy. Innocent. In something over his head. And now here was this nice fellow willing to help him out. And he wasn't even asking for a cut.

"Of course, I'd want to compensate you and your friends," Eddie said.

"We won't take much, less than a thieving lawyer's third, we'll do it for twenty-five percent? Fair?"

Eddie grinned. "Fair." Inside the shell that was Eddie Ricky also grinned.

Pat turned on him. Cold. Menacing. "You wouldn't be a narc, would you?"

Eddie recoiled, stepping back. The look on his face was that of an innocent babe. "No way, man. Why would you say that?"

"Then you won't mind taking off your shirt."

Eddie hesitated, then slowly unbuttoned his Hawaiian print shirt revealing nothing but bare skin.

"Or your pants."

"Do I really have to do this?"

The look in Pat's eyes answered the question for him. He slid his pants off. Pat grabbed his crotch, checking for a wire. Nothing.

"Get dressed. And try to understand my concerns."

"Sure," Eddie said, shaken, heart pounding in his throat.

Lynn called them to supper. It was a quiet meal.

"I should get an Academy Award," Ricky thought, on his balcony again, another glowing butt dangling from his mouth. Eddie might be afraid of Pat, as Ricky used to be. Ricky wasn't anymore, and never would be again.

They had set the plan, everything contingent on both Pat's and Eddie's people. But it was a starting point. Eddie was nervous, afraid. Pat cool, confident. Ricky was eager, impatient for what he'd waited seven long years for. Lynn was innocent, at least in this case. But then, he thought, there are no innocents in war. Only collateral damage.

It had been planned with the preciseness of a military operation. One that John Wayne could have pulled off. The plane flew low and lonely into a desolate field south of Miami. There were no lights on the plane. Only six heavy-duty flashlights to mark the landing strip. Eddie could have used a GPS system - and in fact had, he just didn't tell Pat about it. The flashlights were just for show. The pilot was actually being guided to the landing spot by a global positioning satellite signal. The pilot didn't know either Ricky or Edmond. He knew another of Ricky's false identities.

Eddie and Pat waited for it to land, slapping at mosquitoes, while spraying repellant on themselves. The plane circled the field once, tipping its wings. Eddie flashed a light up to him. There were three other people here with Eddie and Pat. One was Pat's partner, Jay. The other two were muscle men. They would move the drugs from the plane to a van and they would transport it to the city. That way Pat couldn't get stopped with it - if anyone got in trouble it would be them.

The plane made a smooth landing. Pat and Eddie went to it, greeted the pilot, who declined to give his name. He was about the same height as Eddie. Same build. It had taken Ricky a long time to find just the right person.

"Let's see it," Pat said. The pilot showed them the smooth white powder. Pat tasted it. The grin on his face said it was the real thing. He nodded to Jay who gave the orders for the two muscle men to start moving the coke to the van. It was a lot of coke but it didn't take long.

Pat and Jay talked near the van, while Eddie paid off the pilot.

"What do you want me to do with the kid?" Jay said, looking towards Eddie.

"Take care of him. No strings attached."

Pat looked back at the plane. Eddie was gone. Where the hell was he? Without even time to formulate an answer the plane exploded into a ball of white light, illuminating the night sky like a million flares.

"Let's get the hell outta here," Pat shouted.

"What about your pal, Eddie?"

"Fuck him."

The van started off. Pat and Jay got into Jay's Beamer, turned over the engine. The two vehicles headed for the road that would take them to the highway. Heading towards them were a stream of lights, white headlights - also red and blue police lights. The van was in the lead and was going to go past the police cars when a black and white pulled into the opposing traffic lane. The van swerved to avoid the cops, ditching on the side of the road. The Beamer crashed head on into the police car. Lucky the cops were expecting a hit and were saved by their crumple zone, air bags and heavy-duty bumper. The Beamer wasn't so lucky. Neither Pat nor Jay were seriously hurt, but the Beamer had become an accordion.

Burned and dead, Eddie's body was found in the wreckage of the plane, while Ricky motored back to Miami in the small boat he'd moored near the landing strip.

"It's a setup," Pat shouted as police hooked him up and led him to a police car. "A goddamned setup."

"Shut up," a uniform said. "Don't you know you have the right to remain silent? Exercise your rights." He shoved Pat's head below the roof of the car, pushing him into the backseat.

"I'll get you back you little fuck," Pat shouted, staring back at the burning wreckage, as the police car drove off.

The dead body was positively ID'd: Edmond Taylor. Computer records matched. That was enough for the authorities, who didn't believe Pat and Jay's story about the pilot being someone other than Eddie.

The dead pilot had flown Agent Orange missions in Viet Nam. He was dying of cancer. Ricky had made him an offer he couldn't refuse. A million dollars for his wife and his life. The pilot wouldn't live to see the sun rise in the morning. But it was his choice. He could have lived a few months more or he could take a million dollars for his wife and kids' futures. There really wasn't much of a choice as he saw it.

It was Florida. Pat and Jay were given the death penalty for a death - Eddie's - involved in the commission of a felony.

Lynn stood at the curb, watching her life pass out of her field of vision, nothing she could do about it. All of her and Pat's possessions had been forfeited after his conviction. She was a co-conspirator, though she received no jail time.

Ricky almost felt sorry for her. He sat in a black Porsche Carrera he'd bought the day after the airstrip bust. He was parked down the street from Lynn and Pat's house. He watched sheriff's deputies moving the furniture out, including the Bosendorfer grand.

She looked up. Saw the Porsche, headed its way. He started to turn the ignition. Changed his mind.

She leaned down to the window. His face was cool, not even breaking a sweat in this heat.

"Maybe you should take the piano," she said.

"Wouldn't fit in the car." He looked at her - mirror to the past. His eyes showed real warmth. Almost asked her to come with him. "You look worried."

"I'll manage."

"I'm sure you will."

She started to walk off, turned back. "I knew a boy once. He was a sweet kid."

"What happened to him?"

"He was burned so he decided to burn back. I hope he's happy. She walked back to her spot on the curb to watch her life being loaded in vans for the sheriffs to take to the auction house.

Edmond was dead. Ricky knew he'd never come back to Miami, no matter what his identity was. He turned the ignition, the Carrera sped off down the street.

Paul D. Marks is a stealth screenwriter, making his living from optioning his screenplays and rewriting other people's scripts or developing their ideas. Paul has sold short stories to numerous publications. PaulM44908@aol.com

One For My Baby
By JoAnne Lucas

Trouble comes in all shades of ugly, and there isn't a grave deep enough to keep you safe from the cold kiss of unfinished business from the past. You up the ante when that trouble involves a man and a woman.

Sure, I've made mistakes that way - what gal hasn't? But some mistakes come with a heavy fine of regret, like the one I pay on every day of my life. It gets old and dulls your senses. I didn't even realize that lately I'd lost my edge on sensing danger.

"Did you see that guy hanging around back there?" The young gal who works as a hat check girl held the club's door open for me. "Brrrr, gave me the creeps."

I picked up the long skirt of my dress to miss hitting the step and looked back over my shoulder. Street traffic was settling down, there weren't many pedestrians and none that showed any interest our way.

I shrugged it off. "Long as it's not Old Man Trouble, it's nothing to worry about."

People talk a lot about trouble, say it comes in threes. Most people just don't know what trouble is.

In the midst of our opening operations for the Blue Lady Lounge I snagged the right shoulder of my beaded gown against a coat hook. A thread that wove sequins and loops of beads over all the soft and clinging blue jersey material broke. This, after the piano player had turned up too drunk to play and the chef threatened to quit again - just normal problems that precede a regular Saturday night at Fresno's hottest place to be.

I'd designed the Blue Lady from the clubs in those black and white B movies of the forties and fifties. Mine was a classy number in living color complete right down to the cigarette girls with their fishnet stockings and the merchandise trays that hung around their necks. I love it when a SRO crowd packs the lounge and a line is stretched outside, all waiting for a table and preferably one that rings the dance floor and bandstand. I hire six to eight college kids costumed as glamour gals with upswept hairstyles and tuxedoed gentlemen, and as torch singers and gangster types. I seat them throughout the club to encourage the customers to give free rein to their fantasies and come dressed like-wise. Encouraging and playing to the public's fantasies rakes in a better pay-off than just watering the whiskey.

I quickly dealt with the pissed piano player and sent counter threats back to the chef. That left me holding up the broken thread on my gown to stop the run of beads and I couldn't pin on my corsage.

Bill Reynolds, a young pre-med student in a tux, helped me. He was one of the regular Friday and Saturday night crew. "Did you see where both the mayor and the D.A. have reserved tables?" he asked. "Man-oh-man, are we going to have fun tonight! We've got a pool going that says the mayor shows up as a gangster this time. Want in?"

"I'll pass," I said and thought again what a nice, good-looking kid he was.

The new piano player was warming up with *One For My Baby* and played well enough that he would be able to sell it to the crowd later. The corsage was being taken care of and I thought that after I fixed my gown, I would have maybe a half hour to myself. I looked down at young Bill's blond head bent close to scrutinize the corsage pin as he worried it through wired stems and the gown's material. "Thanks for giving me a hand here, Bill."

"Hey, no problem." He finished the job and straightened up. "Can't have our Blue Lady running around without her signature gardenias." He gave me a grin and patted my shoulder.

"Well, now, ain't that charmin'," said a gravelly voice I had hoped to forget. "He's a little young for you, Lizzie."

This was trouble.

"Hullo, Mitch," I said.

"Surprised to see me, babe?"

"It's been a while."

"Yeah, it has. You still look great," he said. "Kinda surprised me that you'd landed in Fresno. What keeps you in this hot hell hole? Got something sweet going with the Italians?"

"Maybe I've got family here," I countered.

"Nah, your sister and her husband still duke it out in Fontana and your ma died - I checked." He moved in close and grabbed my upper arm, "Me and you need to go somewheres quiet and have us a little talk - catch up on old times."

Young Bill tried to intervene before I could stop him. Mitch let go of my arm to punch him in the stomach with his right while he sapped him with his left. The poor kid crumpled to the floor.

Mitch leered back at me. "You want to talk now, or maybe I should work your hero over some more? How 'bout I re-arrange his nose so he don't look so pretty?"

I suppressed a shudder and shrugged instead. "Don't you ever get tired of suckering kids in so you can play with your sap? It doesn't matter whether we talk here or not, but first you leave that on the bar."

Mitch opened his fist to show his buddy sap secured around his wrist and finger. "Sure, baby, just as soon as you drop your bag."

I moved to place my silver satin evening purse on the bar, but Mitch intercepted it and fingered the contents through the fabric.

"Still carrying that old five-shot derringer. Worthless piece of shit." He shook his head. "Always told you it don't have the range to do much good. Know what I mean?"

"Depends on what you're aiming for," I said. "What is it you want?"

"Well, now." Mitch dropped the sap with the purse, "I want what's owed me. You collected two K on your way out of Dallas. That was my pigeon. I figure two thou plus nine years' interest just about makes me and you equal partners in this nice little place."

"You're crazy!"

He backhanded me and I staggered only a couple of steps. *He's losing his touch*, I thought.

My manager, Hal Weever, and a couple of his waiters had rushed over, all eager and pumped. I put up my hand to stop them. "Just trying out some material for a show. Need to get the kinks ironed out," I said and waved them off. The waiters left, but Hal stayed close. I turned to Mitch, "Leave your guns with the buddy and we'll talk in my office."

Mitch sneered as he pulled out a .38 and placed it on the bar.

"I said *all* your guns."

He shrugged and added an automatic. I knew he carried a switchblade and possibly another piece in an ankle holster, but I let him think he got away with it. I turned to my manager and gestured to Bill Reynolds on the floor who was beginning to come around and to the items on the bar.

"Take care of things," I said.

He nodded.

I headed for my office, not bothering to look at Mitch. Once inside he closed the door and shot the bolt. "Hold it, babe. You stay right there where I can watch you. Don't try nuthin' cute and keep away from any drawers."

I looked at him over my shoulder and noted he was getting a little excited. I remembered that total dominance after putting down some sassy resistance was Mitch's big turn-on.

"You want a drink?" I asked.

"Yeah, a drink would be good."

Still holding the gown's broken thread, I awkwardly poured him a generous double whiskey and me a cognac.

"Here's to old times," he said.

"If you say so."

"I do." He clinked his glass against mine, tossed down the drink, and motioned for me to do the same. I took a sip of Courvoisier and deliberately strolled over to the CD player while he was pouring himself another double.

"Did I tell you, you could move? Get away from there -- Now!"

I gave him another long look, sauntered toward my desk and stopped at its side. By now I faced him front on. So I leaned slightly back against the desk while I sipped my drink. Mitch's eyes were all over me like hungry mosquitoes and I let them feast.

He gulped more whiskey.

I set down my snifter and reached across the desk for the red enameled cigarette box. He threw his empty glass right past my head and it smashed against the wall behind me. "You need me to teach you again how it goes? You don't touch nuthin' 'til I check things out! And put your hands on top of the desk where I can see 'em."

Oh, yeah, he was coming along nicely. I gave him a sly "make me" smile, straightened up, and pulled down hard and slow on the broken thread. Crystalline beads started a waterfall from my shoulder, rippled in a race across the bodice of my gown, and sensually rained from the nipple of one breast.

Mitch's breath came heavy as he watched the domino effect. I groped for the office door release hidden under the desk's lip while I leisurely rolled my shoulders and upper body to make the run of beads wantonly drip from the other breast.

He wet his lips.

As he had demanded, I now made a big show of placing my hands flat on the desktop, a little behind me so my bust jutted up like an offering.

"Is this what you wanted?" I asked in a husky voice.

He was on me like a dog on a leg, smashing kisses against my face, and holding my upper arms pinned to my sides in his rough embrace. "Oh, yeah, baby. I've been wanting this for years." He pulled me completely upright so he could grind his groin hard against mine. Then he jerked my head back by grabbing a handful of hair and twisted it in his fist. "You miss me, babe? Tell me how much you want me."

"Mitch," I breathed an invitation in his ear and nipped the lobe.

He plunged his tongue into my mouth. I moaned and sucked it while I held him tight against me at his waist.

He growled, groaned, and after two muffled popping sounds jerked stiffly before collapsing to the floor.

I wiped his spittle from my face and watched him die. Hal Weever still held my .22 at the ready. It wasn't necessary, his two shots to the back of Mitch's head had done the trick. Hal emptied the corpse's pockets while I reached for my brandy and swished some around in my mouth before I drank the rest.

I stared at the wall for a long time.

"How's the Reynolds kid doing?" I asked.

"Bill?" Hal asked. "I talked to him. He'll be okay, just a little shook up. Like you had said, I told him the guy was an out of work actor who auditioned for the role a little too vigorously and we decided not to use him."

I nodded my compliments on his good work. Then I crossed the room to the safe, counted out two-thousand dollars in hundreds, and handed it to Hal. "When you dump him, leave this stuffed in his mouth." Sure, I knew Mitch wouldn't take it with him to the grave, but that wasn't the point. I walked by and gave the corpse a hard kick. I always pay my debts.

After Hal supervised the body removal and clean up process, I changed my gown and let him zip me up. His hands lingered on my shoulders. "You know, Liz, I could almost feel sorry for that poor dead slob," he said. "If he knew you for so long, how come he didn't know you'd kill to protect what's yours?"

"I didn't have much back then," I answered.

"Yeah, but, still. Everyone knows the Blue Lady's your baby and you wouldn't let anyone hurt it."

Wrong, I thought and moved away. The Blue Lady's not my baby . . . Bill Reynolds had been.

JoAnne Lucas is an active member of Mystery Writers of America and Sisters in Crime. She almost always writes about Fresno, CA. Her numerous mystery stories have appeared in several anthologies and in fine magazines.

Unholy Burial
by J.K. Cummins

Edith poured brandy in her morning coffee. Harold would have been appalled at her weakness-he'd borne his own suffering with dignity-but sometimes it was more than a soul could bear.

"El Nino storms continue to batter San Diego," the television newscaster began, "and a surf-advisory has been issued. High tide will be at nine o'clock this morning, and waves are expected to crest at ten feet on all west-facing beaches. Affected residents in Del Mar, Encinitas, and Solana Beach are being urged to evacuate."

The phone rang. Edith pushed mute and struggled up out of the recliner with the help of both canes. She needn't hurry—her friends knew to give her time to answer. On the tenth ring, she picked up. "Hello."

It was Mary, and she'd worked herself into quite a state.

"Yes, I was watching the news."

Mary repeated the advisory anyway.

"No, that won't be necessary…"

Mary insisted.

"I really appreciate your concern, I truly do, but…"

Mary interrupted.

"Just listen a minute, dear. I have no intention of letting the ocean destroy my home and hurl me into the sea."

A mistake-Mary now had a graphic picture of the danger.

"No, not just sandbags...let me finish." Edith took a sip of her cold coffee. "My neighbors obtained emergency permission from the city to put down 'riprap.'"

Mary, poor dear, was hard of hearing.

"No, I didn't say 'riff-raff.' I said, 'riprap'--big boulders." Edith hurried on before Mary could break in again. "Crews have been working like crazy for the past two days, putting down riprap and dredging up sand berms."

Mary, living in a Senior apartment complex in land-locked Vista, couldn't see what good that would do.

"It'll keep the waves from sucking the sand out from underneath the houses and undermining the foundations."

Mary was finally satisfied.

"Of course, I will. Thanks for calling." Edith put the phone down.

The wind shrieking in around the French doors sounded like a keening woman, and it was getting on her nerves. I must not have latched them properly, Edith thought, as she made her way over. But once she'd opened the doors to the balcony, it took all her strength to get them shut and locked again.

She pressed her forehead against the cool glass and looked out. Dark clouds scudded across the slate sky, driving the rain in sheets against her windows. Gusts thrashed the palm trees that lined her patio and whipped the potted ferns on Simon's terrace. The whole house seemed to shudder and groan under the relentless pummeling of the storm...just like it had during that El Nino winter fifteen years ago.

The braces supporting her ravaged legs were cutting into flesh, so Edith made her way back to the recliner and got her feet up. She poured some more brandy in her coffee mug and picked up the silver frame with its photo of Jenny and her horse Beau. As the alcohol warmed her, Edith remembered the day the bottom had dropped out of her world.

The morning of February 22, 1983, had promised sunshine. But it had lied. At noon the skies opened up, sending a Noah-like deluge down on San Diego County. By mid-afternoon, with the storm at its zenith, Edith began to worry because her daughter still wasn't home. Their neighbor Simon Nilsson, an avid horseman, had given Jenny riding lessons for years, and that Saturday he'd persuaded her to join him on horse patrol at the Rancho Penasquitos Canyon.

Pounding on their door. Edith answers it. Simon Nilsson is standing there soaked to the skin...shaking, obviously distraught.

He refuses to come in, starts blathering on with his teeth chattering about how he and Jenny had stopped near the waterfall for lunch...when the rain started...took shelter in a cave...hoped to wait it out...by the time they realized the storm wasn't going to let up, the small creek that meandered through the ravine was a raging torrent.

Harold joins them at the door, handing Simon a towel to wrap around his shoulders. Edith takes her husband's hand as the story continues. Somehow, making their way through deep brush in the pelting rain, they'd become separated. Holding his palms out in supplication, Simon tells them he'd finally had to give up searching for her, had reported Jenny missing to the Park Ranger, then loaded his own horse Ebony into the horse trailer and come home.

Leaving Edith behind in case Jenny called, Harold joins the Sheriff's Department and the Search and Rescue volunteers. In the early hours of the morning, they find Beau wandering at the bottom of the canyon, only bruised and scratched. The ranger says, "a miracle the horse wasn't swept away by the flash flood.... carried all the way to the ocean. Terrible, terrible that poor Jenny..."

Harold had dismissed everyone's fears that Jenny drowned in the raging waters, that would have meant she was dead ...he'd never accept that. A couple weeks later, he'd had a stroke, so his body knew, but he never admitted the possibility aloud. Harold preferred to hate Billy Lawrence, the young drummer the police thought Jenny might have run off with, preferred to wait every day for five paralyzed, paralyzing, years for a note or a call that never came.

But Edith knew that Jenny loved that horse and wouldn't have deserted Beau in the midst of a storm…it couldn't have happened like that. No, Harold was wrong. So Edith had watched the beaches for weeks, waiting for her daughter's body to wash up, determined to know, afraid to find out.

Determination was part of Edith's nature. In 1950 polio had taken over her nerves, her muscles, had threatened to take her life, and she had beaten it. But Jenny's disappearance and Harold's death ripped out her heart, and no amount of exercise or determination could fix that. So when the polio resurfaced a year ago, she no longer had the will to fight. She quit her job and took up her vigil again, watching the incoming waves for hours each day, hoping for a sign.

Edith resisted the urgings of friends to move into an "assisted living" facility. She called it an "assisted dying" facility. When she had trouble managing the stairs, she moved into the second floor bedroom where Harold had lain all those years, listening to the ocean and staring into space. She had a small fridge, a coffee maker, a microwave, and Mary to shop and clean for her. Dear Mary--her friend and caregiver--who worried about her, who told her to get a hand-controlled car, to get a mechanized wheelchair… to get on with her life.

What life?

The storm was making her restless. Edith finished the brandy and made her way back to the French doors. Protected by the boulders and sand berms, her patio was only being splashed by spray, but huge waves were already breaking over Simon's terrace, had smashed the potted ferns and overturned the patio furniture. An umbrella floated upside down in the backwash like a child's bathtub toy.

Simon was in Hong Kong on business, and none of the neighbors knew how to reach him for money or permission to join them in trying to stave off disaster. But Edith knew Simon as well as anyone knew that his arrogant nature would have made him refuse anyway. He'd have scoffed at the idea of berms and riprap, would have said his house was built to last, would have shaken his fist at mighty Neptune.

Edith checked the clock: 8:45. High tide in fifteen minutes. She pulled a chair over and sat down to watch. Her weakness found the unbridled power of nature invigorating; her passivity reveled in its raging fury.

Gulls were wheeling and swooping over the encroaching tide. Maybe they'd spotted a fish caught in the piles of seaweed being thrown up by the surging waves. In the old chest next to the French doors, Edith found the binoculars Jenny had used for watching dolphins play in the ocean. She adjusted them to her eyes and kept watch for the next hour. The rain finally stopped, but the merciless sea continued to lash Simon Nilsson's terrace and the bluff that supported it. Waves were sucking sand away, were eating at the terrace's foundation, undermining it. Soon it would be beyond saving, beyond human help.

A few days after Jenny disappeared, Simon had started building that brick terrace. Edith watched him as she scanned the ocean, wondering what it was that drove the man to labor in the cold wind until long after dark, hammering lumber into place, mixing and pouring cement, loading and pushing a wheelbarrow full of bricks, bending and stooping to lay them, align them.

Now, Edith watched as the bluff collapsed like a child's sand castle. Chunks of cement and brick from the terrace started tumbling into the sea. Bits of lumber floated for a moment on the waves before being carried out like so many matchsticks. Within minutes, a huge wave wrenched the rest loose, and the terrace crashed into the ocean with a resounding splash.

That was when she saw it…something that looked like… Edith refocused the binoculars to be certain. Yes, that's what it was. Caught behind steps that only a few moments ago had led down to the beach from Simon's terrace, was a human skeleton!

She had to know. After all these years of waiting and watching, she had to know for certain. Edith stood up, wanting to rush, but she was a bit shaky, and it wouldn't do to fall, not now. Using her canes like she'd once used cross-country ski poles, she hurried as best she could across the room. But at the stairs she paused. Her difficulty climbing the steps had kept her a prisoner for the past six months. Could she do it?

Every minute she hesitated increased the likelihood that the skeleton would be swept out to sea. She'd once seen a toddler negotiate steps by scooting down on her bottom. Worth a try. Sticking her brace-encased legs straight out in front of her, she bounced down the stairs.

A few bruises on her backside would be worth it if she could find out for sure. But as Edith crossed the downstairs living room, she began to have doubts. What were the chances after so many years?

When she opened the outside door, the cold wind drove stinging spray into her face. Her heart was pounding in her ears and she couldn't seem to get enough air. She knew. The skeleton must have dropped to the sand from Simon's terrace, from where it had been buried all these years.

The wooden steps were narrow and wet. Edith realized she'd fall to her death if she tried to walk down, so she lowered herself and slid to the bottom, splinters tearing at her skirt and legs. When she tried to get up, the canes sunk deep in the wet sand. She couldn't get any leverage on the step, so she rolled over onto her knees and used the banister to pull herself up.

Edith looked across to the steps ripped from Simon's terrace, now leaning like saw teeth against the remains of the crumbled bluff. The tide had crested, was starting to go out, and as the waves receded, they were tugging at the skeleton.

She had to hurry. But how to get across those last thirty feet? Canes and braces would be useless. Another wave nudged the skeleton further out onto the open sand.

Edith dropped to her knees and started crawling. When she was nearly there, a wave knocked her over. For a moment, she didn't think she had the strength to go on, just wanted to lie down and let the next rush of water carry her out to sea. But when she looked up, she saw that the skeleton was free of the steps, would be carried away by the next big wave. Now or never. Like a Marine under barbed wire, she elbowed herself to within a couple feet.

The clouds parted for a second, and a glimmer of sun danced across something shiny hanging from the bones of the neck. When the backwash from high tide's last hurrah swept the skeleton past her, Edith reached for the necklace. She succeeded only in grabbing the charm hanging from it. With a leaden heart, she watched as the skeleton was carried out to sea.

Totally spent, she lay on her stomach in the wet sand, her glasses lost and salt water stinging her eyes. Then she slowly unclenched her fist. Jenny's ankh… there was no mistaking it. The Egyptian symbol for "life" she'd ordered twenty years ago in Cairo with "J E N N Y" written in hieroglyphs.

Edith looked up, her eyes filled with tears. "Thank you, Lord." She kissed the ankh and said, "Good-bye, my sweet girl."

Three hours later, bathed, her wounds dressed, and in dry clothes, Edith could barely remember what a nightmare it had been making her slow, painful way on hands and knees back to her bedroom. She could barely think at all. After forcing herself to eat some soup and crackers, she lay down and slept for most of the afternoon.

Edith woke with the ankh still clutched in her hand. Her sweet girl, her poor, darling girl betrayed by a friend, by a man they all trusted. Had Simon planned it? Or had circumstances huddling together in the cave, waiting out the storm-prompted him to act on his desires? And when he was rebuffed, had his nature-to always take what he wanted-made him go too far?

Whatever had happened, Simon Nilsson must pay for Jenny's death. But how? No one would believe her without the skeleton, without even whatever traces might have been left in the cement.

Edith shuddered at the thought of her daughter's unholy burial.

She knew what she had to do, and the rage that had burned inside her for so long would give her the strength.

The candle flickered as Edith waited in the dark of her neighbor's living room. Simon had given her the perfect excuse. Insensitive to her weakened condition, he'd called to ask her to water his plants while he was away. Her pride had made her accept the challenge, but in the end, she'd had to have Mary do it for her.

He was due back sometime around seven o'clock. Simon had lost most of his eyesight to macular degeneration and couldn't drive any more, so his assistant would be picking him up at the airport and, she hoped, merely dropping him off at home.

Had she thought of everything?

Having turned off all her lights, Edith had made her slow way over on her canes with a penlight held in her teeth. Simon's house was the last one on the cove, and when she flipped the circuit breaker, his living room was plunged into total darkness. The candle would be blown out when all was ready.

She left the drapes drawn, but opened the sliding glass doors. Except for the gentle lapping of waves on the shore, all was quiet. A restless breeze ruffled the curtains, and Edith shielded the candle. Her only worry was a full moon that threatened to peek through the clouds.

A car door slammed. Some harsh words for the assistant before the car drove off. A key turning in the lock and the door opening.

Edith moved toward the front hall.

The sound of suitcases being dropped and the click, click, click of the light switch. "Damn electricity."

She cleared her throat and said, "Simon, it's me," then she walked into the hall.

He squinted, trying to make out the shadowed face holding the candle. "Edith, what are you doing in my house?"

"The plants, don't you remember? You asked me to water the plants."

"Yes… yes. What's wrong with the electricity?"

"The storm, didn't you hear?"

"How could I hear? I was on an eighteen hour flight from Hong Kong."

"Of course, how silly of me."

"Was there any damage?"

"It depends on what you mean by damage."

"Quit talking in riddles, woman." Simon made a move toward the living room. "Give me the candle. You can go home. I'll see for myself."

When he reached for the candle, Edith turned. "I'll lead the way."

Praying that the moon was still hidden behind the clouds, she opened the drapes. As Simon came toward her, she blew out the candle.

"Why did you do that?"

"It was the wind."

"I have a flashlight in the end table. Get it and follow me."

"Be careful." The words were out before she could stop them.

"Oh, do be quiet."

Simon Nilsson stepped through the open doors and into nothingness. His screams were swallowed by the wind, but there was a bone-crushing thud as he hit a chunk of cement left embedded in the sand.

Then all *was* quiet.

Tomorrow's high tide would carry another body away for an unholy burial at sea.

J. K. Cummins teaches Creative Writing at Palomar College and has published over two-dozen stories. She is a book reviewer, an active member of Sisters in Crime and MWA and writes mystery/suspense novels.

Compiled by Babs Lakey

A Made Man

By Warren Murphy

The *sirocco* was blowing hot and fierce out of the heart of the Saharan desert, hopping quickly across the short span of the Mediterranean that separated Africa from Sicily, up the face of the Sicilian mountains, down the other side, and on out into the Gulf of Castellammare.

Danilo Sesta stood in the bow of the *tonnara* boat and stared back over the purple and blue and peacock green waters into the heart of the hot wind, back toward the town of Castellammare del Golfo.

He had been on the boat all day and did not much care for work, for rising early, laboring until after dark, being forced into the company of loud and stupid men. But still, he thought, life was good. *And someday it will be perfect.*

The tunny were running well this spring of 1919 and even though he was just 18, he was making a man's wages. For now. But when the fishing season ended in the autumn, as the youngest of the crew, he would be the first to lose his job and that would not be so good. Perhaps he would go to America. It was cold there, he had been told, and he would not have the sun and the heat that he loved. But there would be work. He could grow rich, as did all who went to America.

And then when he was old -- forty or so -- he would come back to Castellammare del Golfo and build himself a fine villa and stock it with many fine things to eat -- he was always hungry -- and many beautiful women: women of every color and sort, but all of them very, very *bellissima.*

"Hey, Nilo." A voice behind him spoke his nickname.

Nilo turned around and smiled. "What, Fredo?" he asked.

Fredo motioned him to come closer. He was perhaps a dozen years older than Nilo, a short but sturdily-built man who looked like one of the Saracen lords who had ruled this island so many hundreds of years before.

"We've work to do," Fredo said.

He was looking down into the *mattanza*, the chamber of death as it was called, the small room made of fishing nets and hung in the sea between the two boats of the *tonnara.*

Nilo was puzzled. He moved closer to the older man. They were not supposed to be fishing this day, not collecting the tunny or spigola or dolphins or swordfish or sharks that had swum into the chamber, there to be speared and hauled aboard either of the *tonnara* boats.

Indeed, there were only four of them out on the water: Nilo, Fredo, and on the other boat, the two Selvini brothers, Paolo and Enzo. The others of the *tonnara* crew were all ashore, helping to celebrate the wedding of the fleet owner's daughter, and only the four of them had been left behind to clean up the boats and to protect the nets from vandals or thieves.

Nilo did not like the other three men but he had found them useful. They drank too much and when they did, they were careless with their money and some of it found its way into Nilo's pockets. He justified this by thinking, *As well into my pocket as into the purse of some waitress or prostitute.*

"I did not think we were to do any fishing this day," Nilo told Fredo.

Fredo smiled at the boy and put his arm around him. Nilo was handsome, almost to the point of prettiness. He had large chocolate eyes, with thick black lashes, pouting lips and a slim boyish body. At night, several times when the boats had been at sea overnight, Fredo had lain down next to him, gently brushing the boy's back. Nilo had pretended to remain asleep, ignoring him, as if he had not noticed.

"That is not the kind of work I mean," Fredo said.

Nilo looked at him for a moment, then shrank back. He had the fleeting fear that Fredo knew Nilo had been stealing his money and that of the other crew members. He tried to tell himself that it was only his imagination.

"What do you mean?" Nilo asked. Trying to appear casual, he moved a few steps closer to the rack where the great long gaffs that they used to haul in the fish were stowed.

Fredo laughed softly, almost shyly.

"Have I ever told you how beautiful you are?" Fredo asked.

Nilo stopped. He said nothing.

"I dream of you all the time," Fredo said. "You and nothing else."

Nilo laughed and spat into the sea.

"I thought you were a man, Fredo," he said. He was just out of arm's reach of the gaffing poles.

"I *am* a man, and as a man, I must have you."

Nilo felt a shiver run up and down his spine. Where were Paolo and Enzo? He needed help. Fredo was too big, too strong. There was no place to run to. No help could be expected from the wedding guests until late this night at the earliest. And despite the way he made his living, Nilo could not swim. The water had always frightened him.

Nilo called the names of the other two men. "Paolo! Enzo!"

Now it was Fredo's turn to laugh.

"It will do no good, little thief," he said. "They feel the same as I. And we have all paid in advance. With all the money you have lifted from our pockets."

The two brothers appeared just then in the corner of Nilo's vision and he turned toward them but with just a glance, he could see that what Fredo had said was true.

Nilo fought them to keep them from catching him. And he fought them while the brothers held him down while Fredo carefully, methodically violated him. He fought them when it was Paolo's turn and he fought when Enzo did the same. By then he had been beaten and was bleeding terribly and he felt as though his flesh had been gashed open, just as he had gashed open so many of the fish that they had hauled in from the *mattanza*.

They let him lie there on the deck, unconscious, after that. Then, in the heat of the dying late afternoon, they came into him again and again and again, drinking and laughing and singing songs of the sea.

When the sun went down and darkness covered the waters and they were done with him, the three men threw Nilo into the sea, counting on the predators that always swam around the *tonnara* boats to finish him off.

Nilo Sesta wanted to die. He wanted nothing more than release. Release from his pain. Release from his shame. He could not live anymore. He wasn't a man. Not after what had been done to him. He was not a man and he was worse than a woman.

Nilo let himself sink deep into the sea. It made no difference. The sea was warm and inviting. The Gulf of Castellammare would take him into its bosom, hold him there, not let anyone hurt him anymore, not let anyone shame him anymore.

Nilo sank until he could go no further. He was too buoyant. His body was rejecting its watery grave, demanding to breathe fresh clean air. Nilo told himself to open his mouth and let his lungs fill with water and sink even deeper down into oblivion. He wanted to but he could not make himself do it. He began rising, rising not because he wanted to but because of his body's own natural buoyancy.

Something brushed briefly against Nilo's leg, something big and wide and rough. The boy shuddered. Sinking peacefully to the bottom of the bay and dying gently was one thing, but being bitten and hacked and chewed to death bit by bit, piece by piece, by sharks or barracuda was something else again. Nilo kicked out at whatever had bumped into him and began frantically flailing his arms. He rose even faster than he had before. Once he began rising, his body took over from his mind: it had determined to live, regardless of what Nilo's brain had been planning. He kicked even harder.

Nilo broke the surface of the sea at first without even knowing it. He took in huge gulps of air before he realized that he was breathing again. His eyes feasted on the slowly rising moon and stars, thinking that they had never been more beautiful, that life had never been more precious.

He trod water unthinking for almost a minute before he remembered that he did not know how to swim, before he remembered that to fall into the sea was automatically to drown, to die. The thought panicked him and he began flailing the water frantically, desperate for rescue and yet not desperate enough to call out for help lest Fredo or the Selvini brothers hear him and turn back to finish the job they had begun.

In his flailing, Nilo turned in a complete circle and as he started halfway around again, he noticed only a few meters away the dark silhouette of the two *tonnara* boats riding high in the water.

Nilo forced himself to calmness. He could not stop his fear but he could control it, prevent it from becoming panic. He tried treading water again and found that it worked. He was able to remain upright, in place. The only problem now, he realized, was how to get to the boats to keep from drowning.

But if he went back to the boats, Nilo knew he would be delivering himself once more into the hands of his assailants and that was certain death. He would have to, somehow, get to shore. But that too was impossible. The shore was a mile away at its nearest point. He could never reach it.

He felt panic rising in his throat like a swollen lump of flesh and he fought to keep from retching. Perhaps, he told himself, if he could get to the side of the *tonnara* boats and somehow hold on until the rest of the fishing crew returned from the wedding celebration, then maybe he could be rescued.

Nilo forced the top part of his body to lean in the water, toward the boats, and then tried to use his hands and arms to move forward, just as he had seen swimmers do. The distance was not great but it seemed to take an eternity to traverse.

When he finally reached Fredo's boat, he searched desperately for a safe handhold until he came upon the anchor line dangling overboard. He grabbed the coarse rope and held on with a fierce determination.

I am alive, God damn their souls. I am alive.

Time came and went. Minutes passed, then hours. Nilo could hear the sounds of drunken revelry from the three crewmen aboard the boat above his head and while he waited, his determination just to survive grew and changed into an even more powerful desire for revenge.

Finally, Nilo grew aware of a change in the activity on the boat. He listened carefully for what was being said but could not make out the words. Then he knew what was happening. Paolo and Enzo were leaving the *tonnara* and taking one of the smaller rowboats to go back to shore to meet the partying fishermen after they returned from the wedding.

Nilo waited for the Selvini brothers to leave. A few minutes later, he heard snoring from above his head. Fredo had gone to sleep. Or passed out. Slowly, Nilo worked himself around the boat until he reached the stern where he could hoist his upper body onto the gunwale and then pull himself completely onto the deck. He lay there on the wet cold wood, gasping and puffing, fearful that he would wake Fredo and yet, not really caring if he did so. But Fredo did not wake.

Nilo crawled forward to the rack where the gaffs were kept and only then stood up. Most gaffs were hammered into a hook, but throughout the fishing season, Nilo had been using a straight spear with a sharp bladed barbed end. He quickly found that tool in the rack.

He crossed the small deck in three quick steps and positioned himself over the thin pallet where Fredo slept. Nilo gently prodded the older man with the point of his weapon.

Fredo stirred and Nilo prodded again.

"Who is it?" Fredo demanded thickly. "What do you want?"

Nilo did not answer at first. Then he said, "You, Fredo. I want you."

Fredo sat up, still not fully aware of what was going on. Nilo did not give him a chance to say anything. He drove the gaff hard between Fredo's legs. His aim was sure.

As neatly neutered as any capon or gelding, Fredo screamed, a horrible mixture of pain and anguish. He grabbed at the place where his manhood had been. Nilo laughed and slammed the end of the gaff pole into Fredo's face. The burly man collapsed back into unconsciousness and Nilo trussed him up with heavy fishing lines, until the older man was immobilized.

He took his folding knife from his pocket and slowly began to carve away on Fredo. For the first five minutes, the fisherman screamed, begging for mercy, begging for death, begging for Jesus and Joseph and Mary to help him.

By the time his screaming had stopped, there was hardly a strip of skin more than three inches wide anywhere on Fredo's body that had not been sliced by Nilo's knife.

The necessary deed done, Nilo sat back on the gunwale and quietly contemplated his work. Fredo was dead now or soon would be. That left Paolo and Enzo Selvini. The brothers would be more difficult, watching out for each other, protecting one another.

For them, I will need a weapon more powerful than a knife or a hook.

Nilo began looking through all the cabinets and lockers of the two boats. Occasionally, he had seen the owner on board carrying a *lupara* — a sawed-off shotgun -- and that was what he was searching for. He finally found it hidden under the captain's bunk. Now all he had to do was to get ashore and run Paolo and Enzo to ground.

Another dinghy was tied up to the other *tonnara* boat and carefully holding the shotgun out of the water, he worked his way across the death nets to the other fishing boat, clambered into the rowboat, locked the oars in place and began pulling for shore.

Nilo Sesta woke with a start. His tongue was thick in his mouth and he hurt in every part of his body. The ache between his buttocks turned to pain and he wanted to cry out. But that would not do. A man, even an 18-year-old man, did not cry -- at least, not because of physical pain. A broken heart, yes. Other things, perhaps. But not for physical pain.

Nilo carefully scanned the shore. He was still in the rowboat he had taken the night before. He must have fallen asleep at the oars and the boat had run aground on a deserted portion of beach. Perhaps he had passed out. He remembered what happened -- the shame of it, the pain of it -- and for a moment said a prayer that it had all been a bad dream.

But it had not been. Nilo knew that and there was no use pretending.

Slowly, Nilo remembered Fredo and what he had done to the burly fisherman. He nodded politely at the memory.

The sun was coming up, far off to his left. He had drifted to the west during the night, drifted away from Castellammare and the men he had to kill. That was bad.

By now every fisherman along the coast must have learned that Fredo was dead and they would all be looking for him, they and the *carabinieri* and all of Fredo's family.

I should have thrown his body overboard. Then no one would know what happened to him and I could have moved freely. I must be more careful in the future.

It was too late to worry about it. Nilo leaned forward in the small boat and carefully unwrapped the shotgun that he had bound in a piece of canvas sailcloth. He inspected it, and then, satisfied, rewrapped it. He had no love for guns but sometimes they were necessary. He remembered Fredo. The fisherman had loved guns, fondled and caressed them as other men might touch a woman. But not him, not Nilo. *At least, not until now. But who knows? This gun may become my closest friend.*

Nilo set the oars, eyed one of the old Saracen watchtowers more than a mile away and began drawing slowly toward it. After a few minutes, he realized he was hungry. This surprised him. Thirsty he could understand; the body demanded water regardless of what indignities it had suffered. Thirst could not be controlled. But hunger was something else again. What he had gone through the day and night before should have driven all hunger from him but it had not. Nilo thought of his mother's kitchen, thought of the good things she cooked there and wanted more than anything to be back in those familiar surroundings. It was not that he was babied or pampered. On the contrary, Nilo was an only child and often his mother and father seemed to treat him with disdain and indifference, causing him occasionally to wonder if he had been adopted and left with the Sestas as an infant.

Nilo beached the boat, then hid it between some huge sentinel-like rocks at the water's edge. He climbed the hill leading to the road, moving rapidly in the early morning sun. If he was where he thought himself to be, he should make it back to Castellammare by noon, even allowing for keeping out of sight and moving through the brush away from the main road.

As he moved along, Nilo began to hum a tune, something he had known since infancy, from hearing his mother, an old folk song that from its curiously flat melody must have been brought across the water by some of Sicily's Arab invaders.

The farther he went, the more he noticed --as he rarely ever had before -- the intense beauty of his home island. The trail he was following was edged in vines and cactus. Off to the side were clumps of bamboo and small stands of blue-green olive trees. The air around him hummed with the songs of massive yellow-banded bees and thousands of butterflies seemed almost to provide a guard of honor for him. A little way off, Nilo could hear the faint whir of hummingbirds going about their lives, collecting sweet nectar from the flowers which bloomed here in every color and shade imaginable. The sun moved higher into the sky and the air around him grew more and more heavily perfumed with the scents of thyme and other wild herbs.

It could have been paradise, Nilo thought, and could remember no time when he had felt more intensely alive. *I have been treated like a woman and yet my heart is light.*

It might, to some, seem strange, but Nilo understood the reason for it very well. He was Castellammarese. In other places, in other times, he would not have been expected to feel the way he did. But here, among the hills of Western Sicily, there was no need for pretense, especially in Castellammare del Golfo. The town, all said, had an evil reputation, even for Sicily. Somebody had once told him that eight out of ten men in the town had spent time in prison and that one out of three had taken another's life. Those things might or might not be true, Nilo thought, but in his hometown there was, at least, no hypocrisy that prevented one from taking satisfaction from a righteous killing. He had killed once already and was about to do it twice more.

As he walked, Nilo meditated about the pleasure of delivering death to someone who richly deserved it, then hummed another song, this one happier than the last.

Once the parish priest -- and at this thought Nilo crossed himself -- had tried to take him for the priesthood. Nilo was a good boy, he had said and could go far in the church. But Nilo's father would not allow it. The elder Sesta had some private quarrel with God and he had sworn that he would rather be eternally damned than have any child of his go over to the enemy's side.

It was a memory from childhood.

And now I am no longer a child. My childhood has ended.

He hardly noticed that he had arrived at the hill overlooking Castellammare. Trying to keep out of sight, he started down toward the center of town. Almost without guidance from him, his feet automatically led him along the various *viccolos*, the dark and narrow alleyways, leading to his home.

It was fortunate that they had. And it was equally fortunate that his feet stopped him before he turned into the last shadowed way.

Nilo stopped and unwrapped the *lupara* and moved forward with caution. His eyes, he later told himself, must have been directed by San Giuseppuzzi, his favorite saint, father of Jesus, protector of the family, patron and advocate of lost causes. Because, ahead of him, their backs toward him and facing Nilo's house, were Enzo and Paolo Selvini. Each held a shotgun in his hand. They must have been waiting for him, waiting to shoot him down as he came out of the door of his house.

Nilo walked slowly up behind them and spoke each of their names once, softly. They turned and Nilo fired. One shell for each brother. They went down, crying and cursing for brief seconds and then silent. Nilo carefully picked up their guns. Dead men had no use for guns.

Nilo Sesta stood for a moment, looking down at the bodies of the two Selvini brothers, surprised at the quantity of blood that poured from their bodies, streaming now, forming a puddle halfway across the alleyway.

Nobody could ever pay him back for what had happened to him on the *tonnara* boat but Fredo and the Selvinis had made a down payment.

Above him, Nilo heard a wooden window shutter open slowly. He looked up at the window, saw an old woman there, and smiled. Soon, very soon, everyone in Castellammare del Golfo would know what had been done and who had done it. Everyone would know except the police, because no one would speak to them about it.

He thought for a moment about urinating on the men's bodies.

That will make me as much an animal as they. And they are not worthy of my piss. He reached into the pockets of their loose-fitting pants but neither man had any money.

Cradling all three shotguns in one arm, Nilo walked quickly, almost defiantly, across the street into the front door of his home, where his father told him that he would have to flee to the United States.

"What will I do in the United States?" the boy asked.

"You will do very well."

Novelist Warren Murphy has won more than a dozen national awards for his work, including two Edgars from the Mystery Writers of American and two Shamus Awards from the Private Eye Writers of America. Murphy is also a screenwriter with various credits on Lethal Weapon II, The Eiger Sanction, Remo Williams: The Adventure Begins and Murphy's Law (ABC TV series.) A MADE MAN is from a work in progress – look for it and other new books available now at www.warrenmurphy.com

Silver Lake
by Michael Bracken

Bob and Joe hadn't seen each other in many years when they met at the Oyster Bar. They exchanged pleasantries, each asking after the other's wife and kids. Then Bob said, "They're draining Silver Lake."

Joe choked on his coffee. "They'll find the car."

"With Sally inside."

Joe mopped his face with a napkin, then used another to wipe spilled coffee from the tabletop.

Bob waited.

Joe lowered his voice and leaned forward. "There's no statute of limitations, is there?"

Bob shook his head.

A buxom blonde in a low-cut white blouse and short black skirt approached their table. Her teeth sparkled when she smiled. "Are you gentlemen ready to order?"

Bob ordered a filet mignon, medium rare, and a dozen oysters.

She turned to Joe. "And for you?"

He blanched. "Nothing," he said. "Coffee's fine. No, I need a drink. Chivas. Rocks."

"Yes, sir," said the blonde. "I'll have that right out."

As she turned and stepped away from the table, Bob's gaze followed the sway of her hips.

Joe leaned forward, drawing Bob's attention from the blonde, and whispered, "How can you eat?"

Bob shrugged. "A man has to do what a man has to do."

Joe's drink arrived. He downed it and ordered another. When they were alone again, he asked, "What are we going to do?"

"I'm going to eat my dinner," said Bob, "then I'll throw a little charm on the waitress and see if she'll help me work off the oysters."

"You haven't changed, have you?"

Bob smiled. "How's that?"

"You're the same arrogant asshole you were in college."

Bob shrugged.

The waitress arrived with his meal.

"The plate's warm," she said as she bent over the table and provided Bob with a clear view into her ample cleavage. She remained bent over a moment longer than necessary, then straightened and turned to Joe. "Refill that again?"

"Keep them coming," Bob offered. "I'll pick up his tab."

Bob ate. Joe drank.

Bob ate dessert. Joe drank more.

The waitress brought the check and Bob laid a trio of bills on top of it. The waitress reached out to collect Bob's money and he placed one hand on hers, lightly pinning it to the table.

"What time do you get off?" Bob asked.

She winked at him. "Depends how good you are."

"I'm staying over at the Hilton," Bob said, "if you care to find out." He told her his room number.

"Eleven-thirty," she said. "Will you wait up?"

"I'm already up," Bob said. He released his hold on her hand. "Standing at attention."

When the waitress walked away, Joe leaned over. He slurred his words when he spoke. "You're really going through with it, aren't you?"

"What?"

"The waitress. You tell me Silver Lake's being drained and we're only days away from spending the rest of our lives in a state penitentiary and you're looking for a place to stick your dick."

"Better to find a place outside the pen than inside," Bob said. He slid out of the booth and helped Joe to his feet.

"Let me call you a cab," Bob offered. "You're in no condition to drive."

"Neither was she," Joe said. "Not that night. Not after what we did to her."

"What we did?" Bob whispered sharply. "*We* didn't do anything. *You* screwed up and *I* helped cover it up." He tapped one finger against Joe's chest. "Don't you ever forget it."

The two men glared at each other until Joe lost his balance and leaned against the wall. Bob had the valet phone for a cab and waited with Joe until the cab arrived a few minutes later.

The waitress arrived promptly at eleven-thirty, knocked lightly, and then stepped inside the hotel room when Bob opened the door. She pressed herself against him, her heavy breasts flattening against his chest.

"You don't waste time," Bob said. Then he covered her mouth with his, smothering her response. Her lips parted and Bob buried his tongue in the blonde's mouth. She sucked it hard.

When their kiss finally ended, the waitress kicked the door shut, then stepped out of her black pumps. Bob picked her up and carried her to the bed, where they reacquainted themselves with one another's bodies.

Afterward, in the dark, her head on Bob's chest and his arm around her shoulder, the waitress asked, "Do you think he suspects?"

"He didn't recognize you at the restaurant," Bob said. "I think we're good to go."

"Look," Bob explained, "I know a guy says he can get to the car before the water level drops that far. He'll pull out the body, get rid of the evidence."

"How can he do that?" Joe didn't look up when he spoke. Instead he stared at the headline on the *Silver Lake Gazette.* The headline, story, and accompanying photo confirmed what Bob had told him the night before: the Army Corps of Engineers planned to drain Silver Lake so they could repair a major flaw in the dam.

"Doesn't matter," Bob said. They sat in his car, parked two blocks away from Joe's home. "But it'll cost money, more than I can get my hands on. I need to know if you're in or not."

"Of course I'm in," Joe insisted. "I'm not going to jail for something we did twenty years ago."

"Not *we*," Bob said. "*You.*"

"What'll it cost?"

"A quarter mil."

Joe choked. "I can't—"

"You'll have to," Bob said. "You don't have a choice."

"But—"

"You can get it, can't you?"

"Of course I can get it," Joe said. "It won't be easy, but I can get it." He folded the newspaper in half. Finally he looked at his former college roommate. "Can this guy you know guarantee that the problem will disappear forever?"

"It'll be like she never existed."

"Well?" she asked when Bob returned to the hotel room.

"Hook, line, and sinker," he said. He crossed the room to where she sat on the bed, wearing only a black underwire bra and black thong panties. "He'll have the money Friday."

She stood and kissed him. Bob reached for her breasts but she pushed his hand away. "We don't have time. I have to go to work."

"Quit," Bob said. "We'll have the money Friday."

"What if something goes wrong?" she asked. "This hotel isn't free."

Bob released his hold on her and she turned away. After she dressed and left the hotel room, Bob stood at the window and stared out at the parking lot.

In three days, they'd have a quarter of a million dollars. In less than a month, Silver Lake would be completely drained. Among the usual debris at the bottom of the lake would be a 1969 Mustang coupe he and Joe had reported stolen all those years ago--empty because Sally had not been inside the Mustang when Bob had pushed it down the hill into the lake.

It had been a set-up from the start—a prank one frat brother played on another. Bob had set up his virgin roommate with a girl from his hometown, then he'd gotten Joe drunk before the big moment. Joe passed out halfway through his deflowering and when he awoke, Bob convinced Joe that he'd killed the girl.

"I rolled her up in your cover and stuffed her in the trunk of your car," Bob explained.

Joe sat on the edge of his bed, his face in his hands. "Oh God oh God oh God. What are we going to do?"

"We have to dispose of the body."

"We can't," Joe said. "We have to tell someone."

"Not me," Bob said. An hour later, he'd convinced Joe to follow him to Silver Lake. He drove Joe's Mustang. Joe drove his Corvette. When they reached the Lake, Bob stopped the Mustang at the top of a long, steep hill.

"You want anything?"

"My books," Joe said. "My tapes."

Bob cleaned out Joe's car and carried everything back to his Corvette. Then he shifted the Mustang into neutral, released the emergency brake, and gave the Mustang a good shove. It moved slowly at first, gaining speed as it rolled down the hill, finally splashing into the lake. They sat in Bob's Corvette and watched the Mustang slowly sink.

The next day, Bob met Sally at a nearly-deserted coffee shop on the edge of town. He gave her fifty bucks for her performance.

"Hook, line, and sinker," Bob said. "He never even asked to look in the trunk."

Sally took her fifty bucks and returned home.

Joe had reported his Mustang stolen that day and after filing a police report and an insurance claim, neither Bob nor Joe ever spoke of that night again. The next semester, they had different roommates. After college, they went their separate ways.

During a business trip years later, Bob discovered Sally waitressing at the Oyster Bar. He took her for drinks when her shift ended, intending only to reminisce about old times, and they'd wound up spending the night in his hotel room. A few months later, Sally had shown Bob a photo of Joe in the local paper, reporting his most recent promotion.

"Think he remembers what happened that night?" she asked as they lay in bed after trying to screw each other's brains out.

"How could he forget?" Bob said. "I'll bet he still thinks he killed you."

They laughed about it, screwed a second time, and then didn't discuss it again until Bob saw the newspaper article about

Silver Lake and the Army Corps of Engineers' plan to drain it. That night they'd begun making plans.

At the end of her shift Thursday night, Sally returned to the hotel room to find Bob asleep in the bed. She stripped off her clothes and slipped in beside him.

The next morning, Bob rolled out of bed early and paced for most of the morning. Sally watched him for the first hour, then she showered, dressed, and left the hotel room. She said she had shopping to do.

At noon, Bob finally showered and dressed. At three minutes past two, he pulled his rental car to a halt in the parking lot of an abandoned discount store near the Interstate. Two minutes later, a 1969 Mustang pulled into the empty spot to his right. Joe slipped out of the second car and slid into the passenger seat of Bob's rental.

"Do you have it?" Bob asked.

"Every cent."

"And?"

"It's in the trunk," Joe said. "In a duffel bag. Do you have any idea how heavy that much cash is?"

Bob shrugged. He had never stopped to think about it.

"Are you sure this guy of yours can do what he says?"

"Trust me," Bob said. "Have I ever lied to you?"

Joe stared hard at his former roommate.

"Well?" Bob asked. When Joe didn't respond, he said, "Let's see it, then."

The two men climbed from Bob's rental and walked to the trunk of the Mustang. Joe opened the trunk, and Bob reached in for the duffel bag. He opened it far enough to see cash. Lots of cash. He slipped his hand deep into the bag and pulled out a handful of greenbacks.

"It's all money," Joe said. "Top to bottom. One quarter mil, just like you said."

As Bob leaned forward to stuff the cash back in the duffel bag, Joe smacked him on the side of the head with a crescent wrench. Bob collapsed half in and half out of the Mustang's trunk.

Joe glanced around, then grabbed Bob's feet and forced his unconscious body into the trunk. He slammed the lid firmly closed, then quickly slipped into the driver's seat, keyed the ignition, and sped from the parking lot to the frontage road, and then up onto the highway.

Four hours later, Joe arrived at Silver Lake. Twenty minutes after that he found the same steep embankment where they had pushed his car into the water twenty years earlier. Joe stopped the car and climbed out. He pounded on the trunk with the flat of his hand and when he didn't hear any response, he opened the trunk. Bob had not regained consciousness during the trip and he lay half on the duffel bag of money.

Joe tugged the money out from under Bob and dropped the bag to his feet.

Sally stepped from the bushes and Joe turned to face her. "Where's the car?"

"About a half mile back," she said. She wore blue jeans, a loose-fitting T-shirt, and hiking boots. "Nobody'll notice it."

"For twenty years I've had nightmares," Joe said. "Twenty years this son-of-a-bitch has held it over my head and I wouldn't have known any different if you hadn't phoned me yesterday."

Sally stepped forward, away from the trees. "You think it was easy for me?" she asked. "I got screwed twenty years ago, just not the same way you did."

Joe snorted. "You were a cheap slut then," he said. "What are you now?"

"Well," Sally said as she pulled a snub-nosed .38 from the small of her back, "I ain't cheap."

Joe stared at the handgun.

From the trunk, Bob groaned.

"Climb in," Sally said, motioning with the gun's barrel.

Joe glanced in the Mustang's trunk. Then he stepped toward Sally.

She squeezed the trigger and a bullet ricocheted off the pavement at Joe's feet. "The next one goes through your chest."

Bob groaned again. Then Joe climbed into the trunk beside his former college roommate.

Sally slowly walked toward the Mustang, watching for any sudden movement from inside the trunk. As soon as she was close enough, she slammed the trunk closed. Then she walked around the car, and reached inside. She released the emergency brake and shifted the Mustang into neutral.

She walked to the back of the car and leaned her ass against it until the car started to roll.

From inside the trunk, she heard pounding and yelling, but she ignored it. She returned the revolver to the waistband of her jeans, hefted the duffel bag over her shoulder, and began retracing her steps to her waiting car.

The Mustang slowly gained speed as it rolled down the embankment to the lake. Sally barely heard the car hit the water and soon she couldn't hear anything at all.

Sally smiled when she reached her car. She knew she would be laying on a Caribbean beach long before the Corps of Engineers discovered a pair of 1969 Mustangs at the bottom of Silver Lake, one empty, the other with a pair of surprises in the trunk.

Michael Bracken is the author of ten books. More than 700 of Bracken's short stories have appeared in literary, small press, and commercial publications worldwide. Additional information about Bracken, including a selected bibliography is available at: *www.CrimeFictionWriter.com.*

Mirror, Mirror
by Beverle Graves Myers

I'd never believed in spooks and thought anybody who did was stupid, nutty or both. Know that guy who talks to dead people on TV? Pure con man as far as I was concerned. If he stepped in my jurisdiction, I'd run him in as fast as the scumbags who pull pigeon drops on old ladies. To me, the so-called supernatural was just another scam -- until the night of July eleventh, two years ago.

My partner, Joe Dulworth, and I, had been called to a seedy neighborhood east of downtown -- possible homicide. A fuzzy moon hung in the sky and the heavy, stagnant air had set me up for the headache of the century.

I massaged my forehead as Joe pulled the unmarked onto a wide parkway studded with old oak trees. The address was a turreted, gabled monstrosity that had been cut into apartments. The landlord met us on the porch. He hadn't bothered to throw a robe over the short satin pajamas that just brushed his knobby knees. We both flashed our badges, but mine was the one he chose to read.

"Oh my, Sgt. Matthew Reese. I was hoping you detectives would get here soon. I've been trying to help that nice young officer upstairs, but he told me to stay down here." His faded blue eyes bulged with excitement. "I heard the gunshot, you know. That's why I called 911. I don't know much about the couple on the second floor, but you can ask me anything you like. I've got all night. I don't open my antique store until ten in the morning."

I told the landlord to wait in his ground floor apartment and charged up the wide, curving staircase. Joe puffed and panted behind me. With only six months until retirement, Joe had given up on the department's fitness requirements. I couldn't blame him, but my situation was different. If I wanted to make lieutenant, I had to look the part. That's why I'd been sandwiching a couple of hours at the gym in between hitting the books for my promotion test and reporting for regular duty. No wonder Shawna complained that she and the kids barely saw me.

At the top of the staircase, a uniformed patrolman with arcs of sweat darkening his armpits pointed to the crime scene. The apartment had once been a spacious bedroom flanked by a sleeping porch and a dressing room. Now the porch had been walled in to make a pathetic excuse of a kitchen, and the dressing room had been turned into the world's tiniest bath. The only piece of furniture that matched the room's original proportions was a massive wardrobe with an oval mirror set into the door.

The mirror provided a perfect frame for the body sprawled across the sagging bed.

Joe shook his head. "She didn't have a chance. Must've got plugged while she was sleeping."

The young blonde's face did look relaxed. With eyes closed and lips curving in a delicate smile, she might have been enjoying a pleasant dream instead of lying on a bloodstained pillow with a hole under her jaw.

"Neat entry point," I said. "Burn ring around the wound. Looks like he used a small caliber at close range."

"He?" Joe cocked a bushy eyebrow.

"There's always a 'he', especially with a bimbo like this." I bent to examine the tattoo that decorated the buttock spilling out of her red lace thong. "Ronnie. Ronnie in a heart surrounded by roses and ribbons. Ten to one that's our guy."

"You never know. Ronnie might be last year's model. Or the year before."

"Nah, look at the colors -- nice and bright. This tattoo is recent."

The patrolman stuck his head in the door. "Crime scene techs are here." It looked like a good time to talk with the landlord.

Gaylord Portman - his real name, I swear I'm not making any of this up - apologized for his air conditioner being on the fritz and offered iced tea. When we said no thanks, he shooed a fluffy white cat off the sofa and curled back into a pile of cushions.

"Ronnie Bauer and Tiffany Green," he said, fanning himself with the latest copy of Glamour magazine. "Nice couple, moved in last month. They keep to themselves. No partying, no drugs that I'm aware of."

"They have jobs?" That was Joe.

"Tiffany is… *was* a dancer." Gaylord smiled coyly, soliciting a follow-up question.

I bit. "What kind of dancer?"

"Exotic, I believe she called it. Before tonight, you could have caught her at the Mantrap II. *If* that's the kind of place you fellows frequent." His shoulders made a circular shrug. "Ronnie works at that big, twenty-four hour video store at the bottom of Broadway. He's probably there now. Will that boy ever be in for a nasty shock!"

"When did he leave for work?" I asked.

Gaylord couldn't say much about Ronnie or anyone else leaving or entering the building. "I was giving myself a facial, you see, and the bathroom is at the back, no windows. I wouldn't have even heard the shot if I hadn't just turned off the steam machine."

"What time was that?"

"Ah, exactly eleven forty-five. I know because I was timing it. A little steam is good, but too much will absolutely destroy your pores, darlings."

The landlord insisted in walking us out into the dreary entryway. The three of us were forced to cram together by the tenants' mailboxes as Tiffany Green's body was bumped down the stairs on a stretcher.

Gaylord took the opportunity to give my elbow a playful squeeze. He almost got a punch in the nose.

"Sgt. Reese," he practically cooed. "Did you notice the magnificent wardrobe in Tiffany's apartment? It's genuine Eastlake, really too good for a rented room, but I haven't been able to force myself to part with it. I have lots more lovely pieces at my shop. Why don't you stop by and see me, 'er them, sometime?"

I jerked my arm from his slender fingers, and Joe and I started upstairs again. My partner mopped his forehead with his handkerchief. "That old fruit's story smells to high heaven. Who would give themselves a steam facial in this kind of weather?"

We ducked under the yellow tape stretched over the apartment door. The techs had done a quick job. The bedroom was empty and quiet except for a fluorescent light fixture buzzing like a squadron of angry mosquitoes. I pressed my thumb and forefinger over my eyes, willing my headache to pass.

"My money's still on Ronnie," I said. "We need to get over to that video store. It's only a couple of blocks away."

"Keep your pants on," Joe growled, poking into drawers that had already been searched. I sighed and opened the big wardrobe that Gaylord Portman had bragged about. Nothing inside except some men's jeans and shirts hanging on wire hangers.

I closed the door. The oval mirror shone with the image of Tiffany Green's peaceful face on the bloodstained pillow.

I jumped back with a gasp.

My gaze ricocheted from mirror to bed and back again. The mattress on the bed was bare. The coroner had removed the body and the techs had taken the sheets to the lab. Yet, there in the mirror was Tiffany Green, lying on her side in nothing but a red lace thong.

Drawing a deep breath, the nape of my neck tingling, I forced my voice to stay level. "Joe. Come look at this."

My partner lumbered across the room, opened the wardrobe, then closed it without comment. The mirror reflected only his bulky frame and my slack-jawed face peering over his shoulder. "I don't see anything, Matt," he said. "What is it?"

I must've bumbled through some lame observation. No way was I going to bring up a crack-brained illusion brought on by overwork and eyestrain. Joe would just tell me I needed to kick back and chill for a while. Well, Joe didn't have a wife and two kids bitching about living in a crummy townhouse with no yard and no trees, did he?

After giving the kitchen and bath another look-see, Joe was ready to find Ronnie Bauer. I breathed a sigh of relief when he turned off the glaring, buzzing, overhead light and ducked under the yellow tape. For a moment, my head stopped throbbing and I believed that nothing out of a cop's ordinary routine had transpired in that shabby bedroom. Then I caught a glimmer of movement in the mirror.

I slowly approached the wardrobe. Surrounded by gloom, the mirror displayed a close-up of Tiffany's breasts rising and falling. She was alive! She parted her lips and snuggled deeper into the pillow. Then a hand wearing a black glove and clenching a small revolver came into view. A man, definitely, with those bulky muscles and those dark curls on the forearm. He shoved the gun barrel under Tiffany's jaw and pulled the trigger.

My stomach dropped to my knees. It was like a silent movie playing right before my eyes. Only it wasn't there. It couldn't be. As if to confirm my disbelief, the glass suddenly cleared and the mirror returned to reflecting the empty bed and the dirty wall behind it.

Joe called from the doorway. "Matt? You alright, buddy?"

I gulped and nodded. "Yeah, I'm fine, Joe. Just fine."

I didn't tell Shawna either. She was already worried about me, what with the late nights I'd been pulling. Being a cop's wife was no picnic, and Shawna had been a real trooper. I wanted to spend more time with her and the boys, but just then, the most important thing was getting my promotion. With a pay raise, I'd be able to give Shawna and the boys what they deserved -- a nice house in a tony neighborhood with a dog, a tree house, all that stuff.

My prospects for making lieutenant had looked damn good until our last couple of cases had fallen through. So, besides acing my promotion test, I knew I needed to hit a home run on this Green murder. The quicker, the better.

I'd arrived home an hour or so before dawn and folded into my favorite chair to nurse a Corona and think the case through. Joe and I had found Ronnie Bauer at the video store -- a muscular twenty-four year old with a moon face and a scruffy black ponytail. He cried when we told him about Tiffany, but I tended to think the tears were just an act. His manager described him as a "good kid, pretty responsible, but not the sharpest knife in the drawer."

He had that right. Ronnie didn't seem to realize he topped the list of potential suspects. When we told him we needed fingerprints and a firearm residue test to rule out Tiffany's close associates, he agreed to go downtown without even breathing the word *lawyer*.

His coworkers were divided on alibi for the time Gaylord heard the gunshot. One girl backed up Ronnie's story that he'd been shelving returns in the DVD section between eleven-thirty and midnight, but the others couldn't remember seeing him for a crucial twenty minutes.

The murder weapon was still missing. The crime scene techs had dug a .22 slug out of the mattress, but Ronnie denied that he or Tiffany owned a gun of any type. I guessed the case would come down to whatever the forensic lab gave us. Usually did, unless there was an eyewitness.

I grunted and tipped back the last of the Corona. Too bad my little hallucination couldn't be entered into evidence; Ronnie's right arm was a double of the one in the mirror. Oh well, a couple of hours of sleep should grease whatever gears in my brain had gone haywire and that would be the end of that particular brand of weirdness.

Joe and I spent the next morning questioning the babes at the Mantrap II, fishing for leads on any customers who had a thing for Tiffany Green. Joe's idea, not mine. Tracking down every john who'd ever slipped a dollar bill in that lady's G-string could take forever. I just wanted enough evidence to nail the guilty boyfriend and wrap up the case.

By noon, the temperature sign at the bank was flashing 101 soggy degrees and my headache was back in full force. Joe pulled into Corky's Barbecue for lunch, but my appetite was missing in action. Try as I might, I couldn't get that mirror off my mind. I had to satisfy myself that the whole incident had been a bunch of hooey. I left Joe to his platter of baby-backs and headed for Gaylord Portman's place.

The apartment was quiet as a tomb. Ronnie had gone to stay with his folks, and everyone else in the building must work days. I opened the blinds so I could leave the ceiling light off and balanced my butt on the edge of the bed. The dark wood of the wardrobe gleamed in the slanting light; the silver oval reflected my form and no one else's. I waited, listening to the blood drumming in my ears and feeling every beat like a jackhammer behind the eyes.

I checked my watch at a quarter to one, and again five minutes later. At three minutes 'til, I heard it.

A faint scratching sound came from the vicinity of the wardrobe. Was it behind the big cabinet or inside? I strained my ears, but the noise stopped.

When it started again, a minute or so later, I took a few steps forward. The mirror showed no unusual sights, but the sound of delicate fingernails dragging against the planks lining the wardrobe intensified.

Maybe it was the heat, maybe the headache. I don't know, but instead of searching for a rational explanation, my mind exploded with images of a bloody Tiffany clawing at the back of the door. I pictured coffins, premature burials, desperate hands scratching their nails raw. My feet felt like blocks of concrete. I was stuck, too terrified to open the door and too proud to run.

Suddenly, I couldn't take any more. I was in Desert Storm for God's sake. I tossed grenades down the hatches of enemy tanks. I was going to open that door no matter what was behind it.

I leapt to the wardrobe, grasped the brass handle and pulled. A white shape flew at my head, delivering a sharp pain to my upraised arm. My feet went out from under me, and I stumbled backwards onto the bed. I was left sucking my bleeding wrist as I watched Gaylord Portman's Persian strut out into the hall.

Scared by a cat! Acting like a six-year old who thinks there's a monster in his closet. What was I coming to? Matt old buddy, I thought if you don't want to end up in the psycho ward you better head back to reality on the double.

I slammed the wardrobe door. And nearly lost the lunch I hadn't eaten.

There was Tiffany, sleeping peacefully. Even though I stood right in front of it, the mirror no longer acknowledged my existence. I moved closer, put my nose two inches from its flat surface, but there was no Matt, only Tiffany. Then a new figure entered the reflection.

I knew it! Ronnie Bauer slunk in the door from the hallway, a small revolver in his gloved hand. With an impassive expression, he positioned the gun under his girlfriend's jawbone, drew the hammer back and pulled the trigger. I could almost hear the explosion.

After a quick shift back to my reflection, almost like a TV changing channels, the scene replayed. My fear had evaporated. I couldn't begin to explain what was going on, but I knew it was real and I meant to get to the bottom of it.

I opened the wardrobe and ran my hands over the back of the door. The beveled mirror was sandwiched between two thin panels. When I used my pocketknife to open a slit between them, I met layers of dirt and old wax. I'd wager that mirror hadn't been out of that door since the wardrobe was manufactured.

Next, I threw the clothing on the bed and inspected the interior. It was so tall that I could cram all of my five-feet-eleven inches in if I kept my head ducked. That's how I found out the top came off, then that the sides were set into grooves in the columns that formed the corners. If I'd had a screwdriver, I could have removed the mirrored door from the front section at the hinges.

As it was, I had the thing almost completely dismantled when a little cough sounded by the door. Gaylord Portman stood on the other side of the police tape, holding the cat in the crook of one arm.

"It's called a knock-down wardrobe," he said. "It comes apart to fit through doorways. Our Victorian ancestors were very practical people."

"Where did you get it?"

"Oh, I bought it at auction years ago and put it in the shop. I managed to sell it several times, but the buyers always returned it within days. I finally moved it to the house and I confess I've quite fallen in love with it, even though I'm usually more of a Biedermeier man."

"Have you ever noticed anything… well, odd about it?"

"Odd, Sergeant?" He cocked his head. "What could be odd about a wardrobe?"

I scratched my jaw. "Your cat was in it."

He ran his fingers through the white fur. "Pussy has a mind of her own. She's used to going wherever she wants."

"Can Pussy open doors with her paw?"

He answered with a lopsided smile before moving on down the hall.

I put the wardrobe back together and searched the rest of the room for wires, projectors, any high tech equipment that could be producing the images in the mirror. I drew a complete blank -- nothing that could explain the strange happenings. Once back in place, the mirror replayed the murder scene several times, then reverted to its ordinary reflection. I was deeply puzzled, but at least I no longer doubted my sanity.

I began to work out a theory while I drove back to Corky's. With human deceit ruled out, the mirror had to be a genuine supernatural occurrence. Hard to believe, but, I supposed, not absolutely impossible; scientists were discovering unheard of things everyday.

And since no one else had seen the images, they were obviously meant for me. Call it a message from the great beyond or whatever you want, I convinced myself that someone (Tiffany? My dead father, who'd been a cop before me? Some other benevolent Spirit?) was somehow using the mirror to help me solve the case and assure me that I was on the right track about Ronnie Bauer.

Joe failed to turn up any leads at the strip joint, and Tiffany's neighbors at the house all had alibis. While they confirmed the general time that Gaylord heard the shot, not one of them could place Ronnie, or any other possible suspect, on the scene. My partner continued to have a bad feeling about the landlord, but couldn't come up with any motive for him. That suited me. I wanted to stay as far away from the old fruit as possible. His hands were way too grabby.

And no firearm residue had been detected on Ronnie. Not surprising. Hadn't my magic mirror already shown me that he'd worn gloves? I had to admit that we hadn't found any gloves, but I figured they were probably with the gun, wherever Ronnie had stuffed it or buried it. The city provided a million hiding places. We might never find it.

The days rolled by and turned into weeks. Without enough evidence to make an arrest, the case began to cool.

I'm not sure exactly when my plan took root, but it came to full bloom after the captain raked Joe and me over the coals for the second time. "I'm surprised at you, Matt," he'd said. "I know Joe is just going through the motions -- that condo in Florida is calling his name. But I expect more hustle from you. The promotion board isn't going to be impressed with your percentage of unsolved cases."

If he'd still lived, my father would have disowned me for what I was about to do. I wasn't wild about it myself. I'd always been a straight arrow kind of guy, but like some wise man once said: "Desperate times call for desperate measures." Shawna and the boys deserved more than they were getting. I wasn't going to let them rot in that crummy townhouse any longer than I was going to let Ronnie Bauer get away with murder.

When I finally made up my mind, the substitution was pathetically easy. I'd remembered a cold case from a couple of years ago. We had a slug and the Black Widow .22 Magnum that had fired it, but no fresh leads. Hell would freeze before anybody requested the evidence box from that particular case. Luckily, the female sergeant in the property room had always had a thing for me. She was actually grateful when I asked her to do me a favor and run an errand while I watched her desk.

I replaced the slug that killed Tiffany with the one from the revolver in the cold case. Then I went to the video store, poked around until all the clerks were busy out front and planted the Black Widow in Ronnie's backpack that I found hanging in the break room.

When Ronnie finished his shift, I was waiting for him, this time with my partner in tow. I told Ronnie that Joe and I had a few more questions for him and offered to drive him home. We were barely out the back door before the kid slung his pack on his shoulder, wrinkled his forehead and pulled the gun out of a side pocket.

Ronnie protested his innocence loud and long, but he couldn't explain having the gun that matched the bullet that had supposedly severed his girlfriend's carotid. Unfortunately for him, the court appointed a public defender that barely topped him in age and IQ. They both nearly cried when the guilty verdict came in.

Joe presented the only fly in the ointment. He'd been around long enough to suspect a plant, but just like I predicted, my old partner decided to let a peaceful retirement take precedence over a long, drawn-out internal investigation. Even so, I'll never forget the look he gave me when the judge pronounced sentence.

I had to keep reminding myself that Joe hadn't had the benefit of the mirror. That oval glass had made me its sole witness. Some mystical power I couldn't comprehend had chosen me to be the champion of truth and justice. And I'd done my duty, just as I always had. If I ever got up the nerve to tell him the whole story, even Joe would understand. Wouldn't he?

I did make lieutenant, not on my first try, but eighteen months later. One of my first duties was witnessing Ronnie Bauer's execution. Thanks to a string of bungled appeals, Ronnie had ended up on the fast track to lethal injection. The execution wasn't a pretty sight, but I had to give Ronnie some credit. The kid faced it with a lot more courage than I would have predicted.

Another steambath of a summer came and went. All in all life was good. Shawna picked out a nice house. It was in a great school district and even had a pool in the backyard. Now that I was on a desk job, I actually got home in time to grill burgers and watch the kids swim.

One night when the kids had gone to bed and Shawna and I were snuggling on the couch in the great room (cathedral ceiling, built in home theater, etc.), she pointed at the TV. "Matt, turn it up. Wasn't that man involved in one of your cases?"

A still photo of a younger Gaylord Portman filled the screen. The announcer was just finishing, "…an apparent gay bashing. Mr. Portman was wearing women's clothing when the three youths attacked him with chains and lead pipes. He was pronounced dead on arrival at University Hospital."

Shawna burrowed deeper into my shoulder and murmured, "Poor little man."

I didn't much care for old Gaylord or his kind, so beyond a brief flicker of regret for his last gruesome moments, I didn't think about the effeminate landlord again until I chanced to be driving by his house several months later.

It was a perfect late fall afternoon. The air was cool and crisp -- no headache for me that day -- and a few orangey-yellow leaves still decorated the oak trees. The rambling old house was surrounded by contractors' trucks; it must have been bought by one of the yuppies who'd started reclaiming the neighborhood.

I pulled over to the curb and watched some workmen carry out debris and toss it into a dumpster. I wondered what had happened to my magic wardrobe and formed a half-baked idea of entering the house to see if it was still there. As if in response to my idle thought, a plumber's truck backed out of the narrow, gravel driveway.

Was that my wardrobe, sitting in a shaft of sunlight by the tumbledown garage behind the house? As my feet crunched up the drive, I saw the cabinet listing to one side and the door hanging by one hinge. It looked like a very angry foot had kicked the door in.

The oval mirror had shattered, but a few pointed shards still dangled from the rim. I reached for the largest piece; it broke off in my hand with a small chink.

"Well, if it isn't my old friend, Sgt. Reese."

I gasped. Gaylord Portman's face swam in the dagger-shaped fragment of mirror. He was actually speaking to me.

"I hoped I'd get to see you again. I owe you an apology, you see. You and poor young Ronnie."

The sharp edges of the mirror bit into my hands. I could barely catch my breath in the air that had suddenly turned as dank and heavy as July's worst. I ignored the blood dripping from my fingers as Gaylord's image continued.

"I should have let you in on the secret of the mirror. It's a marvel, but not all of its little stories are true. Just like me, it's apt to lie. Truth one day, lies the next. You simply can't depend on it."

"The mirror lies -- what are you talking about?" I forced the question between clenched teeth.

A brittle, silvery laugh drifted up and assaulted my ears. "Only this, darling. Ronnie didn't kill Tiffany. I did. I went up to borrow some moisturizer for my facial and the little bitch laughed me out of the room. Oh, I'd been laughed at more times than I could count and called much worse than the names she came up with, but this time something just snapped. As if that pretty little whore had any idea what I had to go through, how hard I had to work to achieve just a smidgen of her glamour… well, I should have stopped myself, but I couldn't. I went for my revolver, came back up and put an end to her laughter forever. Would you like to see?"

The scene in the sliver of mirror began to shift, but I didn't give it time to play. I smashed the glass to the driveway, and for an instant I was surrounded by hundreds of bouncing, sparkling bits, all bearing Gaylord Portman's laughing image.

I don't remember how I got back to the car, but I can tell you what happened next. I sat for hours in the brilliant sunshine, gripping the bloody steering wheel. I prayed to the god I wasn't even sure existed -- prayed with all my might, that, on this day, Gaylord was truthful on just one point -- the mirror lied.

Beverle Graves Myers writes mystery and horror. Her short fiction has appeared in Woman's World Magazine, FMAM and various anthologies. Her first novel is INTERRUPTED ARIA (Poisoned Pen Press 2004).

Compiled by Babs Lakey

Her Brother's Keeper
by Laurie J. Wood

Ruby Westlake still had the goods for a whore nearing thirty-five. She yanked up her leather miniskirt that had twisted sideways on her thin hips, and rearranged her fake red cashmere sweater cut down-to-there so that more of the gold glitter showed on her boobs. She shoved the sweater nearly off her shoulders under her white rabbit fur jacket that just barely touched her tiny waist. Fluffing her blonde wig with her long ruby-red nails in the reflection of a car window gave her a glow of satisfaction.

She looked good and she knew it. Who cared about her birthday on Boxing Day? Tonight was Christmas Eve and she was still only thirty-four, lookin' twenty-eight. Hardly a wrinkle, firm boobs, legs that went on forever in these boots over her knees, and a tight ass to match. Too bad it was so cold; the john's wouldn't find the ruby in her belly button right off.

Leeza was already warmin' their corner on Warner and Lightguard Streets. It was near the harbor and just south of the respectable part of downtown. Still, there was an all night diner "The Amazon", with a neon red Parrot hanging out front, where the girl's hung for coffee and just to get out of the cold. Raoul was a good guy, even if his tattoos were scary. His neck was surrounded in a tattoo of flames, parrots and vines ran up both arms, and his chest and back were covered in Peruvian fire gods.

Leeza blew into her hands plumes of frost in a swirl around her cinnamon face.

"Oh man, ah cain't believe y'all got that mini skirt *on* girl, yor gonna freeze yor ass off! Y'all never gonna last all night out heah!"

"I don't need all night. Just need till one, maybe two, in the morning. Gotta run for some cigs. You want anything?"

Leeza shook her head no and stamped her feet. Her cheap plastic high-heeled boots slid in the slush. She wore a leather motorcycle jacket over a neon green slit skirt with a leopard print top, draped low in front to her nipples. Huge African hoops swung from her ears and her lips were painted a vivid blood red.

"Y'all got any gloves, girl?" she asked, as Ruby came back and lit up.

"Go get warm. Raoul's put on a Christmas feast for anyone droppin' by. Egg nog, fruitcake, turkey 'n everything. Go on, you can turn tricks later." Fiery ash flicked off Ruby's cigarette.

Still blowing on her hands, Leeza nodded. She grabbed the long door handle to "The Amazon", and Ruby watched the chewed up plastic wreath swing back and forth as other street people crowded out the door. Sated on turkey, and Raoul's bootleg brandy, two men went east on Lightguard St. singing Christmas carols and trying to hold each other up. Ruby took one last drag of her cigarette and considered her options.

One car slowed down to take a look at her, and she waved him off. The Giant Tiger Store was still open down the block. She took a few steps forward and tapped one perfect nail against her teeth, right hand cocked on her hip. Leeza was still inside. Ruby ran across Warner St. all the way to Giant Tiger. All she had with her was a black purse that was empty except for a small roll of dollar bills and a thin stiletto. The other stiletto she carried in a special holder in her right boot.

Once inside, she walked carefully up and down the aisles, keeping her eyes out for other shoppers. The clerks were bored and there was hardly anyone in the store. Ruby knew she needed a special gift for tonight, two if she could manage it. She sidled into Ladies Wear and over towards Accessories. The purse was on backwards and she pushed a pair of ladies winter gloves into it.

Brown leather with a soft lining. The clerks were still talking to each other as Ruby walked out and crossed the street to "The Amazon".

It was a relief to get out of the cold. She grabbed a mug of brandy- laced eggnog as the tray went by, and raised it with a smile of thanks at Raoul. Red and green Christmas lights rimmed the long counter where platters of turkey and fruitcake were laid out. Raoul's patrons were a mixture of drunken street people who would leave here for their grates and cardboard boxes, punked up teens who might find a bed at the shelter if they were lucky, and whores who worked the six blocks surrounding his diner. Someone was singing "Silent Night" and crying in the back corner booth.

"Raoul!" Ruby grabbed his bulky sleeve as he tried to get all 250 pounds of himself behind his counter. "Can I buy a fifth of brandy from you?" She fished a twenty-dollar bill out of the waistband of her skirt.

"Hey, doll, it's Christmas!" His meaty hand slapped her on the shoulder. "And isn't it your birthday soon?" He reached under the counter and tipped a mickey of Napoleon brandy at her.

"Got any more of those really great Cuban cigars, too?" She had to yell in his ear to be heard over the din.

"You don't smoke cigars!" He yelled back.

"It's for a friend! A Christmas gift!"

"Ok, for that I'll take five bucks."

Ruby handed over a frayed five-dollar bill. She tucked the precious cigar into her purse, along with the fifth of brandy. "All right if I take some fruitcake with me?"

"Help yourself! And come back in ...don't stay out there all night, ya hear me?"

"Don't worry!"

Ruby stuffed three pieces of fruitcake wrapped in a napkin into her purse. She couldn't close it and it banged against her hip. She found Leeza sitting with a bunch of whores from Fairmont and Leeds Ave.

"Here honey," she held the gloves in her hand, "Merry Christmas, it's just a little something."

"Oh man, I din' get you anythin', girl!"

Ruby hugged her around the shoulders. "You never mind, just stay out of trouble, ok? I'll be gone awhile, so stay warm till I'm back."

"Where you…"

Ruby was already out the door, and the red neon light from the Parrot drenched her rabbit fur jacket in a bloody red hue.

Two blocks west the harbor turned into warehouses and alleys. Squatters lived there and built their fires, hung their blankets and dragged in cardboard boxes from the delivery trucks.

Ruby scrambled over the snowbanks in her high heels, grabbing at icy chunks to steady her, while holding onto the precious cargo in her purse with the other.

She entered a low car park and went around to the back, through a dingy alley that smelt of rotting meat and urine, and then into the back of a warehouse. The door squealed and two men jumped out of the shadows, lunging at her.

A third man rushed forward in the firelight, tackled them and threw them to the floor.

"This here be Ruby, ya morons. Ya don't never touch her!"

They were younger men then she had thought. She switched the purse to her left hand, leaving her right hand freer for her boot stiletto. In her haste, she'd forgotten to be safe.

"How is Jazz?" she murmured to the giant who'd saved her.

"Not good. He's real sick, Ruby." The man's eyelids were heavily creased from too much booze and hard living. "I don't think he'll last out the week. He won't let us take him to one of them clinics."

Jazz was a tough, street-smart kid she'd met two years ago. She'd found him on Garland St. one summer dawn with the breeze blowing in off the harbor. He'd been counting his money after spending a night turning tricks for old men in luxury cars.

Now he was dying of Aids and choking on his own mucus. Ruby held on to the arm of the man who'd saved her from the punks.

"Does he still know who you are?"

"Most times." He hesitated. "Not always, Ruby."

The man led the way through a maze of blankets, boxes, the side of an open van, fires in barrels, and coughing, fighting people.

The young teen lay in a cocoon of threadbare blankets near the north end of the warehouse. It was actually just two sides of a box, and the older man had tried to position it to keep out the wind. The boy's face was gray, a toque over his head, and he was wrapped in several layers of Salvation Army suit jackets. Ruby put down her purse and began chafing his hands.

"Jazz? Can you hear me?"

His eyelids flickered and a tiny bit of drool dripped out his mouth.

"Could you leave us alone, Frank? Thank you for what you did back there."

"Sure, Ruby." Frank backed away and sauntered off towards a big barrel fire near the center of the warehouse.

"Jazz." She leaned near the boy's ear. "Jazz, wake up. I have fruitcake for you, and brandy."

There was a dirty mug with some water in it. She filled it with a finger full of brandy. Lifting Jazz's head, she poured the tiniest sip in and watched his throat convulse. She talked gently of what a wonderful Christmas they'd have when he woke up, the presents gaily wrapped under the tree, his warm bed upstairs in her house, and the perky dog that would greet him Christmas morning.

Suddenly, his eyes flew open and his hands grabbed her wrist.

"Ruby, is it really you?"

"Yes, Jazz. It's ok, hon, everything's ok."

He took a few more swallows of the brandy and water and then sank back on the backpack he was using as a pillow. He began a paroxysm of coughing and spat up bloody phlegm.

"I brought you a Christmas gift, just like you wanted, Jazz, but I don't know if you should have it."

"You know how I want this, Ruby. Exactly how I want this."

Her hands shook a little as she took the cigar out of her purse. She unwrapped the fruitcake and broke off little pieces of it. Then she held up his head, cradling his lice-ridden hair to her chest, and hand fed him tiny pieces of Raoul's finest fruitcake. Once in awhile she'd give him a sip of brandy and water. It took him nearly an hour, but he finished all three pieces.

"Just like my gramma used to make." His voice was weak and tired. "I want my cigar now."

Ruby reached under his blankets until she found his lighter and a pack of cigarettes with only three smokes left. She sucked on the cigar until it lit, and watched the spirals of smoke float towards the high ceiling. Then she helped him sit up again, and held the cigar to his lips.

He puffed and the sweet, powerful cigar smoke filled the small space like incense.

"I'd like to go to Christmas Mass, wouldn't you, Ruby?"

"Been a long time since I was at Mass, Christmas or otherwise. Don't talk now."

Jazz reached for the cigar again, watched the red tip burning in the semi-darkness.

"I want you to hold my hand when you do it."

"Jazz..."

"You gotta do it, Ruby...it's gotta be tonight." He stared upwards for a few minutes, as if listening.

"They say 'yes'." He turned to look at her. "Can I see your 'ruby'?"

"You can see anything, if you give up this fool plan!" She pulled up her red sweater and pulled down her skirt. The ruby was a quarter carat and winked from a 14k hoop through her navel. Jazz touched it with awe.

"You're the real thing, Ruby Westlake. I won't ever forget what you done for me these last months."

"Jazz…"

"Now. I want to do it now."

He took a long puff on the cigar, another one, and then another one before he started to gag and choke. He handed it off to Ruby, who ground it out on the concrete beside his nest of blankets. She poured another sip of brandy and water into him when he'd stopped coughing.

"Sure you don't want the rest of this mickey?"

"Naw, give it to Frank for Christmas. I want to do it now."

He fixed his murky blue-eyed gaze on her and held out his filthy hand.

"You're the real thing Ruby. And I thank you."

She took his right hand with her left hand. Tears smeared her heavy mascara as she sat beside him and drew her boot stiletto out of its hidden sheath. Ruby leaned over his gaunt face – what was he – sixteen, seventeen? She bent closer and closer until their breath mingled together. Her tears wet his cheeks. His eyes were closed, his hand tight in hers. She could taste the fruitcake and cigar smoke on his lips.

Gently, she kissed him with the soft whisper of a first lover. Her stiletto out now, she gathered all her strength and plunged it into the right side of his neck, hitting the carotid artery dead on. Jazz's body contorted and she felt the hot spurts of blood hit her neck, hair, and chest. She held his hand and the kiss, until the bucking of his body stopped. When she sat up Jazz's eyes were staring at the ceiling with a rapturous look on his face. She reached over and closed them.

Ruby wiped the blade of her stiletto clean, then the handle, with the top blanket. She folded his hands together, and put the mickey beside his pallet. She wiped off the blood on her mouth with the napkin from the floor.

Strong arms jerked her upwards and her feet left the ground.

"Hey Al, isn't it nice when you catch 'em in the act like this!"

The uniformed cop set her down with a bone-crunching thud and shook her by the shoulders so hard her wig nearly fell off.

"What are ya, Vampirilla, or are ya going to tell us you just like to steal from the dead?"

Ruby kneed him in the crotch as hard as she could, planted an elbow in his face, and gave his partner a roundhouse kick to the head. A crowd of derelicts and winos had gathered, armed with bricks and planks of wood. The partner was still face down on the concrete, and Ruby had her stiletto up against the first cop's neck, her lips to his ear.

"First of all, moron, I'm on the job. Badge #501. Second of all, you're about to blow three years of cover. Now get out of here, rookie, before these people give you the beating you deserve."

"Where's your badge." He squeaked out.

"You'll have to check my crotchless panties. Call Sgt. Hubbard." She pricked his neck just a little with the stiletto. Al was starting to moan a little on the floor. "Get your partner out of here."

A monotone of "Ru-*by*, Ru-*by*, Ru-*by*" chanting was starting, as she let the cop stand up straight and then pick his cap up off the floor. He radioed for a Sergeant and an ambulance for the body lying in the blankets. Ruby began walking through the crowd.

"Hey, you...." The cop yelled after her.

She waved, but didn't turn around.

Laurie J. Wood was a Police Officer in the early 1980's, received the Governor-General's Anniversary Medal Canada 125 for Outstanding Community Service. She now writes full-time and takes care of her family while exploring her themes of love, revenge and honor.

Island Ghosts
by David Bain

"I saw the *Time* brief just yesterday," his old friend Mazie said, her voice coming through a couple thousand miles of phone line all the way from Michigan. "You look good in it, about twenty-one, I'd say."

"I feel a hundred frigging years old, but I might have *been* twenty-one in the picture," Will said. "I haven't seen the article -- I *refuse* to read any of them -- and I have no idea where the hell they dug up a photo of me. I haven't talked to any of the media. The bastards. It's all been spokesmen and press releases."

"Yes, I know," she said. "You had a bad experience with the press once upon a time." She paused. "Will, why the hell are you back on that damned island? They give you all this leave, and you go to a place full of ghosts."

"It's Florida, Mazie. The Sunshine State. Where better to relax?"

"Yeah, but it's *Gamer's Key,* Florida, Will. And for you that's hardly Disneyworld."

Will Castleton sucked on his cold Corona, the taste of fresh-cut lime heavy in the smooth beer. Squinting against the sun, he looked out across the deck, beyond the beach and palms to the endless sky-blue water. The glint and glare of the midday sea did not assuage the fact that, for him, those waters were indeed haunted.

"Tell me, Mazie, did *Time* report what, specifically, the guy I killed did to the girl in that motel room?"

"They said she would be in the hospital for months, that she needed plastic and reconstructive surgery, but that she'd be alright thanks to you. That's how they put it."

"They were kind," he said. "And optimistic."

"We've all seen bad things, Will. You get to be there first-hand, but I've witnessed scenes just as bad. I've been there in everything but body. There've been times when I haven't slept well for days, even weeks."

"It'll be months for me, if ever. It was one of the most powerful flashes I'd ever had."

"Will, be glad you at least had the power to do something about it. All I could have done would have been after the fact. After she was dead, Will. Maybe, if I'd had the girl's shirt once it was all over, I could have said she was tortured and died in a motel room. Maybe."

"He mutilated that girl, Mazie. I knew a blood-covered, darkly evil man was in a room somewhere. Somewhere nearby. And I went about my business."

"That's all you *could have* done, Will -- but meanwhile you were beside yourself. I know. You called me, remember? You knew that if you couldn't find it, it would find you."

"I don't necessarily believe that."

"You did everything you could."

"It wasn't enough. I didn't get there in time."

"Will, at the very least she would have suffered even more."

"Here's why I didn't get there in time, Mazie -- because the bastard got what he wanted. He told her sometimes pain was worth than death. '*After you die, you're just dead,*' he said. That girl will be in therapy until the day she dies, Mazie. Scars worse on the inside than out. He got what he wanted."

"Okay, Will, therapy or death? Which would *you* choose?"

Will sighed. "Sorry, Mazie. I gotta go."

Mazie started to protest, but Will hung up the portable phone before she could get it out. He spent the rest of the afternoon in joyless, sun-soaked silence, nursing several more beers.

Here he was, a U. S. marshal, driving his Jeep with his blood-alcohol level surely way over the legal limit, his only passenger a fresh case of Corona.

He was risking it because Gamer's Key was only a few miles long, and at every point but its center, you could see ocean on either side. It was a straight shot from the rented cabin to the 7-11, the closest of only two markets on the entire key.

But now someone was following him.

Not that this was a particularly unusual thing on an island with such limited roadways.

He just prayed it wasn't a cop.

Will pulled the Jeep into the rental cabin's driveway, parked under the cabin itself, which, this close to the water, was up on stilts.

The other vehicle went by.

Will stood in front of his car door, watching the taillights. It was a compact little car, looked like an older hatchback. He felt like the vehicle's shape should have rung a bell, somehow.

Will saw that, instead of turning into another driveway, the hatchback went to the road's dead-end about three-quarters of a mile down, did a U-turn, and came back this way.

The driver suddenly gunned it as he passed. As if Will wouldn't see him if he drove faster.

The crappy little car struggled to gain speed. Will saw by the dim streetlights that the rather loud vehicle was a beat-up blue Chevette from the late eighties.

And that he recognized it.

Shit.

It was Lehman. The reporter for *The Biscayne Beacon* whom he'd had the unpleasant experience with way back when. Seven years and the bastard was still driving the same car.

He had half a mind to get back in the Jeep and follow him.

But why bother. Now that Lehman had confirmed Will Castleton -- failed lifesaver at twenty-one, undeserving national hero at twenty-eight -- was here, he would surely be back.

But Lehman wouldn't be back tonight.

Will drank, listened to the waves out there in the dark.

New U. S. Marshal watches best friend drown

Left alone, the headline for the story Shane Lehman wrote seven years ago could, perhaps, have been read from a sympathetic angle, depending on how forgiving one was. The subhead, however, nailed dead-on the accusatory tone of the article: *"We'd been drinking,' says rookie cop.*"

It was true, but it had been nothing. They'd been halfway through a case of Bud Light for all four people on the boat.

Certainly not the sort of drinking he was doing now.

As for Will, he'd hardly "watched." He had, in fact, nearly drowned trying to locate Brad, whose calls kept getting further and further away.

He'd woken up with this "gift" -- which hadn't given him any inkling of how wrongly Lehman, the one reporter to whom he'd granted an interview, was going to slant the story.

Nor had it told him that the story was going to be picked up by a couple of wire services.

Cold moonlight sparkled off the rhythmically pounding Gulf. Somewhere out there, Brad's spirit still wrestled with the unforgiving water, calling out Will's name. Somewhere out there, the ghost of the man Will could have been still churned through endless water, searching, searching.

If Lehman came to the door tomorrow, Will would punch him in the mouth.

For starters.

It was noon when the doorbell woke him. There was a hammer in Will's head, pounding at his eyes. At least the day was overcast, with no sun to aggravate the hangover.

It was Lehman, of course.

Will did not punch him in the mouth. He made the sack of shit wait though, let him watch through the mostly glass door as he got a beer from the fridge, opened it, took a good long slug. Will examined the man briefly as he swallowed.

Lehman, who was maybe five years his senior, hadn't aged well. He had a paunch and wispy hair combed over a bald spot. The hair of his cheesy mustache was just as thin. He wore ugly gray polyester slacks and a cheap rayon shirt, which was a nauseating shade of green.

Then again, Will himself was only wearing a pair of boxer shorts.

He opened the door. "The hell you want, Lehman?"

"You actually remember me?" The guy seemed honestly startled.

"How could I ever forget? I lost my best friend and the police cleared me before I even woke up. But still you tried to crucify me. I lost my girl and a bit of my reputation, too, no matter how vehemently my superiors defended me."

Lehman shook his head as if bewildered. "You're back here. After that nasty bit of business in Texas, you come back *here* of all places. Care to tell me why?" The guy was apparently unfazed by Will's near-nudity.

"Because I wanted to see your smiling face," Will said. "Care to tell how you found me?"

"My uncle owns Real Estate Sails, you gave him the check for this rental. Seriously, we got bought out by a different publisher. There's a different editor now, too. It wasn't my choice back then and, for what it's worth, I apologize.

"Apology not accepted. You gleefully twisted around every last word I said."

Lehman frowned. "Seriously, Will -- "

"Marshal Castleton, to you. I'm a full-fledged U. S. marshal now, Lehman, despite all your efforts. I have as much power as any sheriff, except my jurisdiction is the entire United States."

Lehman's frown was even deeper this time. "Okay, sorry Marshal. But seriously, I wouldn't have to write things that way again. Listen, can I take you out to lunch, talk about the past few weeks of your life? Literally the whole world wants to know. You could look at it before it's published, make suggestions, take things out. Seriously, I won't bring up what happened last time you were on the island."

"Look, I'll just be polite and ask you to leave. Now."

"You're not even going to offer me a beer?" he said, looking with mock longing at the Corona in Will's hand.

"No, I'm not. Goodbye, Mr. Lehman."

Lehman looked at Will silently for longer than Will felt he should have allowed.

"Your loss," Lehman finally said, turning to leave. "It would have been a great article this time. An award-winner for sure."

Will gave Lehman the finger once his back was turned. But the gesture made him feel small and rather hollow. It was something a kid would do. He finished his beer as Lehman's little car putted down the drive, and he downed two more for breakfast.

Will spent the afternoon on the deck, drinking and watching the steadily increasing clouds turn heavier shades of gray. Around five-thirty, it had gotten cold enough that he went inside for a windbreaker.

Fifteen minutes later he found himself still barefoot but wearing his coat, half a mile down the beach, being pelted by sharp pinpoints of icy rain, a heavy wind whipping his hair and moving the low, full, pregnant clouds rapidly in from the sea.

He turned his face up to the rain. The rain was a feminine thing today. There was, in fact, a woman in the clouds directly overhead. This woman, she had lots of hair and a very small nose. The contours of her pretty face were etched in the darker gray of the clouds. There was a pink edge to her cloudy form that was slightly painful to look at. Now, as he watched, Will felt her essence slowly bleeding from her; the cloud was dissolving.

And suddenly there was no cloud-woman.

The clouds were actually getting much, much darker -- fast -- not lighter at all.

It had been one of his damnable visions.

There was no question about what it meant. Somewhere, probably nearby, a woman's life was in danger of fading, of bleeding away. Sometime before this storm ended.

He was sure of it.

And he would be the only one able to stop it.

He sprinted back to the cabin.

Out of breath, Will picked up the portable phone, set it down.

No. This time he would not call Mazie.

"Okay," he said out loud, though in his mind it was still Mazie he was talking to. "I'm on an island, there's only one bridge to the mainland. If there's any sense to these visions, any rhyme or reason to them, she's got to be somewhere on this rattrap.

"So, do what? Call the local cops, tell 'em you're a U.S. Marshal with a vision?"

The vision wasn't specific enough for that, even if he said he was a psychic, even if he were to give the tip anonymously.

Okay then, just get in the Jeep and drive into the descending night. That's all there could be to do. Just a few streets on this island. If it's even possible, if this is even real, you should find her quickly. Five minutes and you've covered the main strip, five more and you've covered the few blocks of central Gamer's Key.

Will quickly retrieved his handgun.

Ten minutes and he'd find her.

Fierce winds whipped lashed at him as he raced down the deck stairs, the storm seeming to pick up intensity even as he jumped into his vehicle. He realized as he floored it that he was still barefoot.

Ten minutes.

The wind was thrashing the palm trees now. Big fat drops of rain splattered his windshield faster than the wipers could work to throw them off.

He was almost at the end of the island closest to him, where he had seen Lehman turn around the night before. The alcohol was swimming in his brain, adding sparkle to the luminescent sheen the wet windshield and his high beams gave the night.

Lights on in a few of houses, all up on stilts. Rain-blurred shadows visible in one or two. No one visible underneath any of them. Some of the houses throwing weird blue light, TV on, lights off.

He was driving far too fast for conditions, but much slower than he wanted to.

A string of restaurants.

A school playground.

No figures fighting, no shadows of a woman in the throes of death.

Eight minutes.

His first pass through town. The storm-swept streets empty.

Lehman's car and a red Beretta -- the attendant's no doubt -- at the 7-11, the shadow reading the paper and drinking coffee at one of the booths undoubtedly Lehman.

Fuck Lehman.

Seven minutes.

The park. Damn. He had forgotten about the park. He swung the jeep in, whipping through the suddenly muddy dirt trails twining around the mossy trees.

Shadows jumping everywhere in the rain as his high beams swung back and forth down the twisting paths.

The limbs of the trees swung as if challenging him.

The alcohol not helping.

Was that a person? A man leapt at the Jeep from the trees and Will had no time to swerve. No, just a statue of Wilford Gamer, the city's founder, Will's headlights giving it the illusion of motion as he turned.

Back toward the main road.

Two minutes wasted.

Will turned, stamped on the accelerator, once again hurtling through the storm at a speed too slow for his comfort.

Businesses at this end of the island. Mostly rental agencies. All dark.

Real Estate Sails, where Lehman's uncle had snitched him out. Also pitch dark.

Four minutes.

No woman.

The marina. He slowed.

Boats rocking in the waves, tugging at their moorings. Deserted.

The historic fort at the tip of the island. A vast, empty parking lot. The heads of palms peering over the fort's wall, tossing like the manes of wild horses.

Three minutes.

Where the hell was she?

He was nuts. She didn't exist.

Flooring it back to the center of Gamer's Key.

Lehman still sitting in the 7-11.

Will's equilibrium sloshed just slightly when he turned hard at the corner past the convenience store. Houses only up one or two bricks above the ground here. Dilapidated, used furniture on warped porches. Trailers raised on concrete blocks.

One block over. Nothing.

Another turn.

One minute.

A figure in the road ahead.

A man.

Jeans, boots, denim jacket, thick hair, beard, no hat.

In the middle of the road.

Walking forward through the driving rain. Not planning on making way for the Jeep. Big splash with every determined footstep.

Something in his hand.

Light glinted from it.

A knife.

And not just any knife. A big kitchen knife.

Will parked the car crosswise in the guy's path and dialed 911 on his cell phone.

"U.S. Marshal Will Castleton," he told the dispatcher. "I'm reporting a possible 10-zero or attempted murder and a man with a knife. Send an ambulance. I'm on -- damn!" He hadn't noted the names of the streets. "I'm one block west of the Gamer's Key 7-11, at the north end of the street."

“Sir, could you -- ?”

Will pushed the END button and got out of the Jeep. He was instantly soaked, even before he fixed his weapon on the man, which was within seconds.

“U. S. Marshal,” Will said. “Where is she?”

The guy stopped his pissed-at-the-world stride, cocked his head. “Kimmy?” he said. “Hell, Kimmy’s dead, man. You’re too damned late.”

"I *am not* too late."

The man stood there a minute, assessing him.

"You one of them cops afraid to use his gun?" he asked Will.

"No," Will said.

The man nodded.

Will held steady.

Then it went down fast.

The man roared and charged, the hand with the knife pumping.

Will knew instantly what the guy wanted, and he was not going to give it to him. The question had given the guy away.

Suicide by cop. That's what they called it. The guy couldn't face up to what he'd just done, but didn't have the guts to do himself in, so he was going to make a cop do it.

Will stayed calm, took a second to aim low, shot the man in the thigh.

In the movies he might have kept going or got right back up.

In real life he tumbled, dropped the knife and was grabbing at his wound, writhing in pain in the middle of the flooded road, making incoherent growling and whining noises.

Will kept the gun on him.

"Roll over onto your stomach and put your hands behind your back."

"Man, you shot me!"

"I told you I would. Now do as I say or I'll do it again."

"Where is she?" Will asked after he had cuffed the guy. A trickle of the man's blood was already heading for the gutters.

"Can you at least put me in your car or something, out of the rain? You got me lying in the middle of a fucking river."

"You'll live. Where is she?"

The man growled in protest, then added, "Man, everyone on this island knows where we live. She's on the porch."

"Which house?"

"The red one." He motioned with his head.

Will's bare feet sprinted through the cold water on the hard asphalt and through the flooded lawn. He leapt up the three tall steps to the porch.

The woman was there. She was sprawled on her back, wearing a short, rather pretty navy blue dress of some summery material, now soaked with rain.

And blood.

She was dead. Had to be.

There were numerous wounds.

Blood and water mixing all over the porch.

Will heard a rasping breathe over the hiss of the rain, and she moved, tried to sit up, couldn't even come close.

He hastened to her side.

"You hang in there, Kimmy. Help's on its way."

She clutched his hand with her good hand -- the other was badly cut.

She tried to form a word.

"*Shhhh*," he said.

Her panic-stricken eyes found his and seemed to settle just a little.

Will held her body in his arms, held her eyes with his.

"It'll be all right," he said.

Her lips quivered. She moaned, and it ended in a cough, a thin mix of spittle and blood appearing on her mouth.

He kept eye contact, stroked her hair.

They sat that way, and seconds, minutes, hours, didn't matter.

Will believed he felt her soul move through him as she passed.

He looked at her another moment or two. The rain let up a bit, the gray brightening a bit -- then there was a sudden flash of lightning.

But no thunder.

Will looked up. It was Lehman. He'd snapped a picture, using a flash. He'd obviously been listening on a scanner at the 7-11, got here before the cops.

Will decided he didn't give a damn about the picture.

Lehman shook his head. Perhaps there was even real emotion in the gesture. "Hard luck, Castleton. Looks like you got here too late."

Will held Lehman's gaze a long moment.

Then he looked back down at Kimmy's closed eyes.

"I'm not so sure of that, Lehman," he said "I guess ... I don't know if I got here in time or not."

"What the hell do you mean, Castleton?" the reporter said, pointing at the girl. "She couldn't be any more dead, could she?"

"Sometimes all we can ask is that someone hold our hand as we die," Will said. "Or even after."

Will believed that if he listened just right he could hear ghosts whispering their cold, clear assent in the diminishing hiss of the rain.

Then the sibilance was drowned out by a siren, approaching fast.

Lehman, who had been looking at Will, befuddled, pulled a notebook from his back pocket and began scribbling down the quote.

David Bain has published stories in many publications. He is editor/partner with Cyber-Pulp, and the editor of Whispering Worlds, a large e-book of speculative poetry, which received an "Internet Hot Spot" nod from Ellen Datlow. *http://www.geocities.com/davidbainaa.*

Compiled by Babs Lakey

Dead Wife Walking
by Earl Staggs

I was enjoying my after dinner vodka martini when I glanced up and saw her. Her auburn hair was longer and she was deeply tanned but she was still quite attractive and moved with the flowing grace of a runway model. There was no doubt in my mind. The woman who had just entered my favorite restaurant in Tarpon Springs, Florida, was Janice Whitmore.

Four months ago, Janice Whitmore died in an automobile accident in Fort Worth, Texas. Her car went over an embankment and exploded. The car blazed for thirty minutes before emergency equipment arrived. She was not thrown from the car and she did not escape from it. There was nothing left of her but ashes. I know. I watched.

"Would you like me to remove those, sir?"

In that moment of shock at seeing Janice Whitmore alive, I hadn't noticed Paul. He had finally come to clear my table. Paul was a replacement for my regular waiter, Mario, who was sick, according to the owner of the restaurant. In his clumsy attempt to shell my lobster, Paul nearly dumped the entire plate in my lap. My slacks cost more than he made in a week. The owner would hear from me about it.

"Yes, Paul, I would like it very much if you would remove the dirty plates and silverware from my table. I would have liked it even more if you'd done it five minutes ago when I finished eating."

"Sorry, sir," Paul said. "We're busy tonight."

"No busier than usual," I said. "Just hurry." I didn't try to hide my dissatisfaction. Paul was not only incompetent but was now blocking my view of Janice Whitmore as she followed the hostess in a weaving path between tables, coming straight toward me.

I leaned to the left and peered around Paul to see where the hostess would seat Janice. The restaurant was only half filled, mostly with snowbirds down here to escape the February snow and ice up north. The hostess continued to lead Janice in my direction, passing by several empty tables.

Paul finished clearing my table and, true to form, dropped my silverware on the floor. After he picked it up, he asked, "Would you like me to bring you another drink now, sir?"

"No, Paul, I would *not* like you to bring me another drink now. I'd like you to go stand where I can see you and I will beckon when I want you."

I waved Paul away as the hostess walked past me with Janice Whitmore two steps behind her. Janice nearly brushed my shoulder. The hostess seated her at the table right behind mine. For a second, I wondered if she had recognized me, but only for a second. In the twenty years I'd been in the business, I'd never been made. Never.

Paul asked her if she'd like a drink.

"Chablis," she told him in a soft voice with barely a hint of Texas. "Pinelli Blanco if you have it."

I thought about leaving but I couldn't. When you're the best at what you do, you take pride in doing it exactly right. No mistakes. Ever. I had to make sure she did not know who I was. I turned in my chair to face her. She was studying the menu. I smiled. "Excuse me," I said.

She glanced over at me with a pleasant look. There was no hint of recognition, no coy smile to encourage conversation, only the bland expression a woman of breeding gives when approached by someone she doesn't know.

"I'm sorry to bother you," I said, holding my friendly smile, "but aren't you from Fort Worth?"

She lowered her menu and shook her head. "No, I'm not," she said. Her smile was small and quick, not meant to be rude but also not meant to be friendly.

"Please forgive me," I said. “It’s just that you look familiar and I was sure we'd met before."

"That's quite all right," she said. "People tell me that all the time. I'm sure we've never met." She returned to her menu.

I turned back to my table. I had made no mistakes in Fort Worth. I’d considered everything, calculated and planned every detail. Janice Whitmore was dead but she was here, sitting at a table right behind me, waiting for a glass of wine.

Paul brought her wine and I heard him ask, "Would you care to order now, Miss?"

“Oh, I haven’t quite decided yet,” she said. “I’ve heard all your seafood is good. How is your baked halibut tonight?”

Before Paul could respond, I turned around again. "Try the smoked salmon," I said.

She glanced at me, pursed her lips and thought about it. "I love smoked salmon but sometimes it's too salty."

"Not here," I said. "It's excellent and I recommend it."

She smiled and said, "Thank you." She ordered smoked salmon and artichoke salad with vinaigrette.

Paul started to walk away but I held up a hand to stop him. “Paul,” I said, “I want you to go into the kitchen and tell Raymond to be sure not to overcook the lady’s salmon so that it’s too dry. Perhaps you’d better write that down.”

“I’m sure I can remember it all the way into the kitchen,” he said. There was a note of insolence in his voice.

“See that you do, Paul, and...” I looked at Janice Whitmore. “...tell him to go easy on the seasoning.”

Janice nodded her approval of the light seasoning. She was grinning now, glancing from Paul to me and back again.

“Will that be all?” Paul asked. He gave me a forced smile. The red bolero style waiter’s jacket didn’t fit him. He must have borrowed Mario’s but he was more muscular than Mario. It was too tight and he looked totally unprofessional.

“Yes, Paul,” I said. “You may bring me another drink now and another glass of wine for the lady. And there’s one more thing. You need to work on your attitude and learn to pay attention to details. Details make the difference between doing a job right or not, even if it’s only waiting tables.”

I saw the muscles in his jaw tighten. “I’ll try to remember that, sir,” he said. He turned and walked away at a brisk pace.

“You don’t seem to like him,” Janice Whitmore said from her table behind me.

I turned toward her again. “It’s nothing personal,” I said. “It’s just that I come here quite often because the food is excellent and the service has always been first rate. I’ve come to expect that and Paul has been a disappointment.”

Her face widened in a full grin. “It seems to be personal to him. I don’t think he likes you either.” She added a quick wink.

Something in her voice, along with the wink, seemed almost flirtatious. I’d noticed how attractive she was back in Fort Worth but I never let such distractions interfere when I’m working. I wouldn’t let it distract me now. I had to know how she could possibly be alive.

I picked up my drink and moved over to her table. She stared at me for a moment, then looked around as if to see if there was someone close by to rescue her from this sudden intrusion.

"Don't be alarmed," I said. "I know who you are. All I want to do is talk, all right?"

She stared at me for a second, then looked away. She raised her glass and swirled the wine in small circles, watching the liquid slosh back and forth. "You know the movie Casablanca?" she asked.

“Bogart at his best,” I said.

"This reminds me of one of Bogart's lines. How did it go? Something like, 'Of all the gin mills in all the world, she had to walk into mine.' Ironic, isn't it, that I had to walk into this place and you're here?"

"Ironic," I said.

A look of resignation crossed her face. She took a sip of wine and looked into her glass for another few seconds. "You're not going to let it go, are you, Mr. Hardin?"

She knew my name. Not my real name, of course, but the one I’d used in Texas. Only her husband would have known that name. How could she have known it? I’d come back to that later but I couldn’t be too pushy right then. "So you do know who I am," I said. “No, I can't let it go. I have to know how you pulled it off?"

"Of course I know who you are. I should. You trailed me everywhere I went for three days."

"You knew I was there?"

"Oh, you're good, I'll give you that," she said. "It was even fun figuring out where you were without you knowing I knew."

That irritated me. I'd never been made. Never. "I'm glad I gave you some amusement for those three days.”

She narrowed her eyes and studied me for a moment. "You should let it go," she said. "It's not too late. You should just walk away right now.”

"No,” I said. “I can't."

“Is it because of a sense of pride in your work, Mr. Hardin? You can’t stand the thought of failing to carry out a contract?”

“Failure is a sign of incompetence,” I said. “Failure is due to not considering every possible detail, of not planning for any eventuality. No, I never think about failing. Anyone who does is destined to fail before they begin.”

Paul delivered our fresh drinks and her salad. He didn't seem to notice or care that I was sitting at her table now.

"I always deliver on a contract," I said after Paul left us. "Yet, here you are. I need to know how that's possible."

"What difference does it make, Mr. Hardin? You were paid well, quite well, as a matter of fact. It's not as if I'm going to ask for a refund." A grin played across her lips. Apparently, I was providing amusement for her once again. That irritated me even more.

"Obviously, I was conned somehow and I don't like being conned. I think I deserve to know the truth."

She finished her first glass of wine and picked up her second one. "Maybe you do deserve to know. It certainly won't do any harm now. But first, you'll have to satisfy *my* curiosity."

"About what?"

"My car went over a cliff on a tight curve. How did you make that happen? A blowout?"

I shook my head.

"The brakes then. You tampered with the brakes."

I thought about it. Why not tell her? She'd never tell anyone. I knew I'd have to get rid of her now. She could identify me and that was a possibility I never allowed. Not even her husband had seen me. He and I talked only by phone and he left my payment at a prearranged drop point. It was my turn to be amused. I'd never killed anyone twice before and the thought intrigued me. After all, it would be risk-free. Officially, she was already dead.

"Those tricks are for amateurs," I said. "And you can't be a hundred per cent certain tampered brakes will do what you want them to at the right time. The only sure method is the steering mechanism, all controlled electronically. A little wiring work, a remote control device, and all you have to do is push the right button at the right time. The steering locks and the car goes straight even if the road curves."

"But wouldn't that leave traces or wires or something?"

"Poof," I said. "It all went up in smoke."

She nodded. "I see what you mean. Then I'd say you were lucky the car exploded and the fire destroyed the evidence."

"Never trust to luck," I said. "People can walk away from the worst car accidents you can imagine. The fire is the finishing touch."

Her eyes widened. "Then...the fire was...?"

"Electronics again. A tiny spark in the right place and...poof!"

She smiled and raised her glass in a toast. "Brilliant," she said. "It's no wonder you're the best. I'm sure the insurance companies have paid out millions as a result of your work."

I toasted back. "If only they knew." I laughed. I was actually enjoying this. I'd never talked about my work before with anyone. With her, of course, it wouldn't matter. I decided to take her out on my boat and get rid of her in the Gulf of Mexico. I knew it wouldn't be difficult to get her to go. There was definitely a flirtatious nature in her glances now, in the way she leaned forward when we clicked glasses, generously showing more cleavage than necessary. I'd do what I had to do but there was certainly no reason not to accept what she was offering first.

"Now it's your turn," I said. "Someone was in your car that day, someone who looked enough like you to be your twin. Who was it?"

"Her name was Sandra Wallace and you're right. We could pass for sisters up close and from a distance as twins, I suppose. You only saw me -- or her -- from a distance, as you recall."

"Who was she?"

"Sandy was my cousin. That accounts for the resemblance. It also helped that I copied her hairstyle before you started following me. Oh, it was me you followed for those three days it took you to decide on the time and place for my, uh, accident. But on that final day, it was Sandy."

"She came out of your house that morning and drove away in your car. How did you manage that?"

"Why, Mr. Hardin, you're not the only clever one, you know." She leaned toward me again, showing her cleavage again, and touched my arm with her hand. She was definitely offering and I would definitely accept. But there was more I had to know first.

"Go on," I said.

"Sandy always did what I asked her to do," she continued. "After you told Roger when and where you were going to do it, he went off on one of his business trips and I asked Sandy to do me a small favor."

"A small favor."

"I told her I was spending the night with a gentleman friend but I didn't want anyone to suspect I wasn't home where I belonged. I asked her to drive my car to my house that night, spend the night there, then meet me the next morning to give the car back. Anyone who might have been looking would think it was me, the faithful and dutiful wife, home where she was supposed to be while her husband was out of town. I made sure she took the route you expected me to take that morning."

I was beginning to agree. I wasn't the only clever one at that table. "How did you know Roger had hired me?"

She laughed. "Oh, Mr. Hardin, you really must keep up with the modern woman. Any wife who doesn't bug her husband's phone is a fool. You'd be amazed at how many do it and how many of them keep their husbands in line because of it."

That explained how she knew my name and why I was in Fort Worth. "So let me understand this. You knew Roger hired me but instead of blowing the whistle, you decided to let your cousin act as stand-in. Why?"

She leaned back in her chair and took a sip of wine. Her expression grew somber. "Do you know what Roger did for a living, Mr. Hardin?"

"Sure. He was an attorney who did high finance negotiations for big money people. He moved money around, made the deals, and took home a percentage for himself. He was quite successful, I understand."

"Very successful. But did you know some of his success was for ventures that were, shall we say, frowned upon by the authorities?"

"If you mean his money laundering operation, yes, I knew about it but it meant nothing to me."

"We lived quite well, Mr. Hardin. So well that even his legitimate enterprises plus his illegitimate ones weren't enough to pay our bills. He started skimming off the top, I think they call it, and some of his clients found out about it. They wanted their money back and he didn't have it. I'm sure I don't have to tell you what those kind of people do if you can't pay up. As a matter of fact, I believe it was one of those business associates who recommended you to Roger. You must have had dealings of your own kind with them."

"It's very possible," I said. "And you're right. I know exactly how they deal with people who cross them."

"I'm sure you do," she said. "That's probably what keeps you in business, right?"

I smiled. "Could be."

"Anyway, after listening to his phone conversations with you, it wasn't hard to figure out that Roger had found a solution to the problem, for himself at least. We had two million dollar life insurance policies on each other. He decided to collect on mine to pay them off."

"Tricky boy, that Roger."

"Yes, very tricky. You're lucky you got your money in advance. That two hundred thousand he paid you was all he had and he had to scrounge real hard to come up with that."

"I always collect in advance," I said. "But why did you let me go through with it?"

"I considered all my options. I thought about running away, just disappearing, but I didn't like that at all. I also thought about going to the authorities but I liked that even less. Sure, Roger would have been ruined and out of my life, but I'd be left with nothing. Then I decided I had to look out for myself. I decided to let Roger collect the two million dollars insurance on me, then I'd show up and take it from him. What could he do to stop me? I'd threaten to go public and let the world know I was still alive. He'd be really finished then but I wouldn't be left with nothing."

"You'd take the money and disappear, leave Roger to face the consequences with the people he still owed."

She gave a little shrug and smiled. "A girl's got to do what she has to in this cold, cold world, Mr. Hardin. Besides, he deserved it, don't you think?"

I sat back and thought about it. They were quite a pair. They deserved each other. "The only part of your plan that didn't go right was his heart attack. I read about his untimely death in the newspapers."

She picked up her glass of wine and drank it down in one gulp. "The sonofabitch. Right after my memorial service, he decided to drown his sorrows at the craps tables in Vegas. He died right there on the casino floor before he could collect on my insurance policy."

"So he got nothing, which meant you got nothing."

"Absolutely zero. I couldn't even collect on his insurance policy because I was legally dead. Now, that's truly ironic, don't you think? If I showed up alive, they'd figure out how I pulled it off and connect me with Sandy's death. I'm sure not even you could have planned on a detail such as Roger having a heart attack."

"Probably not," I said. "Sometimes even the most careful planning can be undone by something that could not possibly be foreseen."

She raised her empty glass and held it toward me. I met hers with mine in a hollow toast to the unforeseeable.

"And here you are," I said. "Legally dead, broke, and in hiding."

She sighed heavily. "Turned out disappearing was my only option available." There was a certain sadness to her now. I almost felt sorry for her.

I raised my glass and drank the last swallow. I knew all I had to know and it was time to move on. "Instead of having another drink here," I said, "why not have one on my boat? It's docked not far from here, easy walking distance. Maybe a little salt air will help us both put this whole thing behind us."

She looked at me and shook her head. "I'd like nothing better, believe me, but I'm afraid *they* have other plans."

"They? Who're they?"

She glanced over my shoulder. "Them," she said.

I turned and looked. Paul stood there. He had replaced the red waiter's jacket with a suit coat. In one hand, he held a badge. In the other, handcuffs. Behind him stood two uniformed police officers.

"Stand up," Paul said to me, "and place your hands behind your back. "You're under arrest for the murder of Sandra Wallace."

I stared at Paul and his companions, then turned back to the table. Janice Whitmore was standing now and one of the police officers was placing cuffs on her. Janice mouthed "Sorry" to me.

I watched another officer reach into Janice's purse and pull out a tape recorder. They'd taped our entire conversation.

Paul recited my rights as he put cuffs on me. He was rougher about it than necessary. When he finished, he said, "I'm sorry my performance as a waiter didn't measure up to your standards, sir." He emphasized the *sir*. He stepped around in front of me and gave me an arrogant smirk. "I'm sure the inmates who serve you where you're going will appreciate your instructing them on how to do it properly."

I ignored him. Something else was more important. I looked at Janice Whitmore. "Why?" I said.

The female officer beside her started to lead Janice away. I stepped in front of them. "I think you can give us a minute here."

The officer looked at Paul. He shot me a look of disgust but nodded.

Janice Whitmore said, “It was one of those details you talked about, the kind you can’t account for. That stupid cousin of mine told her boyfriend about staying at my house that night and driving my car the next morning.”

“Of course she did,” I said. “You should have foreseen that.”

She shrugged. “I guess I’m not the professional you are. Anyway, he reported her missing, told them what he knew, and they put two and two together.”

“So that sent them looking for you.”

“It took them a while to track me down but they did.”

“And you gave me up. They offered you a deal, I suppose.”

“It took them even longer to find you. Even when they did, they had no proof against you. They needed to hear it from you. They offered me a reduced sentence for doing this." She gave me a sad little smile. "What else could I do?"

I couldn't blame her. Like she said, a girl's got to do what a girl's got to do.

The female office led her away. Paul took a firm grip on my arm and pushed me into step behind Janice. She looked back over her shoulder at me.

“You should have walked away," she whispered.

She was right. I should have walked away as soon as I saw her but I had to know. It was her failure to plan for every possible eventuality, to calculate every detail. I couldn’t have foreseen her tapping her husband’s phone or sacrificing her look-alike cousin. I took some small satisfaction in knowing I had not made any mistakes. Very small, under the circumstances.

Earl Staggs lives and writes his short mysteries and novels in Fort Worth, Texas. His stories have appeared in many magazines. He has served as Senior Fiction Editor for FMAM and as President of the Short Mystery Fiction Society. EarlStag@juno.com

Fired
By Stephen D. Rogers

She woke to confusion at 3:17, panic, sheets drenched by another series of screaming nightmares. She heard sirens and yet again was dwarfed by her attacker as he shrank her world to a cell of pain and then turned off the light.

She sat up and fumbled for the side table drawer. With heavy hands she withdrew the gun purchased but never fired. What need had she for lessons? She'd learned her lesson when the stranger broke into her apartment.

She shook her head in an attempt to clear the roaring in her ears, the smell of danger that stung her eyes.

She brought her knees up to her chest, laid her arms between them and pointed the gun at her bedroom door.

Never again.

The door crashed open and she fired until the gun was empty.

She slumped back against the headboard.

A second fire fighter entered the room.

Tea For Two, Scones For One
Stephen D. Rogers

The boy from next door came up to me and placed his right hand on my left breast. I say "boy" but he must have been sixteen. I say "breast" but of course he rested his hand on a patterned fabric that complemented his blue eyes.

I don't know what I should have done but thanking him was probably a mistake. From such small beginnings does a garden grow.

Women my age -- they say -- should not be thinking about sex. We should be pouring tea and buttering scones, waving at the grandkids scampering on the lawn. We should be doing good works.

They do not have a sixteen-year-old boy at their disposal. They probably wish they did.

He is a young man, bored and contemptuous, who requires constant feeding. Nothing comes without a price and I would never expect otherwise. Even roses need to be pruned and their thorns draw blood.

Yesterday I gave him a rifle.

That present excited him more than all the previous ones put together. What is it about boys and their guns?

Dime I

Did he believe I thought any more of him because he strutted around the room dressed only in jeans pretending to aim and fire at my family heirlooms? Did he think any more of himself?

Daddy was killed on a hunting trip. The stag broke left and bounded between them. Mum, unaccustomed to shooting, lost her head and pulled the trigger.

My young lover pointed the gun and me and went: "Bang, bang, bang."

He laughed, raucously.

Today he wants to use it for real, wants to rob a pub he can not legally enter to drink, even though he didn't know enough to fake recoil.

People, too, must sometimes be pruned back. My mother understood that and so do I.

A Conversation Over Drinks
Stephen D. Rogers

I sat at the hotel bar sipping whiskey, listening to the gossip and the weather, trading nods with anyone who dared to look my way. Out at the edge of things was where I liked to be and people in town understood that.

Over at one of the tables, however, was a stranger with an untouched drink. I could tell by his manner that he was taking it all in. He wasn't giving nothing back though. He wouldn't even meet my eye.

When I'd stood his rudeness as long as I could, I grabbed my whiskey and wandered over.

"Passing through town?"

He blushed like a young girl. "In a manner of speaking."

I hooked a chair with my leg and joined him. "The name's Ross."

"R-Ross?" He stared at his hands, which lifted his glass and drained it. After sputtering like one of those new automobiles, he added, "I'm Joe Edwards."

"What brings you to town Mister Joe Edwards?"

"Research."

"Sounds fancy." Edwards was fancy himself, nattily dressed in new clothes, his hair and fingernails trimmed as though he was getting married this afternoon to the minister's daughter.

"Not really." He glanced at the bar and raised his empty glass but that's not how Al operated. After a minute of being ignored, Edwards turned to face me. "Do you ever think about time?"

"Only after last call is announced."

He tried to smile but I could tell it was a strain. "Just imagine that traveling through time was as simple as walking across town, that it was possible to visit the past."

"And why would we want to?"

Edwards waved as he talked. "To see how it really was. To broaden our understanding of human history. To change something."

His last reason sounded the most heartfelt. Some people did have a hankering to tinker. "I figure it's best to leave well enough alone."

"But what if you could go back in time and kill the grandfather of someone who was going to do evil. You could make the world a better place if you kept the evil-doer from being born."

"You mean like Henry Ford and his infernal engine? I should go back fifty years and plug his kin?"

Edwards blinked. "Hypothetically. Wouldn't you agree that keeping an evil person from being born justifies the expense of time travel?"

"I'm not so sure it even justifies murder, but then you're the researcher."

"Yes." Edwards ducked his head, scraped his chair against the floor as he stood. "You the only Ross in town?"

"The one and only." I shifted to expose my gun belt.

Edwards licked his lips. "It's nothing personal."

"I could say the same thing myself."

"Your grandson is going to commit a horrendous crime against humanity."

"Why don't we step outside."

He was sweating now, ruining his wholesome appearance. "I'm not normally a man of violence."

"In that case, you should have traveled a little further back in time." I nodded towards the door. "After you."

Over three hundred of Stephen Roger's stories and poems have appeared in more than a hundred publications. His website, www.stephendrogers.com, includes a list of new and upcoming titles as well as other timely information.

THE ONLY GAME IN TOWN
by N. S. Wikarski

You ever seen one of those true crime TV shows where they interview hardened criminals? The ones that are dumb enough to get caught anyway. The interviewer always asks why somebody would turn to a life of crime, and the criminal always gives some bogus excuse like lousy parents and poverty but nobody ever mentions boredom. As far as I'm concerned, boredom is the best reason to want to go on a killing spree. At least it was for my friend Slick and me.

We come from a really small town. Cheatham, Vermont. Population - 1,000 morons, and that's including the livestock. Actually most of the livestock are smarter than the residents. Slick thinks that's because of too much inbreeding. After all, nobody ever leaves Cheatham. Leaving would mean that they had enough brainpower to figure out how to get to the other side of the city limit sign. Instead, all the locals ever do during those long winters when they aren't baying at the moon is eat, sleep, and crank out a new generation of morons even dumber than the last bunch.

That was never true about Slick and me though. By the way, my name is A-Boy. Actually that's my nickname. It's not a flashy name like Slick but it's better than my real name, which is Theodore. You know, like in "Leave It To Beaver." Since I wasn't too keen on the idea of 1,000 morons calling me "Beaver", A-

Boy is fine by me. I got that name because I was a straight-A student all through high school. So was Slick for that matter. The two smartest guys in Cheatham, he always used to say. That actually isn't saying much but we had big plans. We were going to prove that we were the two smartest guys in the world.

I remember it started the summer after our senior year in high school. Even though our grades were good, our parents couldn't scrape together enough money to send us away to college. We had two choices. Either stay in Cheatham and bay at the moon like everybody else, or come up with a plan to get the hell out of there.

But we didn't just want to get out. We wanted glory. So Slick started to think about what we could do. He laid it all out on paper and it made sense to me. We were going to become career criminals. We'd cut a swathe through Vermont just like Dillinger did through the Midwest. Before we were through, we'd have a bigger rep than Dillinger. Hell, we'd have a bigger rep than Eminem. And nobody would be able to catch us because we'd be too smart for them. After we'd pulled together a decent nest egg, we were going to jump a tramp steamer headed for Australia and never be heard from again.

One other thing though. It was important not to leave any loose ends. Take no prisoners was Slick's motto. That made sense to me too. It was just simple logic but I think Slick was into killing. He definitely had a mean streak. From the very start.

By the time he could walk, he was pulling the wings off of bugs. By the time he was ten, he was twisting the tails off of kittens. He was hanging stray dogs at fifteen. Last Halloween, he managed to catch a live bat and he was going to bite its head off, only it bit him on the lip first. He had to go in for rabies shots. I thought that was pretty funny. He didn't.

But getting back to our master plan. For me the killing was just cleaning house. For him it was fun. A game. He really liked games. Especially con games and he was good at them too. Slick had this angelic face that the neighborhood moms always fell for.

He could bust a window and break into tears on cue and say he was sorry. They always believed him. Like I said, morons.

Anyway, about a month ago we picked our first target. Slick said the main thing was to find someplace isolated. Out in the country. Not hard to do since anyplace five miles outside of Cheatham was way out in the country. Farmhouses with no close neighbors were our best bet. Especially if the farmers were old and lived alone. Slick said no guns because somebody might hear so we ordered ourselves a couple of top-of-the-line hunting knives off the internet. Personally, I think he was planning on skinning somebody at some point in our criminal careers but I never asked.

The plan was simple. Pick a target, fake car trouble and ask to use the phone. Once we got inside we would look around for anything worth stealing, take care of the loose ends, and be on our way.

It worked like a charm. We found an old guy who lived alone on a farm about thirty miles away from Cheatham. He was a little suspicious at first. I got nervous when I saw a shotgun propped up against his back door but it didn't faze Slick one bit. He just turned on the angel act and we were in. I love farmers. None of them believe in banks. We found a stash of money in a cookie jar on his kitchen counter. A cookie jar, for God's sake! Like I said, no imagination. So anyway, Slick got to road test his knife and we were out of there in under a half hour. No witnesses and about five hundred bucks in small bills. It was a good start.

We laid low for a few weeks. Got a big kick out of reading the local papers about this terrible crime and no clues as to who could have done such a horrible thing. I clipped out copies of all the articles because I was going to put together a scrapbook.

Slick decided we should try another local farm this week before leaving Cheatham for good. We scouted for a while. Had to drive farther to find the right place. About forty miles in the opposite direction from town, we found it. There was an old couple who had a huge spread. Big white farmhouse set up on top of a hill. Lots of livestock. Pigs and dairy cows mainly. They must have been worth a bundle. No kids around that we could see because we staked out their house with binoculars for a few days just to be sure. A nice easy target. We came back late the following afternoon, parked our car at the bottom of their driveway and walked up. I could see from the expression on his face that Slick was going to have fun with this.

The old lady was out in the yard, hanging her wash. She looked like the Pillsbury doughboy only without the cap. Her hair was some wispy shade of grayish blond. She was humming to herself when we walked up to her.

"Good afternoon, ma'am." Angel face was in top form.

She turned around and took the clothespins out of her mouth. "Hello, boys." She smiled and the corners of her eyes crinkled up. I was wrong about the Pillsbury doughboy. When she talked, she sounded like Mrs. Butterworth. She glanced behind us down the driveway. "My goodness you've walked a long way. Why didn't you just pull your car up to the house?"

Slick scraped the toe of his boot in the dirt. Perfect "aw shucks" routine. "Sorry to bother you, Mrs...?"

"Oh, forgive me. My name is Maisie McDonald." She held out her hand.

Slick took it. "Pleased to meet you, Mrs. McDonald. My name is Errol King and my friend here is Theodore Parker."

I stepped up to shake her puffy hand.

"Do you prefer to be called Theodore or Teddy?" she asked me.

"Neither actually, ma'am. Most people call me A-Boy and they call him Slick."

"My, my." She tittered. Honest to God, she actually tittered! "What names you young people have nowadays."

Slick decided to get to the point. "We've had a bit of car trouble, Mrs. McDonald. We'd really appreciate it if we could use your phone."

She shot us a cherubic smile that would have given Slick a run for his money on a good day. "Why, of course. Come on up to the house." She paused as a light bulb went off over her head. "My husband's pretty good with cars. Maybe I could just have him take a look at it."

Slick jumped in. "No, ma'am. I'm afraid we've put you to enough trouble as it is. I'm pretty sure it's the transmission, anyway. We'll just call a tow truck and be out of your way in no time."

That was close. If her yokel husband actually knew anything about cars, we'd be in big trouble.

Mrs. Butterworth nodded and motioned for us to follow her up the path to the farmhouse. I took a look at the outside. No peeling paint. The whole place had a nice, prosperous feel to it. There had to be something worth taking inside. I could see Slick eyeing everything too and smirking a little bit. He must have had the same idea.

She brought us into the living room. Lace curtains and lots of flowery chintz. Knickknacks and doodads everywhere. Just like I expected. Lots of photos on the wall too. Only it was odd because most of them were teenage boys and they didn't look like they were family.

"Why don't you two have a seat and I'll get you some refreshments." She pointed to a phone on an end table. "You can call from there." As she bustled off to the kitchen, she added, "I'll just let my husband know we have company. We don't get many visitors."

"We really appreciate your kindness, ma'am." Slick was laying it on with a trowel.

"What about the old guy?" I whispered.

"It's better if they're both in the same room. That way we won't have to hunt him down." Slick fingered the knife in his jacket pocket and grinned wickedly.

My eyes slid to the phone. "You better make your fake phone call loud enough for her to hear."

Slick nodded and picked up the receiver. I swear, if he hadn't chosen the life of a career criminal, he might have had a great future on the stage. He was so convincing, I almost believed he was talking to somebody on the other end of the line.

Mrs. Butterworth waltzed back in just as he was hanging up. She had a plate of sugar cookies and two glasses of milk. I eyed the liquor cabinet. When this was over I was going to have to wash the taste of milk out of my mouth with Scotch. I smiled politely and took the glass she held out.

"Growing boys need their calcium."

"Yes, ma'am. Thank you very much." I was actually going to enjoy killing her. "Speaking of boys, Mrs. McDonald, you must have a large family of them." I motioned toward the pictures on the wall.

She giggled. "Gracious, me. They aren't all ours. Some of them have just been visitors like yourselves."

"You sure must get attached to people quick," I mumbled.

At that moment, in slouched Gomer Pyle's grandfather. At least that's what he looked like to me. Tall, gawky and gray.

"Al, say hello to our company. This is Slick and A-Boy."

Gomer Senior scratched his head as if he couldn't fathom nicknames any better than his wife. "Alvin McDonald's the name. Pleased to meet you boys." Handshakes all around. We sat down together in a cozy little ring. "Have any trouble getting a tow truck?"

"No sir," Slick hurried to reassure him. "They should be here in about a half hour."

I was wondering how long he wanted to string out this freak show. We needed to know where they kept their money.

"This is a real nice farm you've got here." I hoped that might jog them along.

"Yes, we're very proud of it," said Gomer. "Been in the family for generations."

"It's not every farmer these days who can make a good living," Slick chimed in.

"Oh, we do all right. Don't we, mother?" He patted Mrs. Butterworth's arm as if they shared some kind of secret. She beamed back at him.

"We've been lucky but I think that's partly because we don't believe in banks."

My head jerked to attention. Slick swallowed a whole cookie. "You don't?"

"No indeed." Mrs. B put her serving plate down on the coffee table. "My family lost everything in the depression because of banks. Mr. McDonald and I vowed we'd keep our money right here where it would be safe."

I started adding up columns of numbers in my head.

Slick smiled like he'd just struck the motherlode. "But you wouldn't keep anything valuable in plain sight, would you?" He tried to sound shocked. "After all, you must have heard about that poor old man who was robbed and killed about a month ago."

"Oh, we heard all right." Gomer pursed his lips. "Can't trust anybody these days."

"That's right," added Mrs. B. "You boys really need to be careful as you go through life. You're still young and innocent. No telling what might happen to you if you trust the wrong people."

"You're absolutely right, Mrs. McDonald." Slick was doing his best Eddie Haskell impersonation. "It's gotten so that you never know who to trust." He stood up like he was about to go somewhere.

I wasn't sure what he had in mind. I slid my hand into my coat pocket and gripped my knife.

"Since we have to wait a little while for the tow truck, maybe you wouldn't mind giving us a tour of your farm."

My hand relaxed its grip on the knife handle. Good one, Slick. Get them to show us where they stash their little horde.

"Oh, of course, boys." Mrs. Butterworth stood up and dusted crumbs off her apron. She walked over to a desk in the corner and picked up an old camera. "When we get to the wishing well, I'll take a picture of you both."

Slick smiled. I nodded and we followed them toward the stairs to the upper floor. They meandered down memory lane from one boring room to another. Jesus Christ! They had a story to tell for every stinking closet in that goddam house! I didn't see anything that looked like a good place to hide cash. Maybe there was something in the outbuildings.

We walked out through the back porch. The sun was starting to set. We'd have to wrap up this tea party before dark. Didn't want the headlights on our car tipping anybody off.

Midway between the house and the barn, I saw something that looked like an old well. It had one of those roofs over it with weird flowery vines crawling all over the place. The stonework had been cut away on one side and a plank floor had been laid across the opening so you could actually stand in the middle of the well. Mrs. Butterworth steered us toward it.

"Is it safe to step in here?" I asked. The planks looked pretty solid but you could never be sure.

"Oh, my yes! It's been boarded up for years. We take lots of pictures in this spot because it's so pretty. We call it our wishing well."

I looked at Slick. He was trying to wipe a sneer off his face. I couldn't believe these two saps!

Slick whispered to me, "Let's play along. They might have something tucked into the roof or in the stonework. I want to get a closer look."

I nodded and followed him to the boarded up well.

"Oh, that's perfect," cooed Mrs. B. "With the sun setting behind you, this will be one of our best shots. Now just stand right there on the boards in the middle of the well."

Gomer Senior was positioned a ways behind her leaning against an old iron pump handle. It seemed kind of odd to me that somebody would put a hand pump about twenty feet away from a well but like I said before, morons.

Mrs. B focused her camera. "Now make a wish boys. Then smile and say 'cheese.'"

I rolled my eyes. I couldn't take more than another five minutes of this crap. Slick nudged me. He looked up at the roof above our heads. Then I saw it too. A hundred dollar bill tucked into one of the rafters.

"Holy!"--

Slick cut me short. "Smile for the camera, A-Boy." I knew that tone. The real game was about to begin.

Mrs. B had us in her viewfinder. "Now say 'cheese.'"

Gomer pushed down on the pump handle.

"Ch...!"

The floor opened right underneath us. It was a trapdoor! Christ almighty! We were falling! Falling! We were--

Mrs. McDonald lowered her camera and smiled radiantly up at her husband. "Do you suppose they got their wish, Al?"

Mr. McDonald puzzled a few seconds before replying. "Don't hardly see how, mother." He squinted up at the darkening sky. "I'll get the tractor out and haul the bodies up tomorrow. Too late to get started today."

"You'll have a full day of it what with grinding them up for pig food and all."

Mr. McDonald laughed grimly. "I expect that providing a meal for our livestock is just about the only useful thing those boys have done in their entire lives."

"I think you're right, Al." Mrs. McDonald looked down at the developed photo in her hands. "They did take a nice picture though. It'll look good on the wall."

"These two didn't have guns," her husband observed.

"No, but they did have hunting knives. Big nasty looking things. Pretty easy to see the shape through a coat pocket." She peered down the driveway as a new thought struck her. "Will you have time to take care of the car before dark?"

"Eh-yep. I'll drive it into the machine shed tonight. Break it down for parts later."

"Well, that ought to keep you busy for awhile." She sighed. "How many has it been?"

Mr. McDonald rubbed his neck, thinking back. "I'd say about eight cars in the past five years."

"Yes, that's what I make it too." She drew her arm through his as they walked up the hill toward the farmhouse.

"You know, mother, I've been thinking. We're not getting any younger. Maybe next time we should just call the police and let them handle it."

Mrs. McDonald stopped dead in her tracks. She folded her arms across her chest and scowled up at her husband. "Why, Alvin B. McDonald! I can't believe my ears. Do you have any idea what a criminal trial ends up costing the taxpayers of this country? Not to mention if they get life, then that's 30 or 40 years of feeding and clothing and housing those youngsters all at taxpayer expense. Worse yet, if they're acquitted they'll be back on the streets to prey on innocent folk! The way I see it, we're just doing our civic duty."

Mr. McDonald's face spread into a broad grin as he looked down at his wife. "Unruffle your feathers, woman. I was just having some fun with you." He wrapped his arm around her shoulder. "To tell you the truth, the day the two of us can't manage a couple of piss ants like that is the day we ought to sell the place and move ourselves into a retirement home!"

Mrs. McDonald chuckled. The couple resumed their stroll up the hill. "Where do you suppose these two came from, Al?"

"We'll know soon enough when I haul 'em up tomorrow and check if they got IDs in their wallets. But if I was to venture a guess, I'd say they come from the same place as all the others--Cheatham."

Mrs. Mcdonald tapped her chin as she paused to consider that fact. "Maybe it's something in their water supply that makes them all go crazy."

Her husband nudged her up the steps toward the back door. "I blame them whatchamacallit video games. They start out pushing a button and blowing up a cartoon. Next thing you know, they're pulling a trigger and shooting a man."

Mrs. McDonald squeezed her husband's arm affectionately. "Maybe so, Al, maybe so." She glanced back briefly toward the well. "All I know for sure is that as long as there's been people on this earth, boys will be boys."

Nancy Wikarski's short mystery fiction has appeared in *FMAM,* her reviews in *Murder: Past Tense* and *Deadly Pleasures*. She made her novel debut in 2002 with *The Fall Of White City*--the first installment in her Evangeline LeClair historical mystery series set in 1890s Chicago.

No Sale
by Elizabeth Dearl

Hannah pushed a limp strand of hair from her eyes and leaned against the doorframe, allowing the young couple to share private whispers about the corner fireplace. In deference to her, they did not discuss sheepskin rugs, chilled champagne and blazing logs on a winter evening, but she knew they would later. They were such obvious newlyweds; the girl still flashed her tiny diamond ostentatiously, and the young man used the phrase 'my wife' as often as conversation permitted.

Hannah's heart ached as she watched them, remembering her own days as a newlywed. She hoped their marriage would be far different from her own. Sneaking a peek at her watch, she gently cleared her throat. The husband started, blushed.

"I'm sorry, Miss Bates. We're taking up too much of your time."

"Not at all," she lied. "Do you like the house?"

The bride gazed at her husband and breathed a dreamy sigh.

"It's just perfect," she said. "But I don't know if we..."

Hannah's lips relaxed into a sympathetic smile. "If you'll follow me to the office, we'll set your mind at ease, Mrs. Neil. Interest rates are low, and I'm sure you'll have no trouble qualifying for a loan. Are you sure you wouldn't like to tour the two-story model again? You seemed so set on that one when you first came in."

The couple exchanged an uneasy glance and Hannah could have sworn they shuddered in unison.

"We're sure," Tony Neil said firmly. His wife nodded.

Forty-five minutes later, Hannah closed her office door behind the beaming pair. They had kept her late, but the looks on their faces when her computer approved their loan had been worth the extra time. Plucking a ring of keys from her desk, she stepped into the scarlet glow of sunset.

Having inspected and locked up the first two models, she hesitated before venturing into the third. Ignoring the stiff breeze that had risen to tear the pins from her neat chignon, she stood gazing at the darkening facade of the two-story house.

Styled after a New England Cape Cod, its lines were crisp and pleasing to the eye. Hannah herself had been entranced by it from the moment the framework was raised. But the Neils were not alone in their reaction after walking through the house—in the three months the models had been available, no one had purchased a home based on this design.

"And I know why," Hannah said under her breath. "Even if I can't explain it."

Bracing herself, she unlocked the door and entered the elegant foyer. Dread settled onto her shoulders with tangible weight.

Her steps heavy, she headed for the kitchen. The weight persisted, straining the muscles of her neck. Her fingers groped for the switch, and bright fluorescent light dispelled the settling gloom of evening, but the cheerful pattern of cherries on the wallpaper looked more like blood spatters, and the fake-brick tile felt slimy beneath her feet.

"What is it about this place?" she wondered aloud. The cell phone clipped to her belt let out a piercing chirp and she jumped.

She grabbed it. "Yes?"

"Hannah? You sound out of breath."

She sank onto a bench of the built-in breakfast nook. "Wally. I'm fine, the phone just startled me."

Her boss chuckled. "They scare me, too—even more when they're set on 'vibrate. 'You're there late. Any sales?"

"Two. Mr. Farnhum decided this morning, and I had a walk-in couple this afternoon. They qualified easily."

Good girl! Which houses?"

"Mr. Farnhum bought model A and the Neils want C."

She listened to dead air for a moment, then Wally said,

"What the hell's wrong with B? Hannah, we've got thirty lots set aside for that plan, and they're too small for the single-stories."

"I know. There's just something—" She stared at the blood-stained walls, biting her lip.

"What?"

"Nothing. Maybe the new generation is too lazy to walk up and down stairs all the time."

Wally hooted. "Right. So they spend a fortune on aerobics classes. No, Hannah, that's not it. Look, push B for a while, will you? We're in trouble if it doesn't start selling."

"I'll try." She paused, choosing her words carefully. "Wally, you must have noticed how different this house is."

"Sure," Wally joked. "It's taller."

"Seriously. It has a quality missing in the others. The single-story models are what you'd expect to find in a modern subdivision. This house seems, well, displaced in time. It stands apart."

Wally breathed heavily for several seconds. "So you think it's too old-fashioned? Damn. Seemed like a great idea at the time."

"What are you talking about?" Hannah asked, more sharply than she had intended.

"Interesting story behind this design. I'll tell you all about it tomorrow, okay?"

"Tell me now."

"But—"

"Now." Hannah was surprised by the unrelenting tone in her voice. Apparently, so was her boss.

"Well, in the late 1960's, a young couple lived in a house on that very site. According to the story, the husband returned home one evening to find the place on fire. Just as he reached the yard, his wife, flaming like a torch, came crashing through an upstairs window, trying to escape. She was cut to shreds by the glass. Nasty. The young man couldn't afford to rebuild, didn't really want to keep the place anyway, I expect, after all that. So he sold the land to my company. We've held onto it all this time, waiting for the suburbs to stretch out that far. Our little subdivision used to be farmland, you know."

"And you decided to build a similar house?" Hannah guessed uneasily.

"Heck, we built the same house, actually. We found the plans and thought it would be an attraction. Nostalgia is big right now." He sighed. "Or so we thought."

Hannah looked at the cherries-cum-bloodstains again. "Are you sure she didn't die in the kitchen?"

"Hey, kid, what's the matter? It's not a ghost story, for Pete's sake. I guess no one can be sure, but the upstairs window was broken, and she was all cut up— Look, I've got to pick up my wife at work, her car's in the shop. Go home, will ya?"

"Wally—" She was talking to a dial tone.

She hung up slowly, torn between curiosity about the house and sheer envy. Even dumpy, cigar-smoking little Wally had someone to go home to. Hannah grimaced. Happy marriages had been thrown in her face too often today. Still, dinner for one in front of a television was preferable to a husband's angry face, angry fists. Don't, she told herself. Don't let yourself slip back into the self-pity routine. It's been ten years. You have a good life.

Dark had fallen quickly and she still had to explore each room before she could lock up and go home. Several months before, a small boy had been accidentally locked in another builder's model home for an entire weekend. The story had gained nationwide attention and the bad publicity had nearly sent the builder into bankruptcy. Hannah started up the back staircase leading from the kitchen to the master bedroom. A clever idea, she'd always thought. Lets Mom and Dad slip down for a midnight snack without waking the kiddies. Now the narrow passageway and steep, dark walls seemed unbearably oppressive, snatching her breath as she climbed.

When she was almost to the top, she heard a phone ring. Her hand instinctively flew to her belt, but she knew without checking that this wasn't the cell phone's electronic chirp—this was the deep ring of a desktop telephone. The sound seemed to emanate from the master bedroom.

Hannah eased into the room and pressed the switch, but the overhead fixture refused to respond. She felt her way toward the queen-sized bed, following the edges of the mattress to the bedside table. She fumbled to turn on the lamp as the phone jangled again, and when the light flared she saw an outdated Ma Bell device; chipped black plastic with a rotary dial.

Pulse pounding, she grabbed the handset. "Yes?"

"It's over," a woman said, her voice quavering. "Don't you get it, Mark? I'm filing for divorce tomorrow."

"Who is this?" Hannah demanded.

A man's voice cut in.

"Listen to me, Julie. I am not giving you a divorce."

"I'm not waiting for you to give me anything," the woman responded, her voice trembling. "You've given me plenty over the years as it is, you bastard. Broken bones, split lips, bruises. I've had it. Marcie says—"

"Marcie! I'm sick of hearing about Marcie. If it wasn't for her—"

"I might be dead by now," the woman, Julie, replied. "Leave me alone, Mark, or I'll have you arrested, I swear I will."

Hannah drew in a ragged breath and raised a hand to her face, feeling the slight lump beneath the skin where her husband had once broken her cheekbone. She shook the memory away.

"Try it, woman," Mark said softly. Hannah remembered that deceptive softness well. "You belong to me, and no judge is going to tell me otherwise."

"Goodbye, Mark."

A dial tone drilled into Hannah's ear, and she dropped the receiver as if it were a snake she had accidentally picked up. Well, she thought wildly, Dr. Thorne will be surprised to hear from me again. She didn't understand it. Five years had passed since she'd required tranquilizers to get through the day, three since she'd flushed the last of her sleeping pills down the toilet. Recently, she'd even begun dating again, though another marriage still seemed an impossibility. Yet, apparently, the hallucinations were recurring. Next she'd be back to seeing her ex-husband's face everywhere, hearing his growling voice in her dreams. Shaken, she turned around. And gasped.

A bare mattress, half covered with a gaudy, velour spread, sprawled across the bare, wooden floor.

A young woman bent over a battered suitcase, prying at the clasp. Her long, stick-straight hair fell over her eyes, and she shrugged it back impatiently.

The phone at Hannah's feet began honking angrily, and the girl started. She stared in Hannah's direction.

The older woman straightened her shoulders, her initial bewilderment replaced by indignation. "Who the hell are you?" she demanded. "What have you done to this room?"

Ignoring her, the young woman sprang around the bed and ripped the cord from the wall, hurling the phone through the closed window. Glass shattered.

Hannah's jaw dropped.

"You'll pay for that window!" she shouted. "You'll pay for all of this—" She stopped.

The girl had returned to her struggle with the suitcase, never acknowledging that Hannah was in the room. Was she deaf? Obviously not. A transistor radio blared *The Green Tambourine* from atop a cluttered dresser, and she'd certainly heard the phone's disgruntled beeping. Hannah advanced, tapped her on the shoulder.

The girl whirled, eyes wide with such obvious terror that Hannah took a step backward.

"Look, I'm not going to hurt you, I just want to know what-"

The girl looked through Hannah, searched the air around her, then shrugged and, giving up on the suitcase, began throwing wadded clothing into a threadbare duffel bag.

Hannah sank onto the sagging mattress, which shifted alarmingly under her weight.

"You can't see me," she breathed. "You can't hear me. But you can feel my touch. Dear Lord, what is happening?"

For the first time, she took a good look at the girl's odd outfit. A wide, white leather belt secured a pair of hip-hugger jeans to her slender body. The bell-bottomed cuffs of the pants were ragged above her bare, dusty feet. Her knit shirt was emblazoned with a hot pink peace symbol, and enameled daisies dangled from her earlobes, tangling in her long hair as she moved. Hannah almost smiled. The child looks for all the world like a hippie, she thought. An extinct species.

A crash from downstairs brought the girl to her feet. Hannah struggled to roll off the bed, which seemed to have her trapped between a lump and a protruding spring. By the time she managed to stand, the girl was halfway down the stairs to the kitchen.

"Julie!" a rough voice from below roared. "You come back here, bitch!"

Julie? Oh, God, Hannah thought. No wonder nothing makes sense. This is the girl I overheard on the phone. I'm just continuing my hallucination. She clutched her head between her hands. Dr. Thorne, you have your work cut out for you.

Julie appeared in the doorway, her face pinched and white. She slammed the door and bolted it, then pelted toward the other door that let to the upstairs hallway.

"Key, key," she mumbled under her breath, sweeping small objects off the battered dresser in a frantic search. "Where is the blasted key?"

Hannah flinched as something heavy struck the stairway door.

"Go away, Mark. I'll call the cops!" the girl yelled.

A malicious chuckle was audible through the closed door. "Oh, yeah? With what? I found the phone outside. You really ought to control your temper, Julie." He hit the thin wood again. It began to splinter.

Julie moaned in terror, and Hannah promptly forgot that the entire episode was a figment of her diseased imagination. She stamped her foot. "Listen, you stupid girl, don't lock yourself in here, you'll be trapped. Run for it while he's busy breaking the door down!"

Julie sank to the floor and began to rock back and forth, whimpering. "Mark, please, just leave me alone."

The pounding on the door stopped abruptly. After a pause, a much altered voice drifted into the room.

"Ahhh, Julie, sweet Julie, my best girl. I won't hurt you, I just want to talk. I love you, sweetheart, you know that. I never meant to hurt you. Please, baby, just let me in. Let me hold you."

Throughout this sickening litany, Julie had slowly stopped her aimless rocking. She was now rising slowly to her feet.

"No!" Hannah screamed. "Don't believe him! Haven't you heard all this before? I know I have. Julie, listen to me. Run while you have the chance, get as far away from him as you can. Julie!"

The girl, of course, couldn't hear her. She moved like a sleepwalker toward the stairwell door. Hannah lunged forward to stop her, but her feet tangled in the tacky velour bedspread. By the time she regained her footing, Julie had the door open.

The man outside took one step inside the bedroom, giving Hannah a fleeting glimpse of tattooed arms and a dirty T-shirt before he grabbed Julie by the hair and yanked cruelly, pulling her down two steps. Hannah's eyes widened as she caught sight of what he held in his other hand—a long butcher knife.

Hannah extracted herself from the spread and followed in time to see Julie wrench away from her captor at the base of the stairs. The girl flung herself toward the back door and rattled the knob frantically. Mark grinned, holding up a key. He circled his shrieking wife like a cat teasing a mouse, making playful little jabs now and then with the wicked knife. Still smiling, he used his free hand to turn a knob on the stove—which wasn't, Hannah noted dully, the sparkling electric stove recently installed in the model home. A gas burner whooshed to life.

"I think," Mark whispered, "you could use another lesson in manners."

Julie screamed.

Hannah raced to the back door and knelt beside it, fumbling to unpin her name badge—HI! I'M HANNAH BATES—from her jacket lapel. She'd never manage such a trick with the modern dead bolt that should have been here, but this flimsy lock should prove no problem. That is, if she could make her hands stop shaking long enough to get her name badge loose.

Mark growled a curse, and Hannah turned in time to see Julie make a break for the stairs. As she brushed past her husband, he slashed out with the knife, laying the girl's arm open from shoulder to elbow. Blood spattered the dingy white-painted walls, and Hannah felt faint. Cherries, she thought. Mark's arm, completing the momentum of the swing, made contact with a coffee can, tipping it over. Grease, smelling pungently of bacon fat, cascaded over the edge of the stove, puddling on the wooden floor. As Mark took a step toward his cowering wife, his boot made contact with the oily patch and he sprawled flat. Julie stood where she was, gazing stupidly at her wounded arm, watching the blood drip to mingle with the spilled grease.

It was clear to Hannah now where Wally's story differed from the truth, although she could see how Mark had gotten away with his wife's murder. The broken window upstairs, the fire, the wounds inflicted by his knife…

Limbs waving like those of an over-turned turtle, Mark struggled to get to his feet, but his leather-soled boots could find no purchase on the slick floor. Hannah gave up on the stubborn pin and ripped the nametag from her suit, wincing as a chunk of mauve wool came away with it. She jammed the plastic card between the door and the frame, and sighed with relief at the prompt click of the lock.

Mark caught the handle of the oven door and hauled himself to his feet. A vein throbbed in his temple as he swung toward Julie, who was still obliviously contemplating her bleeding arm.

With a wordless snarl, Hannah flung herself at the man, knocking him against the stove. The grease-soaked sleeve of his T-shirt made contact with the flaming burner. Howling, he dropped to the floor and rolled, just as firemen teach schoolchildren to do. But rolling in a puddle of grease has never been a recommended method for extinguishing burning clothing, and the fire spread down his back like an emblem on a biker's jacket.

Flames licked at her ankles and melted her pantyhose as Hannah rushed to Julie's side. She managed to drag the stunned girl to the door and throw her outside, not sparing a backwards glance to determine Mark's fate. As Hannah grabbed a towel from the clothesline to bind Julie's arm, the roof of the back porch collapsed into flaming rubble. The girl noticed neither the noise nor the towel, which must have appeared to be mysteriously wrapping itself around her gaping wound. Her eyes were unfocused. Shock, Hannah though grimly. Not entirely a bad thing. She won't want to remember much of this.

Headlights flashed from the dirt road near the back fence, and Hannah heard men's voices raised in frenzied speculation. Thank God. Neighbors to the rescue. The entire rear wing of the house was ablaze now, it could probably be seen for miles.

Julie sat down quite suddenly, like a rag doll with its stuffing pulled out. Hannah lost her grip on the girl and stumbled against a garden stake. The back of her head cracked against a fence post as she fell, and her last conscious sight was of a burly man in overalls lifting Julie into his arms as easily and tenderly as if she were a small child.

Hannah awoke to the sound of a blue jay scolding her from the branches of the minuscule sapling the landscaper had planted in the postage stamp-sized back yard of the model home. The sun had not yet made its appearance, but the eastern horizon was pink with approaching dawn. Fluorescent light still glowed from the kitchen window above her head.

Groaning, she rolled to her feet and gingerly probed the base of her skull. Quite an egg.

Her head ached, but her steps were light as she entered the kitchen of Model B and started a pot of coffee from the supplies kept for potential clients. A glance at her watch showed it to be 6 A.M., and she hesitated only briefly before dialing a familiar number on her cell phone.

"Wally? Yes, I know what time it is, sorry I woke you. Just wanted to let you know I'll be a little late this morning. I have to go home and change my clothes. Wally, you idiot, quit cackling. No, I did not have an all night date, as if it's any of your business. Listen, when the Neils show up, don't let them sign the final papers on C yet, okay? I'd like to show them B one more time. I think they just might change their minds."

She sipped her coffee and gazed complacently at the innocent cherries decorating the wallpaper. Only cherries.

Now we're both survivors, Julie, she thought as the morning sun slanted through the window and warmed her face. Good for us.

Elizabeth Dearl is a former Texas police officer, and author of the award-winning Taylor Madison Mystery Series. This story won the 2003 FMAM Annual Fire To Fly Award. Visit her at http://www.elizabethdearl.com

Addio, Mia Madre
By MJ Jones

One afternoon last May, I interrupted my secretary at her computer. "Time for a break, Dawn. Get something to drink and come in the office."

Dawn nodded at the screen. "You know Judge Poplawski wants this tomorrow morning."

"What I've got to tell you is more important," I said.

And it was. Because I'd finally found a way to save my law firm—and make Dawn and me filthy, filthy rich.

In short, I had found Dawn's mother.

My name is Susan Llewellyn and for six years Dawn was my secretary and bookkeeper. My *administrative assistant*, she wanted me to say. As if my law firm were big enough to employ anyone with so lofty a title. But Dawn had worked for me since she was in high school. Why should I care if she liked her business cards to read: *Llewellyn & Llewellyn , Attorneys at Law/Dawn Renee von Stade, Administrative Assistant*.

She liked her name, too, and the opera stars she built it out of. They were her role models, even if she couldn't sing a note. Maybe she needed them because she never had a mother. I mean a real mother, not that series of foster moms Milwaukee County Social Services stuck her with until she was eighteen.

I often wondered why Dawn never looked for her real mother. I know she didn't because she would have told me. Like she told me about the boys she dated or how she felt when she saw Puccini's *Suor Angelica.* But whenever the subject of her mother came up, she'd laugh it off with some crack like, "What if she wasn't Tiri Te Kanawa after all?"

Then, last winter, I found Dawn's mother.

The original Llewellyn & Llewellyn were my father and his younger brother. But about the time I finished law school, Uncle Frank died and Daddy took me on. I'd been reluctant, of course. Pride, though, doesn't fill an appointment book and I knew very well that Smiling Jack Llewellyn had never lacked for clients.

He's been dead for almost three years, but his office—my office now—hasn't changed much. Except for the oriental rug, which I added, the room has the same view of Lake Michigan, the same law book-lined walls and leather wing chairs, the same old-fashioned partners' desk. Daddy used to say that desk was big enough to play nine holes of golf on. A good thing, because under my proprietorship it teems with every office gadget known to man—and, in its middle drawer, the snub nose .38 Chiefs Special my ex-husband claimed no desk was complete without.

I was at the desk when Dawn came in with coffee for me, Pepsi for herself. While I fussed with some contracts, she pulled one of the leather chairs over to the window and gazed into the grey Milwaukee spring.

Finally, I set aside the papers, picked up my coffee, and said, "Hope you and Mike don't have plans for tonight. I've got a lot to tell you."

"We broke up. Tell me what?"

"Sorry about Mike," I said, though I didn't feel very sorry and wasn't so sure Dawn did either. The guy was a real jerk.

"Tell me what?"

I folded both hands around my cup. "You've met my friend Claudia, haven't you?"

Dawn heaved a dramatic sigh and said, "Why does it take lawyers so long to get to the point?"

"My friend Claudia?" I repeated.

"She the tall one with the salt and pepper hair and the million dollar suits?"

"These days, Claudia gets most of her clothes at—" I named one of the city's classier resale shops. The same one I buy at, though Claudia says designer labels never look quite right on stubby redheads.

"If she's that cheap," Dawn said, "what about the handmade pumps? And the top donor's seat at the opera?"

"Ever notice how much you and Claudia look alike? Except for the hair, of course."

"And the shoes."

"What are you now? Twenty-three?"

"Pert'near twenty-four," Dawn said. "What's all this about?"

"I've known Claudia Pfeiffer since University School and at your age she could've been your sister. Same height, same dark hair. Your eyes are even shaped the same."

"What're you leading up to, Susan? That they're finally going to disbar you but I can maybe get a job with Claudia Pfeiffer?"

I told her I was not going to be disbarred and, furthermore, Llewellyn & Llewellyn, even with just one Llewellyn, was not going out of business. Nor would I be cutting her hours or her pay. Not when the firm's future looked so very bright.

"We've got some very important trust work coming up," I said. "And the Office of Lawyer Regulation's inquiry is headed nowhere—for all the scary legal words it threw our way. You know the ones I mean. *Misfeasance, embezzlement*. And, oh yes, *accomplice*."

Dawn blinked, then took a slug of Pepsi before she said, "So what's all this about Claudia Pfeiffer?"

"Claudia's father was my client. Daddy's client, really." Another operatic sigh, then, "Big construction guy, right? Real estate developer, too."

"Biggest in the city. Julius Augustus Pfeiffer, monarch of all he surveyed, as Daddy put it."

"Doesn't he like own that ugly high-rise they blew up everything north of Juneau Park to build?"

"Owned," I said. "He died last December."

Dawn's brows drew together. Perhaps she was puzzled as to why none of Julius Pfeiffer's documents had crossed her desk.

I said I'd taken care of his will and all its etceteras personally. "But they're not important. Not when you see what else I found in the Pfeiffer file."

I held up a piece of paper. It read "Certificate of Birth."

Dawn came and took the paper. She stared at it for a long time. Finally, she said, "Me? Claudia Pfeiffer's daughter?"

She began to grin like she was holding a ticket that hit all five numbers and the PowerBall.

Later, I called Claudia Pfeiffer.

"She bought it," I said.

There was a long pause. Then Claudia laughed. "You're kidding," she said. "Nobody could be that stupid."

"They could be that greedy, though. Dawn already thinks she's the second coming of Princess Di. On the way home tonight, I had to stop her from picking up a brand-new BMW."

"Thank God for greed," Claudia said. "By the way, Susan, please tell me you mean *your* home. That you didn't leave her alone someplace with her cell phone, proclaiming the good news to everyone she ever knew, along with Channels 4, 12, and 58."

"Dawn's asleep in the guest room with half a bottle of Absolut in her."

"I hope that later on she'll be just as easily...uh...dealt with."

"That, mommy dearest, will be up to you."

"Yes, well, when do I get to meet my bouncing baby girl?"

"She wanted to drive the Beemer right over. But I said you'd probably need some time to get used to the idea of her."

"Just have the kid on my doorstep soon," Claudia said. "Swaddling clothes optional."

And why was the highborn Claudia Pfeiffer so anxious to claim a proletarian orphan as her own flesh? And would her enthusiasm last once she saw the piercings and the tattoos?

The answers lay with Julius Augustus Pfeiffer. He wasn't satisfied to build a city. He wanted to found a dynasty.

Unfortunately, his two offspring seemed in no hurry to cooperate. Year after year and marriage after marriage—nothing. He begged them; he threatened them. Until finally three of the best doctors in the state verified what everyone but Julius already knew. The Pfeiffer twins could not have children.

Furious, uncomprehending, and quite possibly mad, the old man struck back the only way he knew how. He placed all his assets in a trust, then had Daddy draw up a will that stipulated nothing would go to Claudia or her brother until they had children. These children, the will made clear, could be within wedlock or not, just as long as they were Pfeiffers, proven so by law and science. Otherwise, his estate would go to the zoo.

Daddy claimed Julius' mental state was such that the will would never hold up in court. But for once Jack Llewellyn turned out to be wrong and, suddenly, at the age of forty-five, Claudia and Julius II were broke.

Broke, though, is a relative term. Claudia had some investments of her own, the booty of various divorce settlements. And, after her last divorce, she'd moved back into the family house, one of those lavish Lake Drive piles built a hundred years ago by the local robber barons and coveted by every financial upstart since. Julius Pfeiffer had bought it even before he made his first million.

That's where, at lunch one June day, I introduced a grinning Dawn to her mother.

Claudia met the door herself—the poor waif was down to only a yardman and a cleaning woman. We would eat, she said, in the library. As we trailed her through the vast foyer, Dawn's grin grew even broader. The Italian marble floor and pillars clearly impressed her.

"This sure is some place," she whispered. "Like the set of *Aida*. All it needs is a couple elephants."

The library held an extensive collection of books, beautifully bound and largely unread, along with portraits of Julius and Virginia, his consort. There was also one of Julius II. When Claudia saw Dawn staring at the pictures, she said, "My parents and my brother. All of them gone now."

Virginia Pfeiffer had died in the early nineties and Julius II right after he heard the contents of his father's will. He'd promptly gotten drunk enough to drive his Lamborghini into a bridge abutment. The car exploded on impact.

Lunch was simple—fresh lake trout, some nice wine, and a lot of chatter, mostly between Claudia and me. Dawn kept quiet, from nerves maybe. She didn't eat much either, though dessert, Spanische windtorte, was fabulous. Claudia could still afford a good caterer.

After we finished, she suggested Dawn take a peek at the grounds. Dawn, looking both grateful and greedy, bolted for the door.

"Well," I said when she was gone. "What do you think of her?"

"I think you'd better be sure that new birth certificate looks real."

"Of course it does. Remember all the birth certificates I used to forge in school so we had I.D.? It's the same now as it was then. All you need is the right form, a good pen, and a steady hand."

"You've got chutzpah, I'll say that for you. And friends in high places."

In low ones, too. Like a clerk in Vital Statistics who saw no harm in letting me do research there, nor in leaving me alone to do it. After all, I was an officer of the court—and an old friend of her boss. Thus, in a few strokes of key and pen, the facts of Dawn's birth were altered *in perpetuum*.

Dawn's original birth registration had listed her mother as Kathleen Anne Siegert. Her father was Unknown. The child's name read Janis Melanie Siegert, the same as on her high school diploma. She'd changed it when she turned eighteen. Had me register her new name with the state, though I told her that wasn't really necessary as long as she didn't use it for purposes of fraud.

Claudia opened a second bottle of wine and filled our glasses. "About the girl's mother—"

"I told you before. No problem."

And there wasn't. Nor would there be.

In the first place, from the moment she'd entered into the adoption agreement, it was as if Dawn's real mother didn't exist. Still, Claudia and I had wanted to be sure the woman would never cause trouble. For all we knew, she might have kept up with Dawn somehow, watched her from afar, and would come swooping down on her newly rich daughter. It didn't seem likely, but the devil is always in the details. I launched a search for Kathleen Siegert.

Once you have someone's Social Security number, she's in your cross hairs; no thicket of married names or criminal aliases can hide her. Kathleen's name had changed only when she married, so it took me but a short while to discover she still lived in the city and owned an import shop in the Third Ward. I also found out she was the widowed mother of two teenage girls. She probably wouldn't be looking for yet a third daughter.

It would've been rather difficult for Kathleen to locate Dawn, anyway, because something had gone wrong at the adoption agency. They couldn't seem to find an appropriate placement. Dawn never knew exactly why, but the upshot was she became one of those "older children" no one seems to want. The agency bounced her into the county welfare system.

By grace or good luck, she turned out to be bright, hardworking, and nobody's fool, a survivor rather than a victim.

The kind of young woman anyone would be proud to claim as a daughter.

Claudia agreed. More or less. "Her grammar's a little iffy and eleven ear studs do verge on excess. She's attractive, though. In a K-Mart kind of way. The tattoos, however, are disappointing."

"That's just her generation."

"I mean they're too small. Too discreet. Though I must admit the Valkyries riding across her back have a certain panache."

"So she'll do?"

"What if I said no?"

I threw up my hands. "Come on, Claud. I've worked on this night and day for the last four months. It hasn't been easy."

"Or cheap," she said. "I've seen your most recent expense account."

"A fake DNA is just a tad expensive."

"You didn't need to pick it up personally. Or fly first class. Or stay almost a week in the most expensive hotel in Boston."

"There were complications," I said.

Which was the understatement of the year. The day before the lab technician was to hand over the report, there'd been an accident at the lab and he'd been killed. It was a shame, of course—the poor man was only thirty-six—to say nothing of inconvenient. The lab took five more days to authorize release of his report.

"At least," Claudia said, "you hadn't paid him off yet."

The woman could be so cheap! I knew I'd have to squeeze her hard to collect my "finder's fee." Good thing her new daughter and I had signed a contract that guaranteed the daughter's personal agent, Susan R. Llewellyn, a most handsome retainer.

That's why I fudged it a bit when Claudia asked for reassurance that Dawn knew nothing about Mr. Pfeiffer's will.

"I'd rather not have her appreciate the exact extent to which she has me over the barrel," Claudia said.

Quite truthfully, I said, “She never saw the will. And won’t.”

When Dawn came back, I left the two of them to get acquainted. I’d done all I could.

Did our plan work? Did Claudia inherit her father’s fortune? Did she reward me for my help? The answer to all of the above is: You bet! The DNA test and birth certificate satisfied the terms of Julius Pfeiffer’s will, and Claudia began to collect from the trust that held her father’s estate. Her monthly allowance was, shall we say, generous. So was my income as sole trustee.

As for Dawn, she got both the BMW and a real mother. To everyone’s surprise, she and Claudia bonded almost immediately. It started with their mutual interest in opera, then moved to a genuine emotional attachment. The money helped, of course, but what human relationship is without self-interest? The point is they liked each other and seemed to grow to love each other, too.

They even made up a charming story about how Dawn had begun a search for her birthmother, only to give it up when she discovered who she really was.

“The girl didn’t want to come off like some kind of gold-digger,” Claudia told her friends. “But then I got wind of it and insisted we meet. Now look at us. Can you believe it?”

Speaking of Dawn’s birthmother—in July, Kathleen Kasabian, nee Siegert, was found shot to death in the office of her import shop. The police figured she’d been killed in a late-night robbery—the safe was empty and all the security cameras smashed. When I read about it in the *Journal-Sentinal*, I said nothing to Claudia. Why spoil what was happening between her and Dawn?

So far as I could tell, only one fly hovered over the love feast. Well, two flies—the men in their lives. Claudia had a new fiancé and Dawn was seeing her old boyfriend, Mike.

Though Claudia privately called Mike a creep she wished had stayed in the Marines, she let me talk her into giving him work at one of the Pfeiffer companies.

"He can be...uh...dealt with later," I said.

For her part, Dawn never said much about Claudia's fiancé. But I could tell she didn't care for him. Nor did I, for the simple reason that Nelson Schwann was far too interested in the Pfeiffer Trust. He began sniffing around almost from the moment he loaded the four carets onto Claudia's finger.

As Trustee, I headed him off as long as I could. But the president of the city's largest bank is a hard man to play games with. Finally, I told Claudia that if she wanted Nelson to go over the books, I was ready for him.

A few evenings later, Claudia and Nelson appeared in my office. It was well after business hours and at a time when no one else was in the building. He carried a large briefcase loaded, I assumed, with the heavy artillery of an audit. Claudia had a tartan-topped picnic basket in her hand.

"I brought supper," she said. "Just sandwiches and some wine."

I managed a smile as I took the basket and set it on my new secretary's desk—Dawn had apparently decided her time was now better spent in the opera houses of Europe. I kept smiling as we went into my office.

Nelson, a tall blond man, was groomed and tailored to look ten years younger and fifteen pounds lighter than he really was. Even so, he still came across as middle aged. I suspected he always had.

They sat in the leather chairs, Nelson's briefcase on the oriental rug between them, and I took my place behind the desk—to gaze across its cluttered expanse at my guests and the door to the outer office. Closed now, it still bore a poster touting last year's production of *La Cenerentala.*

When we were settled, Nelson said, "I hear you're a woman of many talents."

"What's that supposed to mean?"

"It's what your ex-husband tells me. We play handball together at the Athletic Club. He also says you're a very gutsy lady."

"I can't believe he'd be so kind."

"Well, he does claim you have the moral sensibility of a wolverine."

After I finished laughing, Nelson said, "Only this time you've gone after prey far too large."

He reached in his briefcase to bring out a thick sheaf of computer printouts. They proved, he said, just how, and to what extent, I had gutted the Pfeiffer Trust.

As I stared at the printouts, Claudia said, "I must admit, Susan, I was very impressed with what you did to the Trust."

She ran a hand through her salt and pepper hair. "Almost as impressed as I was with what you did to my brother."

Now I stared at Claudia.

"Your ex was right about your talents," she said. "Master forger, creative accountant. And demolition expert. The bomb in my brother's car was clever. All he had to do was sideswipe something, anything, and kahboom."

I went cold, then hot, then cold again. "The police never—"

"That lab technician's death was well handled, too. At first I wondered how you pulled it off without blowing up the lab and everyone in it."

She reached over and touched Nelson's hand. "But Nelson tells me that in the workplace, even after 9/11 and the Unabomber, people still open any package with their name on it. He says one could send an IBM. And, of course, a competent bomb-maker can more or less control the explosion."

My throat felt like there was a rock in it. I couldn't speak. I could hardly even breathe.

Claudia said, "You were so resourceful with the bombs, I wonder why you changed your--what do they call it?—your M.O. Why did you shoot Dawn's birthmother?"

I was still unable to speak when she leaned across my desk and began to fiddle with the intercom.

Nelson said, "Is it working?"

"Yes," Claudia said. "Recording every word."

That's when I finally found my voice. "What is this, Claud?"

"Why, it's your confession."

I slapped the intercom—to turn it off, break it, whatever.

"Don't bother," Nelson said. "The whole office is bugged. Telephone, lamps, computer. Real James Bond stuff."

I couldn't believe it. "Do you honestly think I'm going to confess to killing all those people?"

"Even if you don't," Claudia said, "we've got enough evidence to take to the police."

"Evidence of embezzlement, too," Nelson added, patting the printouts.

I said I didn't know anything about bombs. "So how could I possibly blow anybody up?"

Then something occurred to me. "You're the who'd know about explosives, Claud. Your father's whole career was based on blowing up old buildings. Pfeiffer Demolition made him his first million."

Nelson stood up and went to one of the bookcases. He touched a volume. "Well, well," he said. "A book on making bombs."

He waved at the shelf it sat on. "And here's half a dozen more."

Claudia said, "You've a similar collection at home. Which you should have destroyed, by the way. Then there's all that information on bombs you downloaded from the Internet."

I glanced from her to Nelson. How rich and sleek they looked, he in his bespoke suit, she in her handmade shoes. And how smug.

"Now I get it," I said. "I'm supposed to be the fall guy in all this."

"Hardly."

"I think I even know how you pulled it off, Claud. When your father died, you got rid of the co-heir immediately. No trick, that. It wasn't the first time your alcoholic brother'd cracked up a car. Then you did the guy at the lab—Kathleen Kasabian, too—so nobody'd ever claim Dawn's not your daughter."

Claudia shook her head.

"And you want me to take the rap," I said. "I can understand that. What I don't understand is why you don't just blow me away like the others."

Nelson's eyes went to his briefcase. Was there a bomb in it? Or in that picnic basket in the outer office?

Now I was scared. I had to get out of there.

But Nelson was a big man. He could stop me before I even made it up from my chair. And I'd sure need more help than my clever tongue could deliver. I'd need the .38 in my desk drawer.

Hands shaking, I slipped the drawer key from its hiding place under the computer, palmed it, then somehow stuck it in the lock. All this, I made sure, without being seen.

Meanwhile, I said, "I might've cooked the Trust's books, but—"

"So you admit it?" Nelson said.

I yanked open the desk drawer and grabbed for the gun.

It wasn't there.

The office door swung open then and in came Dawn. She held the picnic basket in one hand, my snub nose .38 in the other.

Turning toward her, Claudia said, "Did you hear all that?"

"Over the intercom?" Dawn said. "Sure. But she didn't confess to much."

"She will," Nelson said. "When that gun's to her head."

Revolver still pointed my way, Dawn came over and set the basket on a corner of the desk.

"You better look at this," she said as she pulled back the basket's tartan lid.

Somehow I managed to stand up and peer inside. Except in the movies, I'd never seen a pipe bomb. But a length of capped pipe wired to a clock and a 9-volt battery gives you the clue. I knew it for what it was.

I pulled my eyes away from the bomb just as Dawn turned to Nelson. "You're a greedy pig," she said. "You want my inheritance."

Then she shot him dead.

As he fell next to the bookcase, she shot Claudia, too.

For a while, we both watched Claudia's body slide off the leather chair onto the oriental rug. Silence and the smell of cordite filled the room.

Later, in my Range Rover with me at the wheel and Strauss's *Elektra* on the CD player, Dawn said, "Good thing you never registered the .38. We could of been in deep shit after Kathleen."

As we left the parking ramp and turned onto Wisconsin Avenue, I asked where we were headed.

"Over to Mike's. I am, anyways. But first pull in that alley."

When we were parked, she turned off the music but kept the dashboard clock on. "It won't be long now," she said. "Beforehand, though, I wanna tell you that you were right about Claudia sending the bomb to the lab tech and how come my real mom got killed."

In the glow of the clock, Dawn looked as green as I felt.

"But Claud's brother," she said. "Who knows? Maybe she did it, maybe he was drunk just like the cops thought."

She pulled the picnic basket out of the foot well and held it on her lap. "Mike put this together," she said. "The bomb, I mean. I put it in the basket. There's another one in a file cabinet back at your office."

Mike, she told me, had learned all about explosives at Pfeiffer Demolition. "So aren't you glad you got him the job?"

We sat in silence until we heard the explosion in my office.

Dawn let out a loud "Yes!" then put the basket back in the foot well.

"I'm kinda sorry about this, Susan," she said. "You were always like a mother to me. Taught me a lot, too. But in fifteen minutes—well, it's gonna look like you made a fatal mistake."

As Dawn climbed out of the vehicle, the thought of my being a mother to her must have lingered in her mind. Or maybe it was Claudia she recalled. Whichever, she paused a moment and, turning back to me, said, "If this was an opera, right now everybody'd be going, '*Addio, mia madre, addio, addio, addio.*'"

That was twelve minutes ago. I'm still in the Range Rover, nylon handcuffs still binding my hands to the steering wheel.

Yeah. *Addio.*

MJ Jones is a retired teacher. In 2001, her story, "The Witch and the Relic Thief," won MWA's Robert L. Fish Award for Best First Mystery Story. Her mystery novel, Holy Thieves, is published by The Fiction Works. This story won the 2003 FMAM annual Slesar TWIST Award.

"Henderson, do you mind? We have work to do!"

Printed in the United States
19925LVS00002B/297

9 780974 960869